This was too convenient for his liking.

Jase adjusted his rearview mirror, waiting for Cassie to drive away, but he didn't hear her truck start. A knock on his window surprised him, hardly a good look for one of Denver's finest. "What's wrong?"

"Engine won't start, and pickup time is in fifteen minutes. The school isn't far, and then Penny, Easton and I are expected at the seniors' center right after that. We've got to check on our allotment at their community garden."

Now he wavered once more. There was zero chance she was using car trouble as a way to divert his attention, not when she'd already manufactured another excuse. Besides that, it was obvious how much Cassie loved her children and wanted them involved in as many town activities as their busy schedule would allow.

"I can drive you there. We'll look at your truck later." Her instant smile was his immediate reward.

"I'll be right back with their booster seats."

Jase braced himself. He wouldn't let anything as simple as a pretty smile distract him. At least, that's what he told himself.

Dear Reader,

Welcome back to Violet Ridge! This is the third book about the Virtue siblings and the Lazy River Dude Ranch, but Jase was the first character to show himself to me. He has long followed his own path, which led him to become a police detective in Denver. With a secret from his past holding him back, I knew Jase needed someone to help him reconnect with his family and provide hope for the future.

Enter Cassie O'Neal, a farmer, entrepreneur and a single mother to two adorable children plus the half sister of someone who leads Jase back to Thistle Brook Farm and to Cassie. A patient gardener—unlike me!—Cassie cultivates vegetables as well as relationships with many of the town's residents. Jase sees these strong ties and is jealous, wanting the same for himself. His respect for and awareness of Cassie is also something he knows he can't overlook. And doesn't. Their journey is a special one.

Although, my favorite "character" is Blossom, who sees herself as the heart and soul of the farm, and the true recipient of Jase's affections! I'd love to hear if Blossom also endeared herself to you. You can email me at tanya.agler@tanyaagler.com or follow me on Facebook at Tanya Agler Author.

Happy reading!

Tanya

A FAMILY FOR THE COWBOY COP

TANYA AGLER

Recycling programs for this product may not exist in your area.

ISBN-13: 978-1-335-46009-7

A Family for the Cowboy Cop

For questions and comments about the quality of this book, please contact us at CustomerService@Harlequin.com.

Harlequin Enterprises ULC
22 Adelaide St. West, 41st Floor
Toronto, Ontario M5H 4E3, Canada
www.Harlequin.com

Printed in U.S.A.

Tanya Agler remembers the first set of Harlequin books her grandmother gifted her, and she's been in love with romance novels ever since. An award-winning author, Tanya makes her home in Georgia with her wonderful husband, their four children and a lovable basset, who really rules the roost. When she's not writing, Tanya loves classic movies and a good cup of tea. Visit her at tanyaagler.com or email her at tanya.agler@tanyaagler.com.

Books by Tanya Agler

Harlequin Heartwarming

The Single Dad's Holiday Match
The Soldier's Unexpected Family
The Sheriff's Second Chance
A Ranger for the Twins

Smoky Mountain First Responders

The Firefighter's Christmas Promise
The Paramedic's Forever Family

Rodeo Stars of Violet Ridge

Caught by the Cowgirl
Snowbound with the Rodeo Star
Her Temporary Cowboy
The Triplets' Holiday Miracle
Saving the Rancher

Visit the Author Profile page
at Harlequin.com for more titles.

This book is lovingly dedicated to my grandmother
Jinx Balewski, affectionately known as Gram.
So often we'd walk to our favorite ice cream parlor,
and she'd tell me about growing up in Pennsylvania
and the cowboy movies that held her transfixed
in her seat, while I'd talk about the latest
Harlequin novel she'd brought home for me.
Thank you for those walks and everything, Gram.

CHAPTER ONE

JASE VIRTUE OBSERVED two red minivans pulling into the gravel lot adjoining Thistle Brook Farm while three black trucks left the premises. It seemed as though half of Violet Ridge was here, enjoying this brisk fall day, laughing and exchanging pleasantries as though nothing momentous had happened. Annoyed, Jase maintained full alert, as that was indeed the case. Yesterday convicted bank robber Keith Yablonsky escaped prison, and this farm was his childhood home.

Jase was confident Yablonsky was heading here, and Jase would be waiting to apprehend him along with his accomplice. Finding the money from the robbery would finally bring this case to a close.

Jase emerged from his government-issued, nondescript black sedan and straightened his tie. A crisply ironed, long-sleeve Oxford shirt and navy suit jacket along with the detective badge attached to his black leather belt gave him an air of authority, but it also made him stand out like a fox in a henhouse in this corner of southwestern Colorado. He planned to use that to his advantage today and serve notice to the Yablonsky family that Jase would do his duty and return him to prison.

Jase was positive Yablonsky's sister, Cassie, was harboring the fugitive, here at this very farm. Who else could be the *C* that Yablonsky's cellmate mentioned so often during their interview? It was hard to believe that sweet Cassie Yablonsky, who'd graduated a year behind him at Violet Ridge High School, could be guilty of such crimes, but no one else associated with the case had the same initial and fit the physical profile.

After the interview, Jase's superior, Captain Shields, didn't hesitate, pegging Jase as the detective who'd travel to Violet Ridge and interview Cassie. After all, Jase had grown up ten miles away at the Lazy River Dude Ranch and was a passing acquaintance of Cassie's in high school.

Jase still couldn't believe that the cute teenager who'd volunteered for every committee and baked cakes for fellow students' birthdays was under suspicion of harboring a fugitive. Yet here he was because Yablonsky's cellmate was emphatic in his description of the accomplice, the first new lead about the robbery in years.

A side benefit to the trip would be a warm hug from his grandmother Bridget, the heart of the Virtue family. Over the past few years, she had let him know in no uncertain terms that he didn't visit Violet Ridge and the family's dude ranch often enough for her liking. But Jase had to keep his distance from his grandparents and three siblings, even if he was the only one who knew why. He'd do anything to keep his family intact.

For now, though, he had to concentrate on the case. Duty always had to come first.

Nodding to a couple of passersby, Jase hurried along a dirt path lined with hay. People queued in front of a rustic wooden building, a farmstand of sorts. Shelves lined with jams and jars of preserved fruit occupied one side while baskets of fall vegetables like turnips, chard and kale rested on makeshift tables along the other.

Jase started for the head of the line. Maybe the employee in charge could direct him to Cassie. Once he found her, he'd start his interrogation with casual conversation, asking after her mother and the farm, lulling her into a false sense of security before he asked the direct questions that could end in her arrest.

"Hey, no cutting!" A bald man in flip-flops and shorts waggled his finger at Jase. "Cassie only makes her pumpkin butter in September, and it sells out fast. We got a late start this morning." He glared at the woman standing next to him.

"It's not my fault, Gerald. You were the one who couldn't find his keys." She stared back at the older man while gripping an empty basket before turning her attention to Jase. "You'll get your turn soon enough. Besides, Cassie's turnips are the only ones my husband will eat."

"Becky roasts them with garlic butter and sage. All of Cassie's farm-fresh goods are worth the wait." Gerald smacked his lips. "Next month's jam flavor is pear vanilla. I'll have to remember where I put my keys. Don't want to miss out on that."

The crowd around them laughed and agreed with the man.

The married couple proved a fierce barrier, and Jase fumed at waiting in this long line to find Cassie. Then he cooled upon realizing he had enough time to scope out the farm's layout, although Yablonsky wouldn't be so foolhardy as to hide in plain sight. He scrutinized the closest outbuildings and kept from whistling at the changes.

Unlike in years past, Thistle Brook seemed to be thriving. Someone had hauled away the rusty farm equipment and umpteen wooden barrels that had littered the landscape. In its place, the farmstand was a bustling hive of activity, and the farmhouse in the distance boasted a fresh paint job and new wooden siding.

A gut instinct that Cassie might have had an infusion of money from the bank robbery proceeds wasn't probable cause to access her bank account.

Yet this wasn't the rundown farm it had been fifteen years ago. Had Cassie figured out a system to launder the money from the bank robbery? If so, that would be another charge in a long list of crimes.

The line moved slowly, giving Jase time to figure out how to tread carefully with his interview. Somehow, Cassie had evaded responsibility for eight years. *Wily* and *ingenuous* were two words that came to mind for anyone who was that clever, and Jase would find a way to obtain the truth from Cassie. If not, today, then soon. This was his sole assignment at present.

Finally, he was close enough to take note of the two employees working the booth, their backs to Jase while they advised customers.

"I ship them in a special box, so the jars don't break." A melodious voice floated on the breeze toward him. "My pumpkin butter is popular since it's the first week of fall, and I just introduced a new jam. Rosemary lavender fig enhances the flavor of the scone recipe that comes with the purchase of any four jars of preserves or jellies."

The customer plucked a glass container off the shelf. "There's something different about them this week, but I can't put my finger on it."

"My friend, Amanda, designed a new logo for Thistle Brook Farms, and I started using the matching labels for this batch of jam. She's a marketing genius." The brunette nudged the blonde next to her.

"Aww. It was my pleasure."

Jase's breath caught. That voice sounded just like his older brother's fiancée, Amanda Fleming. If so, what was she doing here on a farm where an escaped convict might be hiding?

At that moment, Amanda turned around, confirming his guess. Her gaze wandered to the line, and Jase resisted the urge to duck out of sight since he hadn't told Grandma Bridget and the rest of his family he was coming to town. For one thing, he hadn't known until midnight that Shields was sending him here, but a trip to Lazy River was next on his agenda.

Amanda gasped and dragged the young brunette toward him, and he knew it was useless to try to hide his presence. "Jase Virtue! What are you doing here? Seth didn't tell me you were coming."

It took Jase a long second to recognize Cassie beside Amanda. It had been over ten years since he'd seen her last, about the same time he'd left Violet Ridge for good. If he were putting out a BOLO on her, the simple language wouldn't do her justice. Her thick dark brown hair fell in waves past her shoulders, framing a heart-shaped face with eyes that looked hazel at first glance but held enough green in them to make them most unusual. True, her face was appealing, but his conversation with Keith's cellmate left no doubt she was her brother's accomplice.

From her apprehensive gaze, he could tell she knew exactly who he was and why he was at the farm.

"I'm here in an official capacity." Jase found his words muffled as Amanda enveloped him in a sisterly embrace before she returned to Cassie's side. "Seth doesn't know yet. After I talk to Cassie, I'll head over to the Lazy River and say hello to Grandma Bridget and everyone else."

How long he'd be at the farm was still unclear. Everything depended on how long it took for

Cassie to slip up and reveal Yablonsky's presence and her part in the original robbery and subsequent escape.

The brunette extended her hand and then pulled it back, wiping it on the large white apron wrapped around her waist before finally shaking his hand. "I told the police officer everything, the one who informed me of Keith's escape. I haven't seen my half brother in eight years, and I'd like nothing more than for him to be behind bars again."

If he didn't know better, Jase would have believed her statement to be genuine. But eight years on the police force, first as a cop, then detective, taught him to search below the surface. She might be trying to get rid of him in case Yablonsky was already on the premises.

Another idea popped into Jase's mind. Cassie might, in fact, be eager for the police to apprehend Yablonsky. Once he was back in custody, Cassie could launder the rest of the money and leave Violet Ridge for good.

"Where can we talk? Preferably in private." Afterward, he'd confer with Captain Shields to find out if a stakeout of the premises was warranted. If so, using the Lazy River Dude Ranch as his home base, even with guests coming and going, would be convenient and allow him the luxury of spending time with his grandparents.

Cassie's gaze wandered to the long line of customers still waiting for service. "More like when. Once I sell out of produce, I have a farm to manage. I still have a full afternoon harvesting crops for the subscription boxes that have to be ready to be picked up late next week. If you had called first, I could have found someone to help at the farmstand this morning."

And given her an opportunity to practice her story first? He preferred the element of surprise. "I left Denver at dawn and drove straight here. It's crucial that I speak with you alone."

A gasp came while a look of alarm shrouded her face. "Why? Is Keith headed this way? The police officer who informed me about his escape assured me most prisoners are apprehended right away." Cassie paled, and she started shaking.

Amanda placed her arm around her friend and then looked at Jase, her concern clear. "I'll manage the stand if you need to sit down in the farmhouse, Cass."

Before Cassie had a chance to answer, Gerald and his wife came over to them with a full basket of produce and pumpkin butter. Becky shot Jase an exasperated look as though he was trying to ruin her day on purpose. "Really. The nerve of some people. First, you cut in line. Now you're monopolizing Cassie, who looks like she's seen a ghost." The woman patted Cassie's hand. "Whatever he said to you, he's wrong. Just remember you're the town sweetheart. Why, when I think of that community garden at the seniors' center… You've given Gerald something to do in the daytime now that he's retired."

"I'm grateful you started the garden." Gerald nodded and then held up the basket. "We'd like to pay for this."

"Gerald and Becky, you both are two of Cassie's favorite customers, but she has to talk to my future brother-in-law. I'll ring you up so you can be on your way," Amanda said.

The pair exclaimed their surprise at Jase's identity. Amanda simply nodded at Cassie and ushered the couple to the rear of the farmstand.

Cassie turned toward Jase. "We'll have more privacy in the farmhouse."

Before Jase could take another step, a petite woman in her seventies tapped Jase's arm. "You're tall. Can you reach that hanging basket for me?" She pointed to one overflowing with royal velvet petunias and then turned toward Cassie. "What type of fertilizer did you use? Do I need to bring it inside at first frost?"

"These are a special type of flower called supertunias, Mrs. Olsen. They're more suited to our growing zone here in Colorado. I used a standard fertilizer with a lot of water to minimize damage to the roots." Cassie answered the questions with that same calm smile that he always cherished seeing in the halls of Violet Ridge High.

Mrs. Olsen expressed her sincere thanks and asked Jase to reach for another basket, the one with pink flowers. "Purple for me, and this one for my daughter's housewarming present. She'll love it."

Cassie thanked her and directed her to the back

of the stand where Amanda was still ringing up Gerald and Becky's purchase.

Jase prepared to escort Cassie to the farmhouse and corralled his thoughts for the interview. Hearing her voice, seeing her body language, those would help him gauge the level of her involvement with Yablonsky's crime and his escape. He was ready to head to the farmhouse when yet another customer approached him.

"Are you wanting that last jar of pumpkin butter? I hope not." The elderly woman scowled. "My morning's not the same without Cassie's jam. It just makes the day a little brighter, you know?"

Catching criminals and keeping people safe made his day brighter, but he humored this woman and kept this to himself. Instead, he reached for the jam and handed it to her. "It's all yours."

The woman nodded in his direction. "Mighty obliged. Surprise me with three more types, young man. I'll make jam thumbprint cookies for the next Adopt a Grandparent Day." She turned to Cassie, her frown switching to a smile. "That's my favorite night of the month. By the way, why does your pumpkin butter taste so much better than what I buy at the store?"

"Maybe it's because I grow my own pumpkins in the hoophouses. You'll be getting a special pie in your subscription box in a few weeks. That's a perk of signing up for those in advance." Rather than trooping off for their interview, Cassie commandeered Jase into service at the farmstand, and soon he found himself wrapping jars in craft paper.

Captain Shields wasn't going to believe this development. Here Jase was, the leading contender to take over Shields' position when he retired early next year, serving as a glorified vegetable stand assistant.

Jase stuffed the box with thin brown crinkly strips of paper so no jars would break while sneaking a peek at Cassie. The woman was well-liked around here and seemed almost perfect in everyone's eyes except his. Was she an excellent salesperson? Or was she keeping him away from the farmhouse on purpose? Considering she'd been focused on her customers and hadn't so much as touched her phone to send a warning text to Yablonsky, Jase was willing to give her the benefit of the doubt about that. He wouldn't be so generous with the rest of his investigation.

The next hour flew by until the final customer waved goodbye with a tote containing the last of the rosemary lavender fig jelly along with three jars of strawberry rhubarb preserves. Almost every basket on the table was empty and the shelves were bare.

Amanda joined them, wagging her finger at Jase. "I texted Seth. He wanted to come straight here from the dude ranch, but I persuaded him to stay with the guests as long as the Lazy River is your next stop."

"I'll be there as soon as possible. Most likely

by dinnertime." It had been too long since Jase had hugged his grandmother Bridget, but he still needed to scope out this farm. "Everything depends on work."

"You're so much like Seth was when we first met." Amanda opened her arms for another hug. "Welcome home, Jase."

His breath caught. Denver was his permanent home, but he didn't correct his future sister-in-law. Amanda took her leave, and Jase turned to Cassie, who no longer had any excuse to avoid his questions.

"Would you prefer talking here at the stand or in your house?" Either way, Jase would start wearing down her defenses until she confessed.

Cassie squinted and directed her attention to the stable. "Can we walk and talk at the same time? I need to check on my horses before lunch."

Jase nodded since she'd provided the perfect opportunity to scope out hiding places and get the lay of the land before that interview. Afterward, he'd drive to the Lazy River, maybe even in time for a late lunch. He kept his fingers crossed that there'd still be at least one slice of Ingrid's apple pie remaining. He sure did miss the cook's baking. "A stable. Is that new here?"

"No, we've always kept a horse or two. At present we have three." Cassie zipped the cash bag closed.

"I visited the farm once in high school to drop

off something for my grandmother Bridget. I wouldn't have recognized the place now."

Cassie shrugged. "There have been ups and downs since my father died, but the farm is self-supporting and a sight more picturesque without the tractor, rusty tools and barrels taking up usable space. I'm proud of that." She glowed at her pronouncement as her gaze went to his shoes. "Be careful where you step in and around the barn and stable. Especially near patches."

"Patches of what?" he asked.

Her smile reached her eyes as she locked the cash bag in the register. "You'll know what I mean soon enough."

With that mysterious warning, he walked beside her to the stable, his guard on high alert in case they did come face-to-face with Yablonsky. He also kept an eye out for patches of poison ivy, but there was nary a weed to be seen. "Ms. Yablonsky…"

"I'm Cassie O'Neal now, but considering you graduated a year ahead of me, just call me Cassie. We're pretty informal at Thistle Brook Farm." She paused at the corral outside of the stable and pointed to three quarter horses in the distance. "That's Hazel, Honeybee and Hickory."

Impatience at how long it was taking to even begin the interview reared in Jase. "Ms. O'… Cassie, I have a series of questions for you about the case." He stopped talking when his stomach grumbled. He hadn't eaten anything since a protein bar before he left Denver, and he wanted to finish the interrogation so he could enjoy lunch at the Lazy River.

"Give me a few minutes to tend to the horses. Then we can head back to the farmhouse for lunch. I need to eat, too." So much for hoping she didn't hear his hunger pangs and for a slice of Ingrid's apple pie. "You can go on to the farmhouse or walk around or stay here if you'd like. I have nothing to hide."

That gave him pause. She'd just allowed him total access to the farm? Why would she do that if Yablonsky was hiding on the property? Still, he jumped at the chance to explore the grounds. "I won't be too far away."

She looked as if she was about to say something but left him and entered the stable without a word. Jase took note of the well-maintained fence separating the barn and stable from acres of farmland. He weighed whether to start with the hoophouses or barn. Cassie's mention of patches near the barn was too intriguing, and he moved in that direction.

He entered the structure, and a gleaming tractor greeted him. Something scurried, and a calico cat bounded up the steps. Jase's breath steadied, and he understood Cassie's cryptic message. Patches was a spotted cat, not a plant.

He followed Patches up the ladder and found hay bales in the loft near the large window opening. The cat peered around a bale. Jase laughed as Patches emerged and licked its paw. "You may just have used one of your nine lives."

Footsteps on the hay echoed behind him, and he found Cassie at the foot of the ladder. "I see you found Patches."

Jase scrambled down to meet her and brushed off the dust and bits of hay. "I should have known a farm would have a barn cat." Had he been in the city that long?

Her impish expression revealed she'd misled him on purpose. He took note of it as a tell for his interview.

"I'm surprised she let you close enough to see her. Patches is a shy calico." Cassie pulled off her apron and placed it in the crook of her arm. "Lunchtime. I'm on a tight schedule. I'd like to harvest the parsnips before it starts raining."

"Ms. O'Neal, er, Cassie, your brother's escape is a serious matter." He weighed his words about how much information he should share with her. He wanted to gain some trust so she'd let down her guard around him, but she needed to understand time was of the essence. "He communicated some information to his cellmate..."

She gestured for him to follow her out of the barn where she observed the sky, dark clouds forming on the horizon. "My farm is a serious matter for me. My day starts at five, and I need lunch and a cup of coffee to process whatever you're going to tell me. Hopefully this will be a short spell of rain, and it might be over by the time we're done with lunch. Come on."

She walked toward the farmhouse. In no time, they were climbing the stairs to her back patio. Its magnificent view of the Rockies almost compared to the majestic sight at the Lazy River Dude Ranch. With him now joining Cassie for lunch, he'd hopefully make it to join his family in time for dinner.

Cassie opened the screen door, and he brushed off the dust and grime from his shoes in the mudroom before entering the kitchen, an inviting area with a large island and breakfast nook. Jase approached the refrigerator covered with bright artwork and examined the drawings. One featured Patches while another had two children hanging on to a stick figure's arms. He looked over at Cassie who was pulling out two mugs from a cabinet. "Who drew these?" he asked.

"My children, Penny and Easton." Cassie poured coffee and set one mug on the island, keeping the other for herself.

He thanked her and breathed in the robust aroma, a true pick-me-up considering he'd been awake ever since he found out about the escape. Eighteen hours was starting to catch up with him, but he'd gone longer without sleep. "How old are they?"

Why was he surprised she had two children? Perhaps because they weren't in the file, and he didn't like surprises on the job.

"Penny is seven, and Easton turned five in May. They'll arrive home from school in a few hours." She sipped her coffee and then opened the refrigerator door. "Are turkey sandwiches with a side of my homemade pesto pasta salad okay for lunch?"

Anything homemade was a treat, and he nodded. "Sounds delicious. Thank you." He took one more sip and then rested his mug next to hers. "How can I help?"

"Find Keith. Make sure he goes back to jail and stays there." She shivered and sighed. "Sorry. He's a sensitive subject. Can you slather some mustard on the wheat bread for me? There are more condiments in the refrigerator."

He did as directed. "Has your brother been in contact with you?"

His gaze didn't leave her face. Her jaw clenched, and he noticed a hint of aggravation in those eyes. "We shared a father, but that's about all. If I had heard from him, I would have called the police immediately. Do you see the police here?" She waved her arm around the comfortable space, the kitchen a cozy spot where he envisioned many happy meals. "Well, except for you, of course."

He noticed she didn't answer with a blunt yes or no. By answering a question with a question, her response struck him as evasive. Another sign she might be the elusive *C*. He chose his next words with care. "There's been new intelligence to suggest Keith hid the money in Violet Ridge, specifically at Thistle Brook Farm, before he was arrested."

Cassie's face drained of color, her hazel eyes wide with concern. So far everything about Cassie seemed genuine, but he'd heard too many lies in the past eight years to accept mere words.

"Are you saying Keith is heading here?" She cupped her hands on the mug. "Why would you think that?"

The cellmate had mentioned Thistle Brook Farm by name, but Jase kept that info to himself. Instead, he stared at Cassie until she met his gaze. "Do you know where he hid the money?"

"No!" This time her denial was explosive and immediate.

What else did he expect? If she revealed the hiding place, that proved she was either the accomplice or an accessory after the fact. Of course she wouldn't admit it. "Could he have hidden the money on the farm somewhere?"

"No." She let out an exasperated breath and stared out the window. "I don't know. I've cultivated nearly every square inch of this place since he was convicted, but two hundred acres is bound to have some hiding spaces."

So much for this being a quick jaunt to Violet Ridge. Shields was right when he said to pack a bag. Jase was looking forward to staying at the Lazy River Dude Ranch, but would he feel more like a guest than a member of the family? He'd find out later, but first he had to focus on finding

Yablonsky. “Cassie, if you know anything, tell me. If he hid the money here, he’s on his way to claim it.” Unless she already spent it on farm renovations. “He’ll be captured trying to make his way here or the minute he steps foot on the property.”

If anything, her face turned paler. “Penny and Easton.” She whispered the names of her children. “Are they safe?”

“He’s never hurt anyone, but I can’t guarantee that for certain. There’s no telling how desperate he might be.”

Cassie covered her shaky left hand with her quivering right. “I’ll send them to my mother, in Florida. Penny will be devastated. She loves her teacher and was looking forward to having a solo in the school recital.” It almost seemed as though Cassie was doing everything in her power to keep from crying. Jase’s resolve took a direct hit. “And Easton is so proud, being named student of the month for September.”

Jase wavered. There was still a very good chance that Cassie was mixed up in all this, and yet, he believed she was a dedicated mother. He paused, his mind racing. If suspicion mounted on her, would it be easier for her to join the kids in Florida, money in hand, and leave the country from there?

“You can rest assured. The odds are overwhelming we’ll capture Yablonsky soon. Like the first officer told you.”

She transferred her gaze from the window to

him. "Would you risk your children's safety on a statistic?"

No, but then again, he promised himself he'd never have children. He didn't need to bring a little one in the world when life was so turbulent and could change in an instant. "I'm not a father."

She tensed, her body coiled and stiff. "I won't let anything bad happen to Easton or Penny."

Jase believed her. He took stock of what was around him, wanting to give some reassurance. "It sounds as though Penny and Easton have good reasons to stay, and you say Yablonsky hasn't contacted you?" He looked at her for confirmation, and she nodded. "What about adding a security system in the house and on the perimeter of your property?" So far, he hadn't seen any signs of a surveillance company or other deterrent.

Cassie nibbled her lip and started cutting up a hearty red tomato for the sandwiches. "I never needed one before."

That was a conversation for another time, as security and peace of mind were essential wherever one went, but especially out here, isolated like she was. "A good security system should set your mind at ease about your children staying with you. I can have one installed tonight."

Cassie finished assembling the sandwiches. "And by tomorrow, I'll have the security company out here on a false alarm, the first of what will probably be many." She let out a wry laugh. "Most mornings, my five-year-old, Easton, forgets simple things like brushing his teeth unless I remind him. With something so outside his ordinary routine? The first time he goes to visit the barn, he'll either fail to turn off the system or forget the code and bam. False alarm. Then there's Penny, who collects the eggs from the henhouse first thing after she wakes up. The same thing goes for her."

Frustration welled in him before he calmed himself. Obviously, she didn't want a security system installed. The more eyes on the place, the harder it would be for Yablonsky to find sanctuary here. "Security companies work with parents of young children all the time. They'll call you before they come out. Precautions and fail-safe tests are the first steps in ensuring peace of mind."

Cassie swiped at the corner of her eyes. "I won't put Penny or Easton in jeopardy, and I can't leave my farm. Not without anyone else to harvest the fall vegetables and tend to the animals."

There was a simple solution to her dilemma. Better still, it was the perfect opportunity to keep tabs on Cassie. In his mind, she was the best conduit to capturing Yablonsky. While he'd have cherished using the dude ranch as his base and spending time with his grandparents, this solution was better for all involved.

"I'll stay here." Jase gave a firm nod. "I'll do everything I can to keep Penny and Easton safe and make sure everyone learns how to use the security system."

Cassie sent a soft smile toward him. "You'd do that for me? I'll feel safer knowing there's a trained detective on the premises. Thank you."

Now, with her permission to be on the ground, he had full access to the property. He couldn't have planned it any better. The minute Keith Yablonsky set foot on Thistle Brook Farm, Jase would arrest him.

And if Cassie O'Neal was his accomplice, she'd be joining her half brother in jail.

THE SCHOOL BUS was due any minute. Cassie O'Neal kicked a pebble off the path and onto the grass near the Thistle Brook Farm mailbox. Seeing Penny and Easton with her own eyes would do her a world of good.

The past twenty-four hours since the police officer informed her of Keith's escape from prison had been a roller coaster, and Cassie wanted off the dizzying ride. The officer questioned her for over an hour before leaving and telling her about the hotline dedicated to tips regarding Keith's presence.

Just like that, all of the gains she'd made since his crime disappeared in the blink of an eye.

Over the past eight years, Cassie had worked hard to be more than the little half sister of the bank robber who'd stolen a million dollars from the Flying Bison State Trust and Loan Bank. And yet the specter of what Keith had done, the pain, the sheer horrific act of his armed robbery, had never gone away. Her chest ached with hollowness from Keith's actions, now even more empty after his escape.

That tightness was exacerbated with Detective Jase Virtue ensconced in her guest room.

Maybe she should send Penny and Easton to Florida after all. But for how long? One day? One month? A lifetime? She took a deep breath and decided to trust Jase and his training to keep her safe.

Besides, if she called Mom, she'd hear the same familiar refrain as Theresa Yablonsky would once again entreat Cassie to sell the farm and move to Florida. Mom meant well, and her heart was in the right place, but this was Cassie's home.

Before yesterday, the nip in the air had made her giddy at bringing thick, chunky sweaters out of storage and stacking logs by the fireplace for cozy nights of reading and family time. She loved every season at Thistle Brook Farm but especially fall with the anticipation of the holidays and the bonus of pumpkin spice creamer in her coffee.

Best of all, this was the first year of her corn maze, the grand opening set for the end of the month. Already she'd stocked up on items from kettle corn to corn dogs for those Friday and Saturday nights.

Now, opening weekend might be in jeopardy. Detective Virtue was adamant she postpone the festivities until after Keith was captured and remanded into custody. So much for feeling like she was in control of her own life after she'd fought so hard for that privilege.

"Cassie!"

Halting at Jase's command, she zipped up her raincoat. A smudge of dirt on her wrist from her afternoon of harvesting turnips and parsnips caught her attention, and she flicked it away. All of this was overwhelming, too much for one day. She'd gone from excitement over fall festivities to heartbreak at yet another Keith disaster.

"Detective Virtue." She faced him, knowing her eyes were still puffy and raw from last night's news about Keith. "I thought you were arranging for a crew to install the security system."

"They'll be here later today. I need a four-digit code for the keypad." He held his phone aloft as if waiting for her decision.

"Oh-six-two-five. That's my ex-husband Brayden's birthday. Penny and Easton both know it." And Keith would never think of it, if he even knew Brayden's birthdate at all.

Jase gave her a look of approval while she considered the man who'd be living with her for the immediate future. Very few in Violet Ridge walked around in a pressed suit and conservative blue tie. Everything about him screamed *police* down to his chunky black work boots.

How was she going to explain to Penny and Easton that this man with closely cropped dark brown hair and cold brown eyes was sleeping in their grandmother's bedroom? Any explanation would be met with only more questions. Until now, she'd never had a reason to tell them about their uncle's criminal past.

She had planned to tell them about Keith someday. When they were much older and could understand everything. Of course, she was twenty-eight and didn't comprehend Keith's actions. She'd visited him once while he was awaiting trial. After he said he'd do the same all over again, she walked out of prison and his life for good. She never looked back or regretted that decision.

Jase stopped looking at his phone. He must have felt her staring at him, and he examined his suit jacket. "Do I have mustard on me? Pasta?"

"Not a speck of food or dirt on you." As if either would dare to stick to him.

"By the way, thank you for lunch." He held up a finger and answered a call with an intensity she envied. He finished the call and pocketed his phone. "It was delicious."

"Glad you liked it, seeing as how you'll be eating with us for a while." She stared at the sky before plunging into her problem. "I imagine you deal with all sorts of family issues as a detective."

He stared at her with a blank expression and folded his arms. "A fair amount. Why?"

"How should I introduce you to Penny and Easton?"

His back stiffened, and then he shrugged. "Detective Jason Virtue, but they can call me Jase."

"Here's the problem. They don't know about

Keith." She scuffed the dirt with her work boot, unsure of whether her frustration lay with her half brother or herself.

"What do you mean?" That stony expression didn't change. "You've never mentioned Yablonsky before? And no one in town has ever mentioned your brother in front of them?"

"Why would Keith come up in casual conversation? He's not someone you discuss with a child." Was it that wrong to want to protect them a little longer? Especially when no one had ever protected her from the glares or cold shoulders.

"I see." His somber voice proved he was giving her problem some consideration.

Before they could discuss it further, the yellow school bus lumbered into view as she tried to find the words for everything she needed to explain. Jase. The new security system. Keith.

She fidgeted next to the mailbox, unsure of how to broach any of these subjects. Somehow she'd have to toe a fine line so Penny and Easton would stay on their guard while not staying up all night with nightmares shattering any chance of sleep.

The bus arrived, and her pair flounced down the steps. The door closed, and Penny flew into her arms for a massive hug, which Cassie delivered while watching Easton run around the mailbox after spending forty-five minutes on the school bus.

"Mommy," Penny squealed, separating from

her. "I got a gold star for reading aloud in class. I knew all the words."

Not to be outdone, Easton came over and tugged on Cassie's windbreaker. "I can count to twenty."

Then they must have noticed Jase as they both turned in his direction.

"Who are you?" Penny asked.

The wind picked up and swirled around them. A strong gust blew Penny's brown hair all around her head. The skies grew darker by the minute, the tops of the trees swaying, leaves falling to the ground. The impending storm must be gaining intensity.

"I'll tell you when we get inside," Cassie said.

Together they trekked past the farmstand, past the hoophouses to the farmhouse. Big fat drops of rain splattered onto them as they raced into the living room. Penny and Easton laughed until their gazes fell on Jase who was taking off his suit jacket. Jase's phone rang, and he talked for a few minutes. No sooner did he end the call, but a text alert pinged, and his fingers flew across the screen.

Penny folded her arms and scrutinized Jase with a critical eye. "It's rude to be on your phone all the time."

"Penelope Anne!" Cassie stood behind her and placed her arms around Penny's shoulders and hugged her. "Remember your manners."

"But, Mommy, his phone's more 'portant than us, and you've always said that's wrong," Easton defended Penny, and Cassie sighed at her own words coming back at her.

Dread about this conversation welled inside Cassie. They were so young, standing there, Penny in her rainbow leggings and pink glittery shirt and Easton in his jeans that were rolled up at the ends so he could grow into them this year.

She winced but knew it was better the truth came from her rather than some busybody in town. She should know that from way back when. Eight years ago, several people crossed the street when they saw her coming while others called her names to her face. That was when she put Operation Redeem Cassie into effect, to much avail until now.

Penny and Easton were waiting, and Cassie drew on her reserve of strength. "This is De—"

"I'm Jase," he interrupted and smiled at her children. He pocketed his phone and loosened his tie. "I'll be helping your mother with the farmwork for the next few days."

Cassie had to hand it to Jase. While evasive, he'd taken Penny and Easton's feelings and innocence into account for his explanation. Being a parent at the best of times was easy; times like these tested her mettle. Still, she knew what she wanted to pass on to Penny and Easton: simple things like satisfaction in a hard day's work, the thrill of eating a carrot fresh from the garden and always taking care of one another.

"Then why are you wearing a suit?" Penny asked, her question pulling Cassie out of her thoughts. "Mommy doesn't let me wear my best dress to collect the eggs."

"I wanted to make a good impression." Jase was quick with his comeback. "It's nice to look your best for an interview."

Cassie felt rather self-conscious in her work clothes, but the horses and chickens had never complained about her overalls and long-sleeve shirt. "And Jase made an impression on me." True words, as he was most intent on finding Keith and apparently the money Jase indicated might be hidden on her farm. She doubted that. She'd have found it by now, especially after clearing out all the junk to make room for the vegetable stand and prep area. Fortunately, she'd found good uses for anything salvageable. "I'm thankful to have help with the harvest."

Although whether he'd be working alongside her or merely disturbing her hard-fought peace was still to be determined.

"You don't look like a farmer." Penny narrowed her eyes and studied him long and hard. "Are you dating my mommy?"

Cassie's jaw dropped, and heat flooded her face. One glance at Jase proved he was equally surprised by the question. She suspected that was a first.

Cassie rushed to correct Penny's misconception. "He's not my boyfriend." She knelt in front of her children, grasping their small hands in hers. "Trust me. Jase and I are not a couple."

"I'm not dating your mother." Jase's strong voice echoed in the living room.

Cassie frowned. He didn't have to deny it that vehemently.

The pitter-patter of rain became a full torrent hitting the window and pounding the roof—a little like the tension headache forming at everything happening in her life.

"Chores can wait until the storm passes. Do you have homework?"

Penny grumbled about some math word problems. Easton started gloating that he never had homework, so Cassie insisted he read his picture book while she made dinner.

With the children occupied in the living room, Jase followed Cassie into the kitchen. He picked up a carrot she'd harvested this afternoon, munched on it and grinned. "I love snacking on carrots." Then he grew serious and glanced over her shoulder as if ensuring only Cassie could hear him. "Because of the storm, the security company is coming tomorrow morning. Captain Shields texted me there are no substantiated leads regarding Keith's whereabouts."

"Thanks for the update." She cut up onions and turnips, fresh from the field, and added some balsamic vinegar and olive oil before setting them to roast in the oven. "I know I have to tell them, but I'm trying to find the right words."

"Sometimes your presence is more important than the words." He removed his tie and rolled up his shirtsleeves, exposing tanned and muscular arms. “What can I do to help?”

Catch Keith before I have to tell Penny and Easton everything. She blew out a deep breath. Even if Keith was back in jail tonight, she owed it to her children to tell them before they found out about their uncle from someone in Violet Ridge.

“Wash the lettuce for the salad?” she asked.

He nodded as she moved on to chopping up a cucumber.

He finished his task, then excused himself to take a phone call in the mudroom, the rain still pouring outside. He returned as a bolt of thunder clapped overhead.

Seconds later, Penny and Easton hugged her sides, seeking comfort, which she lavished before returning to meal prep. Still, Penny and Easton weren’t their bright, bubbly selves. Had someone in town already mentioned their uncle and his escape to them? Not likely. They would have inundated her with questions about Keith.

Before she could ask what was wrong, Jase pulled her aside and asked to speak with her alone. She sent Penny and Easton to wash up for dinner, and Jase waited until they were out of earshot.

“I have to investigate a tip about Yablonsky. So please, stay alert.” He gave her his number. “If you hear any strange noises, call me right away.”

“Of course.” She texted him, verifying she had the correct number before he took his leave. She nodded her farewell and mixed the salad. This fiasco might be over as soon as tonight if Keith was recaptured.

After Jase departed, Penny and Easton acted more like themselves. Once they finished dinner, Cassie checked to see that the rain had relented enough for her and Penny to gather eggs from the henhouse. Easton wasn't happy about having to go with them, but Cassie wasn't about to leave him by himself with a chance that Keith was still on the loose.

Normally, Cassie loved this time of day on the farm when everything was winding down. She often slipped onto the front porch with a cup of tea, the door propped open in case either child needed her. Tonight, though, the shadows may be hiding someone she once held dear to her heart.

A pair of headlights blinded her until the car was close enough that she recognized Jase's sedan.

Easton grasped her hand. "Who's that?"

"It's Jase." Cassie took care so as not to break any of the eggs in the basket.

"Why is he back tonight instead of tomorrow when we're at school?" Penny asked, her steps slowing until she halted altogether.

Cassie's chest heaved at Penny's observation. She and Jase had only clarified that he'd be working at the farm, which was the truth, but not that he'd be sleeping in their grandmother's room.

Before she could explain, Easton gave a startled grunt and released her hand, falling face-first into the mud.

Quickly, Cassie placed the basket of eggs on the ground. "Are you hurt?"

Easton's grin was her answer. He picked himself up and sent a joyful look at the mud. "I want to do that again!"

"No, sir." She reached for his hand, now covered in grimy gunk. "Penny, please carry the basket inside."

Jase approached, and her children assumed a somber attitude, as if she'd canceled Halloween. Cassie watched as his gaze processed Easton's muddy shirt and jeans with an arched eyebrow. She gripped her son's hand. "He needs a bath."

"Looks that way," Jase agreed.

They proceeded back to the house. Her curiosity was piqued about the tip he had left to investigate, but she held back from asking in front of the kids.

Once Easton was splashing in the bathtub with bubbles surrounding him and Penny was picking out her clothes to wear to school tomorrow, Cassie retrieved fresh sheets and blankets from the linen closet. "I'll make your bed and then head to the stable for my nightly chores once the kids are done with their baths."

Jase accepted the linens, and her hand brushed his. No wedding ring. Either he wasn't married, or he didn't wear his ring while he was on a case.

She winced. What was she doing taking note of that detail?

"I can do it. I've made my own bed for years."

Cassie showed the detective his temporary quarters and could no longer contain herself. "Was that a valid tip? Do you have any idea where Keith is now?"

Jase gave a curt shake of his head. "The information didn't pan out." He laid the sheets on the bed and peered at the hallway. "Where are the other bedrooms?"

"On the other side of the house. This was my mother's room, and you'll have privacy for whatever police matters come up." And she'd have a little distance from the man who was disturbing her routine and her inner core, more than she'd care to admit.

She returned to the other side of the house, and Easton emerged from the bathroom. Mud was still caked behind his ears. Cassie plugged the drain with plenty of water still in the tub. She sent her son to finish his bath while she cleaned the kitchen.

Jase joined her, and she checked her watch. "I need to tend to the horses, Patches and the other animals. Can you watch over Penny and Easton?"

His swift intake of breath gave her pause. "There've been no sightings of Yablonsky, and I don't like the idea of you being out there in the dark by yourself."

Someone was concerned about her. She was touched, especially since he didn't hold her connection to Keith against her. "It has to be me. The horses and other animals know me. I promise I have bear spray, and I've taken self-defense classes."

Jase seemed as if he was about to say something else, but he only nodded. "Keep your phone close."

Penny and Easton appeared, all fresh and clean in their pajamas, books in hand for bedtime stories. Her heart tugged at missing out on this important time, and she lifted her gaze to Jase. Thank goodness he was here. "Jase will read to you."

He looked petrified for a second before reaching for the books. "All part of the job."

Cassie excused herself and slipped out the front door with a firm grip on her canister of bear spray.

Somewhere out there, Keith posed a threat to others, but she was determined he wouldn't hurt anything she held dear again. Not long after the news of the bank robbery, her beloved father passed away in front of her. A massive heart attack had claimed him instantly.

She wouldn't let Keith near enough to hurt anyone else in her family.

CHAPTER TWO

WITH DAWN APPROACHING, Jase closed the bedroom door behind him, intent on performing another security check of the perimeter, the same as he had three hours ago. Earlier, he'd had to cut his first one short to duck into a maintenance shed during the worst of a severe storm. The bracing wind and diagonal rain made visibility next to nothing. If Yablonsky was hiding at the farm, he'd be inside and out of the elements. On that note, Jase had returned to bed.

Now, he grasped his flashlight and headed toward the front door with the barn and stable atop his list of places to check by himself so the O'Neal family could start their day without him getting in their way.

Before he turned the knob, voices greeted him. He sniffed and closed his eyes at the aroma of fresh coffee, not the inky stuff at the precinct.

"Jase? Is that you?" Cassie's voice came from the other direction.

He left the flashlight by the door and entered the kitchen, a bustling hive of activity. Cassie stood at the counter, already dressed for work in jeans and a flannel shirt, chopping up broccoli.

"Would you like some of the vegetable scramble? Everything's farm fresh right down to the basil." Her smile was as bright as the noonday sun.

Something inside Jase pinged with guilt about eating her food and staying in her house with the sole intent of implicating her in Yablonsky's robbery. "Thank you, but I have to search..."

"Search for what?" Easton asked, clambering away from the breakfast nook and peering at Jase with wide eyes.

He caught Cassie's expression pleading with him not to divulge anything more to Easton. Guarding his words was something Jase was used to doing at the station but not so much in someone's kitchen, the cornerstone of most homes. Thinking of the good times at the dude ranch, he vowed to visit his family later today. Then he'd determine if it was time to bridge the past and the present.

"Search for my belt buckle." Jase tried to smile. When he couldn't crack one, he headed to the coffeepot and looked around for a cup.

Cassie handed him a large blue stoneware mug. "Thanks for the save."

Jase noticed she didn't ask whether Yablonsky had been apprehended overnight. Was that because she knew he was still in hiding? Or perhaps she simply believed Jase would have awakened her had Yablonsky been captured. That was a reasonable explanation, he thought, as he poured his first cup of coffee, a much needed pick-me-up. "After this, I'll check to see if the hail damaged your crops."

"That can wait until daybreak when they board the bus. Penny should be back any minute with the eggs for the scramble." Cassie checked her watch and frowned. "Where is she?"

"You let her outside by herself?" The hair on the back of Jase's neck prickled, and he rushed to the door with Cassie and Easton on his heels.

"You don't think…" Cassie's voice was full of pain, more than he'd expected from someone who was in cahoots with a convicted felon.

Even if Easton wasn't in the room, Jase wouldn't have told her what he thought. He kept what he'd seen in his worst cases to himself. Jaded Jase, that was him in a nutshell. Some nights he fell into bed, exhausted, waiting for sleep to bring an elusive peace. Too often, the screams in his nightmares would wake him.

Much as another scream had changed his life and the lives of everyone at the Lazy River Dude Ranch in an instant.

"I'll check on her by myself." He headed for the mudroom exit.

"I'm coming with you. So is Easton." Cassie followed him, the screen door creaking behind her.

The rain had ceased, and the first traces of the autumn dawn peeked over the Rocky Mountains. Streaks of purple and pink were overtaking the gray and promised a better day ahead. A stiff breeze brought a nip of fall to the air. Soon the first frost would be upon them, and hail would give way to snow measured in feet rather than inches.

His heart rate skyrocketed as he closed the distance between the house and chicken coop. Seconds later, he breathed a sigh of relief as he heard Penny murmuring soft words to one of the hens. While no harm had befallen Penny, he couldn't say the same about the henhouse. Thanks to the storm, a large oak branch had split the henhouse in half, leaving the roof in a state of disrepair.

Cassie's gasp came from behind, and she hurried to survey the damage.

"Easton, go back to the house. Bring back the lantern and the old towels from the mudroom." Cassie delivered instructions with the efficiency of a staff sergeant.

"I'll go with him." Jase didn't want Easton going into the house by himself.

"Grab a mop, too," she called out. "Please."

Jase stifled a laugh at Cassie remembering her manners in the midst of bedlam. So far she seemed to be the same sweet person she was in high school. Could he and Shields have drawn the wrong conclusion about Cassie being Yablonsky's accomplice? But the cellmate had been emphatic about *C* and the money being hidden at Thistle Brook Farm.

Jase pushed his doubts aside and set out for the mudroom, keeping his guard up in case Yablonsky surfaced. He could come looking for food if he believed everyone was out of the house for a period of time.

Jase and Easton entered the mudroom. To Jase's relief, there was no sign of Yablonsky. Jase gathered the supplies and reached for the box at the same time as Easton.

"I can carry it." Easton puffed out his chest.

Jase didn't want to discourage the young boy. "How about we do it together?"

Easton grinned, and they delivered the supplies to the henhouse where the soft light of morning emphasized the full extent of the damage.

While they were gone, Cassie had found a shovel. With a determined look, she was transferring sodden wood shavings into a trash bin. Penny was doing her best to cheer up the hens, some of whom were gathered together in a tight cluster.

He and Easton set the box on the ground while a most unusual compunction came over him. For some reason, he wanted to comfort Cassie and give her a hug. Yet she was doing fine on her own. Capable and determined, Cassie was demonstrating a sense of resilience, something that reminded him of the strong women in his family. The urge to hug her passed.

"How can I help?" Jase asked.

Suddenly, another hen peeked out of the coop, her dark mahogany feathers plastered to her side.

"Blossom! You're alive!" Penny's relief was evident, and she went to her mother. "Is she okay?"

"Probably just scared," Cassie reassured her

daughter with a smile as she shoveled another scoop of wet wood shavings into the bin.

The brown hen emerged from the henhouse, and she did look as though she was traumatized. Jase couldn't blame Blossom one bit for feeling that way after the storm upended her existence.

"You're safe now." Jase blinked. The words had come from his mouth.

Blossom must have approved of him as she flattened herself on the ground in front of him.

Jase glanced at Cassie for guidance.

She stuck the shovel in the trodden dirt and leaned on the end. "Blossom wants you to pick her up."

"Huh?" While Jase and Seth had tended to the horses at the dude ranch, his siblings Daisy and Crosby had been assigned to chicken duty. His knowledge of hens was sparse at best, to the point of practically being nonexistent. "I didn't think hens liked to be held."

Cassie let out a laugh and shook her head. "On the contrary. Blossom is a speckled Sussex. She must have liked the sound of your voice and decided you're trustworthy. She's quite sweet and likes attention."

Unlike Jase, who preferred for others to take the spotlight.

Cassie motioned for him to hold out his arms. "Give her a cuddle."

Of all the ways he imagined himself waking up this morning when he left for Violet Ridge yesterday, cuddling a hen on Thistle Brook Farm wouldn't have even made the top thousand. Yet it was sort of nice having a hen in his arms.

"Everything will be all right," he murmured while stroking her feathers. Blossom seemed to take comfort from his touch. To his surprise, more hens came over to him while a bemused smile came over Cassie. "Who'd have guessed my new hired help is a hen whisperer?"

Penny joined them. For the first time, Jase thought he saw a slight glimmer of admiration in the young girl's eyes. She faced her mom. "Can Easton and I stay home today so we can help you?"

Easton made the group complete. "I don't want the chickens to feel sad about their home." Then he puffed his chest. "Penny and I are good helpers."

"Nice try, but no. You have to go to school today." Cassie checked her watch, and Jase saw the glimmer of a gold bracelet next to it. "The bus will be here soon, so we need to finish breakfast. Jase and I will repair the henhouse later this morning."

Seemed as though his muscles would be getting a different kind of workout while he was here.

"But..." Penny, obviously recognizing her protest as a lost cause, glared at Jase. "I get time with Blossom when I'm home from school." She gave him a look as if he was stealing her best friend.

One minute he was a hen whisperer, and the next he was a hen stealer.

Wait until he had to arrest Penny's mother.

At the fence, Cassie glanced over her shoulder.

"Blossom is probably okay by now if you want to eat breakfast with us."

Jase lowered himself to sit on the ground, taking care with Blossom resting in his arms. "I'll give her a few more minutes, just to be on the safe side." At that moment, two hens rested on either side of him. As long as they didn't follow him back to Denver, he'd be fine.

"I'll have breakfast waiting for you."

Cassie's children grumbled about school but followed her to the house.

Once they were out of view, Jase reached into his pocket for his phone, trying not to disturb Blossom. The hen was finally calming down. With some effort, Jase held the phone carefully until he was connected to Captain Shields. Perhaps Shields would recall Jase to Denver and replace him with an officer with more farming experience.

Then again, if Shields ordered him back to Denver, Jase wouldn't be here to protect Cassie and her children. Was that a sign he was beginning to believe in her innocence?

Before he had a chance to ponder this possibility, Shields came on the line. "Any sign of Yablonsky?" Shields could always be counted on for his direct approach.

"No, but I have updates about his sister, um, half sister." Preciseness mattered, and Jase prided himself on his attention to detail.

"If it's progress, good. Our tipline is flooded with even more phone calls this morning. So far, most have been dead ends, same as last night." Shields stopped talking, and Jase knew him too well. He waited as Shields barked orders to someone at the precinct before returning to the line. "Update me about Thistle Brook Farm."

"She's given me full roam of the place." Jase hesitated. "I'm not sure my being here is the best use of resources."

"I hear uncertainty in your voice, so I'll reassure you. No one else in Yablonsky's life matches the cellmate's physical description of the accomplice, and no one in Denver has your connection to Violet Ridge." Shields restated what Jase already knew.

Jase held Blossom a bit tighter. "I'll review what I know. She's good at finding excuses to be by herself." Like last night when she tended the horses. That wiggle of doubt was enough for Jase to suspect Cassie once more. "I'm presently outside near the henhouse while she's inside the house with her children."

Shields told him to wait again, then grunted. "I have a breaking development. A trucker hauled a hitchhiker southwest of Denver before the alerts were issued. Hold on." Shields spoke to someone in the office with him. No doubt his boss was examining the map pinned to the wall and doing math in his head.

Blossom finally tired of Jase's arms, and he let her go. Within seconds, she was pecking at the ground as if her whole world was secure again.

Was his presence part of it? Or was she a resilient little hen who would have been fine without his comfort?

Jase stood and wiped the dirt off his jeans. He preferred the formality of his suit and tie, but while undercover, he had to fit in on the farm. Walking over to the fence, he surveyed the property. Nothing untoward caught his ear or eye. Jase itched to return to Denver and be more active in the search. The sidelines had never suited him, but being a good teammate was a necessity in his line of work.

Personally? He'd decided a long time ago that it was best to keep his distance from his family. He'd caused them pain once before. He'd do anything to spare them more heartache. Yet was staying away only hurting all of them?

When Shields returned to the line, he had nothing new to report. Jase filled him in on everything else from Violet Ridge. "The security system will be installed today."

Shields signed off, and Jase pocketed his phone. He turned to examine the branch and the gaping hole in the henhouse roof. Without repairs, there'd be nothing to protect the hens from the elements. They'd already endured enough. Especially Blossom.

Hadn't he seen some tarps and tools in the maintenance shed during his rounds? Later, Jase would have a talk with Cassie about how easy it was to enter every building. Locks and security were crucial in reducing the risk of harm. Life had enough risk without bringing misfortune where it could be prevented.

With a lingering look toward the farmhouse, Jase headed for the shed. The sooner he covered the roof with a tarp, the sooner he could begin repairs. He stopped at the fence and glanced thoughtfully at the henhouse.

Yablonsky's cellmate said the bank stash was hidden at the farm. Yablonsky wouldn't have hidden money where chickens could peck at it, would he?

Jase wouldn't be surprised at all if he did. Finally, there was a silver lining to this storm.

DESPITE HER CHILDREN grumbling that they wanted to stay home and help with the henhouse repairs, they accompanied Cassie to their bus stop. This morning, given the henhouse catastrophe, wasn't the right time to tell them about Keith and his escape. For one thing, Penny would have questions about why Cassie had never mentioned her half brother to them before. For another, they'd need her solace after such a major revelation.

Once Penny and Easton were on the bus, Cassie let out a big sigh of relief. They'd be safe at school. Maybe that was a sign she should send them to Florida until Keith was apprehended. Her mother loved them, and nothing bad would befall them under Mom's careful eye.

Was it selfish of Cassie to keep them here?

They wouldn't miss anything crucial if she sent them away.

But Jase had promised he'd do everything in his power to keep them safe.

The pros and cons swirled in her mind until the tension squeezed her brain, the tendrils of a headache extending to full branches.

She detoured away from the house where aspirin waited and instead headed to the maintenance shed for the tools to repair the henhouse. Thanks to her father, her carpentry skills were passable. Of course, repairing the roof would come at the expense of baking loaves of fresh apple bread and pumpkin muffins this afternoon to sell at the farmstand tomorrow. Henhouse repairs, followed by tending the horses and harvesting more of her kale crop, would be all she could manage today. It was a shame. Several customers made a special trip to the farm for her fall goodies.

Yet she had to put the hens first. Blossom and company were dear to her heart. The farm animals had provided comfort after the tumultuous events eight years ago caught her off guard.

Her head throbbed at remembering how Keith's robbery, Dad's passing and Mom's move all came so close together. No wonder she'd fallen for Brayden during that stressful period.

Now everything was closing in again. Would her customers stop coming to the farmstand once news of Keith's escape spread around Violet Ridge?

Cassie slid open the door to the shed and gasped.

Her stomach tumbled, and she forced herself not to empty her breakfast into the bushes.

Someone had been here. Her gaze went to the shelves and did a quick inventory. A wheelbarrow was gone. So were a couple of blue tarps and several tools, namely her hammer and wrench.

Keith must have done this. How close had he been to Penny this morning?

Should she call Jase and tell him? Or should she find the officer on patrol and let him signal the alarm?

Her heart raced, and fear took over. Sprinting out of the shed, she hurried to the house where Jase would be eating breakfast right about now.

Running into to her kitchen, she immediately saw Jase's untouched plate of food. She knocked on the guest bedroom door, but there was no answer. With trepidation, she entered, only to find the bed meticulously made. She sniffed, the orangey scent of furniture polish greeting her nose. Somehow, Jase had found enough time to dust the room and leave it immaculate, but there was no sign of his actual presence.

Had Keith hurt yet another person?

She closed the door and took a deep breath, her headache throbbing. Jase had to be alive and well, for his family's sake and Blossom's.

The hen! He couldn't still be holding the scared chicken, could he? She was about to leave the house when she turned and grabbed his breakfast. He'd need something in his stomach when he sent up the alert that Keith was here at the farm.

Cassie arrived at the henhouse and almost dropped the plate of cold vegetable scramble. Her blue tarp covered the damaged roof, and Jase was atop a ladder with a tape measure. The wheelbarrow was close by with her toolbox beside it.

"Cassie?" Jase snapped the tape measure shut and started down the ladder. "Something's wrong. Did Yablonsky contact you?"

Taking care with his breakfast, she entered the enclosure. Some hens pecked the ground while others headed over to investigate her presence. Her heartbeat returned to normal.

"Nothing's wrong now." She extended the plate toward him. "This is for you."

He dropped the tape measure next to the toolbox and sampled some of her vegetable scramble. "This sure beats most of the fare I eat while I work. It's delicious. Thank you." He took another mouthful and chewed slowly, seeming to appreciate the taste, albeit the food had cooled. "What did you mean by nothing's wrong now?"

Another deep breath, anything to try to prevent him from seeing her tremble. "I went to the maintenance shed and found some items missing." Her fears poured out of her. "Then I ran to the farmhouse looking for you."

Cassie gave up any pretense of sounding composed and unaffected by the entire situation. Her half brother was on the run. If Jase's information was correct, Keith had hidden the bank robbery money somewhere on the farm. How had he gained access to the property? Why had he chosen this month to escape? It didn't make much sense. With the unpredictable weather looming, surely it would only complicate his chances of recovering the cash and making a speedy getaway

"Cassie?" Jase's voice sounded like he was in a tunnel.

Cassie's legs wobbled.

Jase emptied the wheelbarrow and flipped it as if it weighed nothing. He led her by the elbow until they leaned against the wheelbarrow.

"Thank you," she said. Cassie glanced at him, his reassuring presence exactly what she needed. "I thought Keith was the one who'd taken the tarp and tools. When I couldn't find you, I worried something had happened to you."

More like Keith had happened to him. The thought of that impacted her more than she'd have liked.

A flicker of surprise came over his face. "The security company should be here soon. That should give you more peace of mind." A muscle in his jaw popped out before he reached for the plate of food once more. "We need to secure the buildings on the property."

Located ten miles from Violet Ridge, she'd never had reason before now to do so. However, Keith was a mighty powerful reason.

"I'm glad you're okay." Cassie moved away

from the wheelbarrow and buttoned her coat, the nip of the fall air passing through the thick fabric, going down deep to her bones. "Just because we told Penny and Easton you're my new hired hand doesn't mean you really work here. You can go and perform your actual job duties. I'll handle the roof."

"Grandma Bridget would have a few choice words if I didn't help you." He motioned with the fork toward the henhouse. "Besides, you are my job right now. I'm here to protect you and your family. Chickens included." He grinned but then sobered quickly, as if he'd caught himself doing something he shouldn't.

Scanning the henhouse again, she admitted this was a pressing matter. His help repairing it before the weather changed again would make things much easier to handle.

"Many hands make light work." One of her mother's favorite phrases. "I'll examine the interior joists while you eat. Then we can take off the tarp and see how many shingles we'll need for the roof repair. The coop's in good shape, considering it's eight years old."

The smell inside the henhouse was musty, but she welcomed the distraction. Protective and confident, Jase was getting past her defenses, and she couldn't risk falling into the same pattern of forcing a relationship during a stressful time. Brayden had broken her heart, and she was determined it would take more than a man being useful and steady for her to trust again, to fall in love again.

Of course, Jase wasn't Brayden. She'd known Jase was special in high school. He always treated everyone, from freshmen to seniors, with respect even if he did seem a touch unapproachable. And now? Seeing Blossom on his lap changed that impression. Anyone who could comfort a hen was okay in her book. Even if that someone had the power to send her half brother back to jail.

She just had to take care and treat Jase the same way she'd treat a resident of Violet Ridge, rather than as a hen whisperer who could possibly take her heart with him back to Denver.

"How's everything look in there?" He popped his head inside the entrance to the henhouse.

She rotated her flashlight toward the roof. It would take some time to sand the area where the wood had splintered. "I'll fix this damage before I replace the shingles on the roof." She flicked off the flashlight and stepped back outside.

Cassie almost bumped into him. This close, he seemed less official and more human in jeans and a flannel shirt. In fact, Jase almost blended in. She reached out and brushed a dark brown feather off his shirt. There was something endearing about a man with a chicken feather hanging off of him.

He watched the feather float to the ground and groaned. "Can you do me a favor?"

Considering he was protecting her children, he

could ask for the moon and she'd get it for him. "Of course. Anything. What is it?"

"Can you not tell Seth and my family that I've discovered my true calling as a hen whisperer?" He plucked another feather off his jeans.

She laughed, perhaps for the first time since she found out Keith had escaped. "Your secret is safe with me." She took a step back and almost rammed into the henhouse. "This is a bigger job than I first thought. Also, I need to check on my three horses."

Jase assessed the henhouse and then looked back at her. "I'll work here while you tend to the horses. The security system crew will be here soon. With so many people around, you'll be safe."

One look at him convinced her he was right. "Am I taking you away from your official duties?"

He glanced at the henhouse once more. "Not at all."

If he fixed the henhouse, she might just have enough time to bake homemade goods to sell at the farmstand tomorrow.

"First, I'll show you where I store the roof shingles. Follow me." She motioned for him to walk alongside her. "I don't know what I'd have done without you this morning."

"You'd have managed." Blossom followed Jase, but he shut the gate before she could escape, bringing a second laugh from Cassie in almost as many minutes.

Maybe having Jase here wouldn't be so bad after all.

"Not nearly as well." She pointed toward the other side of the farm. "I keep the shingles in the barn."

"So Patches and I will meet again."

She liked his dry sense of humor. "If you two become best buddies, I'll keep it a secret from Blossom."

"Secrets seem to be adding up around here." His voice grew stiff as a gray cloud obscured the sun.

"Only small ones." She wouldn't even have classified her joke as a secret. "Those are okay in my book."

They were almost at the barn when he began to outpace her. "Let me go first."

Her heart racing yet again, she watched as Jase went inside the structure before coming out and giving the all-clear. What would she have done if Keith had been inside? She shuddered at the mere thought. "Thank you."

"Just doing my job."

A job. That was what this was to him, and she'd do well to remember that.

Brayden had arrived in town as a tourist and stayed longer than anticipated. His sudden proposal swept her off her feet. Unfortunately, their marriage had been a disaster from start to finish, and Brayden took off for Alaska when the urge to become a bush pilot struck him.

Jase was here for his job, not for his family, not

for her. He hadn't even known she was Cassie O'Neal now.

Jase wanted one thing and one thing only: to find Keith and return him to jail. She hoped he was as good at being a detective as he was at comforting hens. In that case, Keith would soon be behind bars, and she'd have a good night's sleep before the next time she opened her farmstand.

JASE PARKED HIS sedan in the family parking lot of the Lazy River Dude Ranch and grabbed the basket of freshly picked kale and homemade apple bread Cassie sent with him. She wouldn't hear of him going home empty-handed.

He traversed the familiar trails, the sights as comforting as his grandmother's knitted sweaters. The silver aspens swayed slightly in the balmy breeze, which gave no hint of yesterday's deluge but carried the whinnies of the mustangs his way. Jase nodded at passing guests, the mainstay of the dude ranch.

Jase considered stopping at the duck pond to collect himself, but he recognized he was stalling. He quelled his nerves and stepped inside the ranch lobby, basket in hand. He made a beeline for the library where his grandmother held her knitting lessons.

"Excuse me." A voice called from the front desk. "You can't go back there."

Jase froze, backtracked and took off his sunglasses. He smiled at the older woman who guarded the entrance. "I'm expected."

"No one informed me about this." The woman reached for the phone. "Registered guests and family only."

The message punched him in the gut. Jase had stayed away longer than he'd realized if a recent hire didn't know him. He glanced at her employee lanyard, keeping his smile intact. "Hello, Kelly. I'm Jase Virtue." He moved the basket to his left hand and extended his other toward her. "I'm Bridget and Martin's grandson."

Her eyes widened, and she grimaced as they shook hands. "Now that you mention it, I see the family resemblance. You weren't supposed to be here until dinnertime."

He hurried to set her at ease. "I wanted to surprise Grandma Bridget." And he was able to, thanks to the Violet Ridge Police Department, who had sent out an officer to patrol Thistle Brook Farm in his absence.

A dog started barking, and Jase could wait no longer to enter the library.

Sitting behind the long table was his grandmother, knitting purple socks and chatting with his older sister Daisy. A pair of Australian shepherds, Hap and Trixie, reclined at their feet.

Glancing up at Jase's entrance, Grandma Bridget gasped and laid down her knitting needles, grasping the head of the cane resting against the table.

She reached him in no time, tears glistening on her cheeks.

Jase laid the basket on the table where the dogs wouldn't snatch the contents and embraced her.

Even though new wrinkles lined Grandma Bridget's face, her hug hadn't changed a bit. Jase closed his eyes and inhaled the floral scent of her perfume. She only came up to his shoulder, but Grandma Bridget had a mighty big presence. No matter how far away from the Lazy River Dude Ranch he ventured, he'd never forgotten the firmness of her loving embrace.

How he had needed it the year after the accident when the future was so uncertain. His mother's brother had wanted to split up the four siblings, but his grandparents ensured they stayed together, raising them here on the ranch. Jase wouldn't be the man he was today without Grandma Bridget.

He opened his eyes to find his sister standing behind her grandmother. He moved to escape from his grandmother's hug, but she held on a second longer. She raised her trembling hands and cupped his face. "You've stayed away too long this time, Jason Virtue."

Grandma Bridget stepped aside to give Daisy a chance to welcome Jase home. "I keep forgetting how tall you are, Jase," Daisy said. "You have to get here more often. You won't recognize Rosie, Aspen and Lily. They've grown at least a foot since my wedding to Ben."

After Daisy's greeting, Hap and Trixie joined

in the reception before his grandmother slipped her hand in his.

"You look more like your father every day." Grandma Bridget smiled wistfully before chuckling. "Peter had your grandfather's personality but my nose."

Guilt twisted Jase's stomach as he remembered why he didn't visit more often. Everywhere he turned, there were reminders that he'd survived the crash that his parents had not.

Before he could get in another word, his grandfather made an appearance, and Jase found his grandfather's arms as strong as ever when the two of them embraced. Grandpa Martin left Jase and joined his wife at her side. "You know there's a police station in Violet Ridge. Hiring, too."

Jase held up his hands. "Not looking to change positions. There's a good chance I'll be the youngest captain in my precinct's history."

His grandfather grinned. "That's our boy, Bridge." Jase never tired of hearing his grandfather call his grandmother by that nickname.

With that, the ice was broken. Stories flowed during dinner as he and his siblings and grandparents feasted on steak and kale salad thanks to Cassie's contribution.

As hard as it was to break away, Jase took his leave.

"Let me walk you to your car," Grandpa Martin offered.

"No need to do that, Grandpa."

His grandfather insisted, and Jase braced himself for whatever his grandfather had to say to him. He didn't have to wait long.

"Cassie's had a hard time what with her brother's crimes and all."

Jase startled at Grandpa Martin's statement. He'd expected another pitch for why Jase should relocate to Violet Ridge or a polite rebuke about Jase's self-imposed separation, but not about his purpose for coming to town. He treaded carefully, wanting to keep the department's suspicions about Cassie to himself. "Yablonsky will be back in prison soon."

"Next time bring Cassie and her kids to dinner. They're nice folk."

Jase clenched his jaw while the delicious dinner churned in his stomach. One way or another, Jase would get to the bottom of Cassie O'Neal's involvement in the bank robbery. He punched his key fob, unlocking the car, and then looked at his grandfather.

Calmness and trust resided in every wrinkle and crevice. Grandpa Martin was as sure of his pronouncement about Cassie as he was that the sun would rise in the east in the morning. His grandfather had been wrong in a scant few instances, but he was a wise judge of character.

Could he be right about Cassie?

Jase relaxed and opened his car door. "That will depend on the case."

His grandfather pulled Jase in for another hug.

"I love you, Jase. Don't be a stranger." Then he walked away, tucking his hands in his pockets, whistling a jaunty tune.

Tonight had been wonderful, a real homecoming. But while Jase would love to reintegrate into the Virtue family, he couldn't.

His family was loving and forgiving, but how would they react if they learned the truth about what Jase had remembered after a random car accident that occurred while he was training at the police academy? His grandparents and siblings all knew the official police account of the accident that had stolen his parents from them, but they didn't have the whole story. For his sake and theirs, he'd chosen to keep his distance so they wouldn't stop loving him…like he feared they would if they ever learned of his contribution to the fatal crash.

While they might surprise him like he'd surprised Grandma Bridget today, he couldn't take that risk.

CHAPTER THREE

ANOTHER TWENTY-FOUR HOURS had passed without any Yablonsky sightings, and the farm was now fitted with a new security system. The sun was shining directly overhead as Jase hammered the last of the shingles on the henhouse roof, another blister chafing his skin. Muscles he hadn't used in years and forgotten he possessed ached. Grandpa Martin would say he'd grown soft if an honest day's work on a farm caused this much discomfort.

At last, Jase set the hammer down and inspected the repair. The henhouse was as good as new. Still, he couldn't ignore that quiver of disappointment about not finding the money.

When Cassie had mentioned the henhouse's age, he'd almost gasped and wondered if Yablonsky had stored the money inside the walls with his capture imminent. Yesterday evening, Jase searched for any sign of the cash to no avail. It wasn't hidden in the roof or walls. He'd even used a metal detector in case Yablonsky had buried it in a steel box.

Jase would have to get inventive in his search, just as the trackers were having to use ingenuity in their search for Yablonsky. The hotline had received over a hundred calls with tips about Yablonsky's whereabouts. Most of them had been discredited, except for the truck driver. Fingerprint analysis confirmed the driver delivered Yablonsky to Pueblo where they'd parted ways. While the driver continued on to Albuquerque, it was as if the convict vanished into thin air after that.

Why had Shields ordered Jase to Violet Ridge? He could be of more use in Denver. After all, he'd been part of the original case as one of the responding officers to the Flying Bison Bank mere months after he graduated from the police academy. That robbery had been one of the cases that spurred him to become a detective, earning his bachelor's degree online and then passing the exam three years ago.

Yet Shields, convinced Yablonsky was heading to Thistle Brook Farm, insisted Jase remain in Violet Ridge.

At least Jase was no longer working alone. The Violet Ridge Police Department had sent another officer to patrol the perimeter. He'd arrived an hour before Amanda, who was helping Cassie with the farmstand.

All morning, Jase had kept an eye on the parking lot as he nailed shingles to the roof. From his vantage point on the ladder, he could see all the vehicles that arrived and every person who exited each minivan or truck. He'd even chuckled at a bumper sticker on an old gray compact car.

The steady line of automobiles eventually became a trickle. Jase grabbed the binoculars from their resting place and scoped out the property. Only a few customers were picking over the last of the produce.

Jase climbed down the ladder, and Blossom came over and lay on the ground in front of him. Glancing one way, then another, he picked up the sweet little hen, who seemed to appreciate the cuddle.

"Sorry, Blossom, but my work here is done." If only he could say the same for the very reason he was at the farm.

He placed Blossom back on her feet and headed for the fence. The hen followed. It was a good thing none of his fellow detectives or law enforcement officers could see him now. He'd never hear the end of this, and that would be the end of his icy reputation.

And yet he didn't mind. Blossom's sweetness made everything worthwhile.

With care, he opened and closed the gate so Blossom stayed inside the pen. Jase acknowledged the officer who was keeping his distance before Jase wheeled the tools to the farmstand where Cassie was saying goodbye to the last customer.

That left him alone with Cassie, who was taking off her apron. "You just missed Amanda. She's already on her way back to Lazy River. How's the henhouse coming along?"

"It's repaired. Blossom and crew will have a

warm, place to sleep tonight." An unexpected sense of pride traveled through him. He liked knowing he'd helped the little hen who seemed to have taken a shine to him.

Cassie glanced at her watch and gasped. "I have to leave in ten minutes."

Jase's instincts went haywire. Cassie never left the farm while Penny and Easton were at school. Harvesting crops, making pumpkin butter, taking care of the animals—Cassie did all of that and more, as if compensating for her criminal half brother.

Then again, her absence would give him a chance to check out the farmhouse. Since he had her permission to be there, he wouldn't need a search warrant.

In no time, Cassie deactivated the security system, and he followed her through the mudroom into the kitchen. She grabbed her purse off the hook. "I forgot it was Friday, and now I don't have time to change or anything."

"What's special about Fridays?" Was she set to rendezvous with Yablonsky?

"It's early-release day. I pick up Penny and Easton, and then we visit the seniors' center. I'm running late." Out of breath, she faced him and smiled. "It's shaping up to be a beautiful afternoon. Maybe there's time for you to catch Amanda. All she could talk about was her trail ride with Seth and the guests this afternoon. Surely they can fit you into the party."

The hairs on the back of his neck prickled. Cassie was trying to get him away from the farmhouse. Every time he started believing in her, she turned around and acted guilty once more.

He followed her to the parking lot where an older model truck was parked on the opposite side of the lot from his sedan.

"Say hello to Amanda for me." Cassie waved goodbye and headed to her truck while he climbed into his sedan.

For appearance's sake, he'd visit the dude ranch and then also verify her presence at the seniors' center. This was too convenient for his liking.

Jase adjusted his rearview mirror, waiting for Cassie to leave the lot, but he didn't hear her truck start. A knock on his window surprised him, hardly a good look for one of Denver's finest. He turned on his sedan and rolled down the window. "What's wrong?"

"My truck won't start, and pickup time is in fifteen minutes. Penny, Easton and I are expected at the seniors' center right after that." Concern laced her words as her eyes pleaded with him.

He wavered once more. There was little chance she was using car trouble as a way to get him off the property, not when she'd already manufactured another excuse. Not only that, but it was evident how much Cassie loved her children. She wouldn't use them as pawns.

"I can drive you there. We'll look at your truck later."

Her instant smile was his gratification. "I'll be right back with their booster seats."

Jase braced himself. He wouldn't let anything as simple as a pretty smile distract him.

Cassie rushed over and placed the booster seats in the back before climbing into the front.

"Is the school in the same location?" If so, he wouldn't need his GPS.

She nodded and pulled the seat belt across her. "It's the same building, but you won't recognize it. It's been updated. I cochaired the fundraisers that got us the new playgrounds, including features for neurodivergent students. The whole community came together for that." Cassie launched into other changes at Violet Ridge Elementary and brought him up to speed on some of his classmates who now taught there.

In the long car line, Jase spotted Penny before Easton. Her frown was the giveaway she recognized his sedan. Her expression was as disturbing to him as her mother's smile, but for a different reason. He valued each of their opinions of him.

Eventually, the O'Neal children climbed into the car after a teacher confirmed Cassie's presence.

"What are you doing here?" Penny sounded accusatory, and Jase's chest clenched at how little she approved of him.

Cassie turned around and helped Easton buckle into place. "Penny, Jase is our guest."

Penny mumbled an apology. Jase understood

why she was hesitant to accept him. She loved her mom and was trying to protect her.

Jase wanted to protect this family, too. Of course, by the time Penny came around to liking or trusting him, Yablonsky would be in custody, and Jase would be a distant memory. Perhaps Penny was on to something after all.

Once Cassie settled in her seat, she gave Jase directions to the seniors' center. He glanced at his rearview mirror and took in Penny with her arms folded while Easton could barely control his excitement.

"Are you coming, Jase? I like the community garden a whole lot, and so will you. I told everyone at school today about how Blossom likes you this much." Easton flung his arms wide.

The young boy kept talking as Jase flitted his gaze to Cassie, who shrugged. "Easton is easygoing while Penny reserves judgment. You have to earn her trust." She kept her voice low, so he'd be the only one who could hear.

Jase chewed on Cassie's words at one of the few red lights in Violet Ridge. Easton and Cassie were alike in that they trusted people easily. Penny sounded more like him than he'd care to admit. Being reserved was a definite plus in his job, but in his personal life? There weren't that many people in Denver outside of work he could call if he needed a lift or a favor. Yep, he and Penny could both use a course in trusting others.

Easton kept chattering away about his school

day while Jase turned into the busy parking lot for the senior citizens' center and found the last remaining space.

Penny unbuckled both her and Easton's seat belts, and the young boy could hardly hold his excitement. "They're here for Mommy."

Jase looked at Cassie who gave a wry chuckle. "Hardly. The community garden belongs to everyone."

"What's that?" Jase asked.

"I suggested it as a way to get the seniors more involved in gardening. They choose a lot and decide whether to grow vegetables or flowers. It quickly grew into a community effort with the extra vegetables helping out the local food bank and the flowers spreading cheer at the hospital and memory care facility. Once a week, I answer questions about the latest organic techniques while Penny and Easton tend our lot. They've grown close to many of the seniors, which is good. It's a win for everyone."

Without another word, they headed toward the rear of the facility, and Jase controlled himself from gasping.

This wasn't a small backyard undertaking. A vast acreage was divided into small rectangular plots with gravel dividers as far as the eye could see. Chrysanthemums graced the closest raised garden while others contained wooden lattices where climbing vine tomatoes were ripening. "I'm impressed."

Three older gentlemen approached, and each removed their Stetson hats, placing them over their chests. A thin man looking like he was in his late seventies, with a brown bandanna tied around his neck, greeted the group. “Hello, Cassie and mini Cassie and Easton.” He squinted in Jase’s direction. “Good gracious me. It’s Jase Virtue. I remember when you were knee-high to a grasshopper. You’d always trail after me at the Lazy River whenever I tended the mustangs. Always thought you’d become a vet, but you’re with Denver’s finest now. Martin and Bridget didn’t mention you were back in town.”

Jase remembered the days when he shadowed Doc Jenkins during his rounds. “I saw Grandma and Grandpa the other night. They’re doing well, but there’s no room at the inn.”

Beside him, Cassie stiffened as she tightened her grip on Easton’s shoulders. She must not have told Penny or Easton about Keith and their connection yet, but that would have to change later. Maybe even as soon as tonight.

“Cassie did a right good turn in offering me room and board in exchange for helping her at Thistle Brook Farm,” Jase added.

“Why, Miss Cassie, whenever you need help, you can always call on us.” The man on Doc’s left side possessed a salt-and-pepper beard, and he rubbed the bottom strands. “We’ll leave the Silver Horseshoe Ranch and be at Thistle Brook in no time, especially if you throw in a loaf of pumpkin bread."

The man on the other side of Doc Jenkins harrumphed. "Marshall, you're never at the Silver Horseshoe much anymore ever since you started dating Constance Mulligan."

"My brother, Glenn, is just jealous that I got up the gumption to ask her out," Marshall scoffed and winked at Cassie as if he was letting her in on a great secret. "Constance is busy at the Holly Theater today. She's made a real go of it since she bought the place. We have a date at Miss Tilly's Steak House tonight."

Doc Jenkins reached into his tote bag. "Can Easton and Penny have a butterscotch candy?"

Both children faced Cassie, who nodded her approval. "Yes, and thank you."

Doc Jenkins handed each child a butterscotch disc and held out two more.

Cassie accepted hers with a smile, and the cellophane crinkled as she unwrapped it and placed the candy in her mouth. "Thank you, Doc. This is always one of the highlights of my afternoon. Pardon us so we can fetch our gloves and shovels and get to work."

Doc kept his hand extended, and Jase accepted the last one. The candy melted in his mouth. Butterscotch was the flavor of his childhood, and he liked that Doc was keeping up tradition with the next generation of Violet Ridge youth. It was nice to know some things never changed.

On the way to collect their gardening supplies, more residents stopped Cassie and her crew. Cassie accepted lollipops, licorice and a bag of cookies for Easton and Penny that she told them they could have later at home. Everyone seemed to have brought a small token.

In return, Cassie asked each person about their latest gardening updates. Jase tapped his foot after five minutes of her talking to the same man about organic pesticides. Cassie sent him a look of apology, and Jase just shrugged. He was getting used to it.

"Is it always like this?" Jase asked while accepting a pair of leather work gloves.

Cassie shrugged. "At first there were only three seniors who signed up. It's expanded over time, and there's now a waiting list. I'll show you my garden. They allow me one in exchange for helping others."

She led them over to a small rectangular plot. Stakes in the soil let him know she was growing kale, eggplant and onions on one side with herbs on the other.

"How did you choose what to plant?" he asked.

"These vegetables are relatively low maintenance, and kale is a delicious way to add crunch and nutrition to a salad." Cassie directed Penny and Easton to start pulling weeds when Glenn came over and asked for her advice about his beets.

Jase agreed to watch over Penny and Easton, and Cassie hurried along. Easton glanced up, his gloves discarded in the weeds and his hands already covered with dirt. "Mommy won't be back until it's time to go."

Penny nodded. "She helps everyone."

The more Jase was learning about Cassie, the less he could believe she'd be part of an armed robbery. Tonight he'd review the file with an eagle eye, searching for any clue about C's identity that might lead suspicion away from Cassie.

Yet what could he find that Shields and other detectives had overlooked? In eight years of visitors' logs—which wasn't as extensive as it sounded since Yablonsky didn't have many people coming to see him—only Cassie, who'd visited once, had a first name starting with *C* and was a willowy brunette.

After weeding for a long while, Jase stood and stretched his back to see a familiar face headed his way. His brother-in-law, Ben Irwin, smiled and hurried toward Jase. The military veteran turned mayor stopped short of a hug and patted Jase's shoulder instead.

"My father and stepmother asked me to take care of their garden since they're away from Violet Ridge until the end of the month." Ben led Jase to a small plot where riotous pink snapdragons and mums greeted them. "Daisy will be upset she didn't get to see you again. She's still on cloud nine about your visit. Any chance you could make it to our house for dinner tonight? The triplets would love to see their uncle Jase."

One disadvantage of living in Denver was not spending as much time as he'd like with his nieces and nephew. Rosie, Aspen and Lily were no longer babies in the NICU. Instead they were active eight-year-olds whose penchant for acting had been what brought their mother and stepfather together last year. The trio had been cast in the annual holiday production of *The Santa Who Forgot Christmas*, and his sister Daisy had gone along with the endeavor, not realizing she'd have to volunteer her time at the community playhouse. It was there she met Ben Irwin, newly discharged from the air force with time on his hands.

The two had fallen in love, and Jase had returned to Violet Ridge for their wedding. Otherwise, he relied on video calls to keep up with his nieces and nephew.

Jase gestured in the direction of Cassie's children, who were still yanking weeds, and pulled Ben aside so they wouldn't be within hearing distance of the kids. "Once Yablonsky's captured, I'll be able to come over for dinner before I leave town. I'm not here on vacation. I need to stay close to the farmhouse to guard the kids." And Cassie. "Penny and Easton don't know about Yablonsky, and Cassie wants to keep it that way for now."

Ben waved at Penny and Easton when Penny looked over at them. Then he leaned closer to Jase and whipped his gloves out of his back pocket. "I'm well aware of why you're here." Ben continued to keep his voice low and his smile wide while nodding to some passersby. “As the mayor, I work hand in hand with local law enforcement. The police chief consulted me about okaying overtime for patrols in the area. Chief Gutierrez is a recent appointment, and he’s a good man.”

Jase exhaled his pent-up frustration, relieved that Violet Ridge was taking the threat from Yablonsky as seriously as the situation dictated. “Captain Shields is running point from Denver, but even so, I can’t be at the farm all the time.”

Ben donned the gloves and bent to pluck weeds from his plot, his gaze never leaving Penny and Easton. “The force will keep an eye on the O’Neal farm. So you don’t have to feel guilty about visiting your grandparents or siblings.”

Except Jase did feel guilty, but not for the reason Ben suspected. Jase was keeping a wide berth from the ranch where his parents died in an automobile accident when he was six years old, but he couldn’t elaborate on why after all this time. Jase was sure that knowing the true cause of the accident would hurt his grandparents. It was best to keep that to himself for now.

“Thanks for the heads-up.” Jase tugged a long weed from the dirt.

“Daisy, Crosby and Seth miss you.” Ben pulled out one of the snapdragons, its roots exposed, and winced. “Pretty obvious I’m not a gardener, huh?”

“Just a little.” Jase reached for the flower and set it aside to ask Cassie if it could be replanted or if it was beyond hope. “Guess you have to make an appearance at the community garden since you're the mayor. Or do you have an ulterior motive for talking to me alone?"

Ben raised his eyebrow and stared at Jase. "Wrong line of questioning, Detective Virtue. Today I'm here for my dad and my stepmother, Evie. No ulterior motive." He exhaled a long breath. "Although I'm guessing from my efforts, Dad and Evie will be sending my sister, Lizzie, in my place next time."

"Then this is just a friendly brother-in-law chat?" Jase asked.

"Okay, you got me. Any chance you could be persuaded to move back here and work for the Violet Ridge Police Department?"

Jase shook his head at Ben's request.

"Can't blame a guy for looking out for his family, can you? Bridget and Martin have taken me into their family and love me. They love you, too."

And that was why Jase had to remain in Denver. If Jase lived here, he'd accidentally let slip details about the accident. Staying away was the best way to ensure he wouldn't lose their love or respect. "Captain Shields is retiring next year. I have a shot at his position."

Ben removed his gloves and whistled. "That's quite impressive at your age." He looked at the small plot of land and grimaced. "Daisy or Lizzie or even one of the seniors will have to take over before I do irreparable damage."

Jase reached for the flowers and nodded. "Thanks for the chat. Message received, Ben."

"If you think that was a message, watch out for Seth. He takes his job as the oldest Virtue sibling quite seriously." Ben kept his tone light, but they both knew he wasn't joking.

Jase chuckled, glad Daisy had married Ben. He was the perfect foil for his loving sister. "And we all know who I really have to watch out for."

"Grandma Bridget," they said in unison.

Family. The idea of it stirred strong feelings in Ben that went both ways. The good and the maybe not so good. Ben asking him to join the local force was a true kindness, and Jase felt a twinge at his decision to forego relationships. Maybe there was something in attaching yourself to someone else.

Penny and Easton were getting restless if the sound of bickering was any indication. "I better get back to those two. See you around."

"Don't be a stranger." Ben focused on the plot but looked as though he was about to throw in the towel.

Jase returned to the O'Neal children in time for a mound of dirt to fall onto his boot tips. Easton had the good sense to look regretful since he'd been the one throwing dirt at his sister. "Sorry, Jase."

Jase brushed the dirt off his boot. "I won't tell your mom." Maybe she was right about light, inconsequential secrets. "If we work together, we can finish tending to the patch in no time."

He began working alongside Penny and Easton, making sure he stayed between the two. Easton was quite content with Jase's presence, although Penny looked as though she wanted to be back at the farmhouse.

Jase looked up just as Cassie arrived at Ben's side, turning her attention to the snapdragon and other flowers. Jase watched as she guided Ben through the proper way to tend the plot.

Attentive and caring, Cassie served others here at the seniors' center out of love. Dare Jase believe that Cassie was someone who had seemingly earned the respect of every senior citizen here?

Or was this an act so no one would suspect her role in the robbery?

THE SMOKEHOUSE, A CASUAL hamburger joint with a warm ambience, was Cassie's favorite restaurant in downtown Violet Ridge. She swirled the last bite of her cherry cobbler in the melted ice cream and savored the sweetness while laughing at the joke Aspen just finished telling Easton. Ben and Daisy had talked Jase into eating dinner with them and the triplets before extending the invitation to Cassie and her children as well. It was beyond sweet of Daisy to include her and Penny and Easton, even if it was only on account of Jase.

The restaurant manager had pushed two tables together to accommodate their large party, and Aspen kept Easton entertained throughout the meal. Even Penny was happy, giggling over something with Rosie and Lily, Daisy's daughters. Cassie reveled in the good company. Meals like these reminded her of when her father was still alive, with Mom and Dad laughing through dinner and life itself.

She made a mental note to call her mom. Even though Cassie had more in common with her father, she loved her mom. In fact, Cassie was proud of how her mother had devoted herself to her new job at a department store, finding something that excited her in much the same way as farming appealed to Cassie.

She was the third generation of her family to form a deep connection with the acreage of Thistle Brook Farm, and she relished the feel of the dirt in her fingers. She hoped at least one of her kids would grow up to share her passion and keep the tradition going.

Her cell phone alerted her to an incoming text. Cassie groaned. It was never a good sign when Bert asked her to call him rather than letting her know her truck was ready via a text message. She excused herself and headed outside.

Rubbing her neck, she listened to Bert's drawn-out description of her timing belt and the cost of repairing it. The cowbell on the restaurant's front door jangled, and she found Jase by her side. Cassie held up a finger while Bert wrapped up his explanation of the estimate.

After authorizing the repair, Cassie faced Jase and winced. "Hope you don't mind being my driver over the weekend. Bert is waiting on a part, so my truck won't be ready until Monday."

"If I'm called back to Denver, I'll arrange with someone at Lazy River to make sure you have transportation." Jase pointed toward the restaurant's interior.

"If you return to Denver, I'll talk to Amanda myself." She arched her eyebrow, worried she was giving off a damsel in distress vibe. Just because her half brother was on the lam from police, her truck had broken down and her henhouse had taken a hit didn't mean she was helpless. Far from it.

"Point taken. I'm sorry." Jase's jaw clenched as if he wasn't used to apologizing often.

"Thank you," Cassie said.

They returned to their families, and he pushed in her chair for her. She turned to him to let him know she could do that herself when a spark ignited between them. He met her gaze, and she found herself breathless.

"You're welcome." Jase hurried and sat down while Aspen slurped bubbles in his drink, eliciting giggles from Easton.

Cassie returned her phone to her purse, her fingers rubbing against the zippered section. Her father's watch! She'd forgotten to take it to the repair shop.

"What's wrong?" Jase asked.

"The truck wasn't the only thing that broke today. I meant to go to Mescal's Repair Shop for a new watch battery, but it'll have to wait until the next time I'm in town." Who knew when that would be?

She fretted at having to delay getting her heirloom watch fixed. The reminder to take one minute at a time and appreciate all of them, even the rough obstacles, was especially needed, more so with the detective nearby. Too often during dinner, she had sensed his presence, her awareness of him as a good man taking root deep inside of her.

Daisy looked up from the book her daughter Lily was showing her and Penny. "We're having fun. Why don't you and Jase go to the repair shop and meet us back here?"

Cassie started to protest and paused. Had Daisy seen the look that passed between her and Jase? Was she playing matchmaker?

Jase disappeared, and Cassie worried this was too much emotion for him all at once. A minute later, he reappeared with their jackets. "If we hurry, we'll make it to the repair shop before it closes."

She donned her jacket, grateful for the protection from the cool September air, and they set forth for the repair shop, located two blocks over.

Dusk was beginning to settle upon the town, with the antique lampposts bathing the pastel storefronts in a soft glow. Bales of hay with pumpkins and scarecrows marked each street corner. Signs advertising next week's Harvest Festival dotted several store windows, reminding her she had promised Penny and Easton they would attend that. Other displays featured placards for her corn maze weekends beginning shortly after the festival. Autumn had arrived in all its glory, and Cassie was loving every minute.

"Don't you just adore fall? Which scarecrow is your favorite? I like the bucking scarecrow on the hay horse." She pointed to one nearby sponsored by Irwin Arena, the host stadium for the Violet Ridge Rodeo.

"I don't have a favorite season. Each has its good points and bad." Jase checked his watch and tapped on it before bringing it to his ear. "It seems as though I also need a new battery."

Cassie pounced on the first part of his statement. "How can you not love fall? Apple cider, pumpkin spice, falling leaves." She shivered with delight. "And this year, my corn maze will hopefully become a part of everyone's fall experience."

"I didn't say I don't love fall. I said I don't have a favorite season. There's a difference," Jase said.

"True, but autumn in Violet Ridge is spectacular. The aspens are absolutely gorgeous this time of year with all their vibrant color." She twirled around and drank in the beauty of the distant snowcapped mountains, the window displays with burgundy and orange and the leaves on the steps of city hall. "There's so much to love about this season."

"You love fall. Why doesn't that surprise me?

Is that why you go all out with the seasonal jams and jellies at your farmstand?" he asked.

A tingle of pride passed through her. She'd spent hours perfecting her pumpkin butter and apple bread recipes. Those helped make her stand distinct. "The customers like my products, and I like to make them happy."

"You've succeeded." Jase gave her a curt nod and zipped up his jacket. It was as if admitting his likes and dislikes or even complimenting someone made him uncomfortable.

She nudged him and sent a smile his way. "Thank you." There was something about Jase that stuck with her in a good way.

She lapsed into silence as they walked along Main Street. As much as she enjoyed visiting the downtown district, the farm occupied much of her time. Penny and Easton were getting to the age where they would want to become more active outside of the farm, but for now, she was content with everything as it was. Life could sometimes change too fast and there was something about just living in the present.

"That one." Jase broke the comfortable silence when he pointed at a scarecrow in the shape of a buffalo with a badge pinned to its scruff. "It's different and not like the others."

Somewhat similar to Jase himself. He was independent, almost to a fault, but with a core of strength and determination. She liked that about him. Then she caught herself and backpedaled.

She had once found Brayden's independent streak appealing, so much so she married him after only knowing him for a month. Three years later, after her second positive pregnancy test, that independent streak compelled him to buy a one-way ticket to the wilds of Alaska.

Fortunately, Jase hadn't expressed any interest in her, at least, not in a romantic way. Good thing, as she'd be in genuine trouble if she ever fell for someone like him. She had a feeling it would be nearly impossible to mend her heart if that ever happened.

She felt his gaze on her as if he was waiting for a response. "Good choice. I like the displays where the scarecrows are turned into animals. Like that one." She pointed to a goat scarecrow sponsored by a local dairy known for its feta cheese and handmade soap.

She stopped herself from saying anything else. What was she doing, falling into her old pattern of flirting with someone who was totally wrong for her? Someone whose job was to protect her and Penny and Easton from Keith.

She exhaled. Making small talk about scarecrows wasn't a relationship commitment. It was about forming a friendship, and they could both use a friend.

Something grasped her arm, and she jumped before she realized it was Jase. "It's been a while since I lived in Violet Ridge, but isn't Mescal's Repair Shop this way?"

Cassie nodded and turned onto Maplewood Way, the corner occupied with a scarecrow featured as an artist painting a scarecrow Mona Lisa. She looked at the scarecrow, then at Jase. A hen whisperer, a detective and a master carpenter. Jase was a genuine Renaissance man.

They entered the repair shop just in time to hear the chimes belt out that it was half past seven. Wall clocks of all shapes and sizes, cuckoo clocks and grandfather clocks vied for space in the tight quarters. One timepiece was a fraction of a second late and finished its melody behind the others. And then only serene ticks measured the passage of time.

"Be with you shortly," a familiar male voice sounded from the rear of the shop.

"Take your time." Cassie reassured the owner. Jase groaned, and she rolled her eyes. "No pun intended."

Cassie reached into her purse and pulled out her treasured watch, laying it on the counter. Under the glass, a variety of watches, all with individual handwritten price tags, waited for new owners.

Jase removed his watch as well and placed it next to hers. "Nice."

She ran her hand over the leather strap and the gold plating. "It was my father's. My mother gave it to me after he died."

"Why you and not your brother?" he asked.

"Dad died after Keith was already in jail." Cassie swallowed until that boulder in her throat went away. "Keith and I have Dad in common but different mothers. Dad divorced Keith's mother, who ran off when he was two. Dad never intended to fall in love again, but my mother's a truly genuine person."

"How did they meet?"

Cassie craned her neck toward the back, but Mr. Mescal was nowhere in sight. "She was visiting Colorado when she met Dad. He was reluctant to get involved, both because of his first wife and the age difference between them. Fifteen years." Cassie answered the question before he had a chance to ask. "It was a genuine love match, and I was born five years later."

She tapped her fingers on the glass, wondering if she should remind Mr. Mescal they were still here.

"Tricky fix," Mr. Mescal called out once more. "I'll be out in just another minute. Thanks for your patience."

Mr. Mescal had been installing new batteries in this watch for years. She wouldn't trust anyone else.

"Were you and Keith close? Especially considering he's thirteen years older than you." Jase didn't lose step with the conversation, and she admired his attention to detail.

"Sometimes." There had been good times that made it hard to reconcile the gawky teenager with the hardened criminal who showed no remorse for his actions. Even harder was seeing Keith's mannerisms in her children, like the way Penny gnawed on her pencil or the way Easton wrinkled his nose, shaped just like her father's and Keith's. "I think Keith felt left out when I came along. The three of us were close, and Keith stayed on the fringes for most of my childhood."

"It doesn't sound like you and Keith had much of a connection at all." Jase leaned on the counter, giving her his full attention.

"For a while, when I was in high school, we were." Cassie paused. That was the first time she trusted someone at face value only to have that trust betrayed. "Keith left for a long time and then came home, thin and scrawny, without a word of where he'd been or what he'd been doing. He and Dad had a long overnight ride, and then Keith started working at the farm."

For those months, Cassie had followed Keith around like a hound dog, seeking his approval and relishing it.

"What changed?" Jase seemed to be hanging on her story.

The memory of how the relationship between her father and his only son deteriorated left a bad taste in Cassie's mouth. "Turns out Keith expected his share of his inheritance early. Dad told him he couldn't spare any money. He was tapped out from paying back a loan he'd taken after losing his crop to hail and the tornado."

Jase nodded. Everyone in these parts was impacted that year. "One of my classmates lost both her parents in that tornado."

"I remember that. Well, Keith seemed to take Dad's statement in stride, but a week later, he and Dad had a major row. Turns out Dad had been saving to buy me a car for my high school graduation present. The money was gone, and Dad accused Keith of taking it." Their raised voices would always be imprinted on her memory. "The next day after school, I found a card on my pillow from Keith. He'd stolen the money, and he was gone."

After that, Cassie had accepted any requests to be on a school committee and work on behalf of others. Her father beamed when she told him about something she'd done at school and tell her how proud he was she wasn't anything like Keith.

Mr. Mescal emerged from the rear, wiping his hands on a rag. "Cassie, my favorite customer." He looked around her and brought out a jar from behind the counter. "Where are Penny and Easton? I stocked up on their favorite lollipops."

Cassie smiled. "They're with Daisy and Ben Irwin and their family at the Smokehouse." She looked around and pointed at Jase who was bent over and looking at the display case. "Jase and I walked over so I could get my watch fixed."

Jase waved at Mr. Mescal, who pushed his glasses up on the bridge of his nose. "Why, Jase Virtue. Long time, no see. Welcome home."

"You two know each other?" Cassie regretted the question as soon as she asked. This was Violet

Ridge. One way or another, most of the residents knew each other.

"Jase knows almost as much about clocks and watches as I do." Mr. Mescal opened the lid of the lollipop jar for the detective. "Grape still your favorite?"

To his credit, Jase accepted one. "Yep." Then he faced Cassie with a slight smile. "The machinery is like a puzzle. I still repair clocks and watches for fellow officers and detectives. It's a good way to relax my mind while I focus on a case."

Mr. Mescal offered Cassie her choice.

"None for me, but can I take two to Penny and Easton?"

Mr. Mescal nodded, and Cassie chose cherry for Penny and lime for Easton, placing them in her purse for later. Then she changed her mind and plucked out a grape lollipop for herself.

"Say hello to them for me," the shopkeeper said.

"I will." She laid the watch on the counter and zipped her purse, only to find her bracelet land on the zipper. Picking it up, she spotted the problem. The clasp was broken. She handed the gold chain with a *C* in the middle to Mr. Mescal. "Can you fix my bracelet clasp and replace the watch battery?"

"Hmm. The clasp will only take a minute." Mr. Mescal donned a pair of white gloves and reached for his tool kit. After testing the battery, he shook his head. "I thought I'd just replaced it, and it still registers as good. I'll have to keep the watch here, but I'll take good care of it."

She accepted the repair claims ticket he offered her and nodded her thanks.

Jase purchased a watch battery and chatted with Mr. Mescal, as he installed it himself. While they were busy catching up, Cassie wandered around the small space, examining the numerous clocks and other items.

While she preferred living in the present, committing to everything and everyone so each minute counted, she couldn't help but regret what had happened between her father and Keith. Telling Dad the car didn't mean anything compared to losing his relationship with his son would have at least offered a bit of perspective, but that wasn't the crux of the matter. Trust was broken, and her father's health had deteriorated from there.

Cassie reached out and brushed the front of an old-fashioned wooden clock. She still missed the grandfather clock that once stood in her foyer. Her mother must have taken it with her to her condo, but Cassie always forgot to ask her about it. The last time she visited her in Florida, it wasn't in the suite, though. Her mother must have a locker or rented a storage space for her dress forms, sewing machine and other personal items that wouldn't fit in the smaller living space.

In hindsight, it was easy to see that Keith's theft of her car money was the moment everything started falling apart for her family and, for a time, herself. Life could change in an instant, and she wondered if she was at that type of crossroads once more.

She peeked at Jase, who seemed fascinated by the inner workings of his wristwatch. There was something about him that was as solid and timeless as these timepieces.

Nope. She had to get past this awareness. This noticing Jase as more than just a detective. All she wanted was for life to go back to the way it was before the cop knocked on her door and told her about Keith's escape.

Yet, minute by minute, that seemed less possible.

CHAPTER FOUR

YESTERDAY HAD THROWN a wrench in Jase's investigation. He'd been positive Cassie purposefully led him away from the farm in order to aid and abet Yablonsky. However, his instincts had apparently misled him—confirmed by his middle-of-the-night search of the grounds that revealed no trace of the convict having been there. More so, Cassie's truck actually needed a new timing belt rather than some cheap, easy fix.

On top of that, nearly every senior citizen in Violet Ridge was a card-carrying member of the Cassie O'Neal fan club. Even his sister and brother-in-law were fans.

Too bad Penny wasn't part of the Jase Virtue fan club. Here they sat in Cassie's kitchen with Penny's hazel eyes, exact replicas of her mother's, trained squarely on his face. It was obvious Penny didn't hold him in high regard, and that was before he delivered more bad news.

"I can't take you to the seniors' center today. I'm helping your mom on the farm." He thought of a solution. "I'll ask your mom if Daisy can drive you there."

"Mom's in the greenhouse." Easton stopped shoveling scrambled eggs into his mouth long enough to pass on the information.

Jase offered his thanks, grabbing a piece of buttered toast from the stack on his way outside. At the greenhouse, he found Cassie using a soft sponge to wipe down the glass walls.

"Easton told me where I could find you." He popped the last bite of toast in his mouth and swallowed. "I'd have preferred hearing your schedule from you."

"I keep forgetting I need to check in with you." Cassie didn't look at him, instead, she remained focused on her task. "I'm a week behind in performing my monthly greenhouse maintenance."

"Penny would like to know what time you'll be done." Jase took in Cassie's appearance. Her flannel shirt was wet in spots, and she pushed the stray strands of her hair back in place with the crook of her arm. While perfect for a day on the farm, he doubted she'd want to wear that outfit to the seniors' center. "Apparently we're supposed to leave in ten minutes."

Cassie faltered and dropped her wet cloth. "Oh no! I lost track of time, and I still need to harvest the late potatoes so I can add them to the winter boxes." She groaned and tapped her forehead with her closed fist. "But it's Adopt a Grandparent Day, and Penny and Easton look forward to it so much." Her face fell.

A healthy respect for what she was accomplishing on her own welled up inside him. Here she was, a single mother, a farm owner and a small-business entrepreneur, raising two sweet kids—Penny's feelings toward him notwithstanding.

"Could someone else pick them up and take them? Amanda? Daisy?" Jase was more careful with his approach so he wouldn't overstep his bounds like he did yesterday.

She winced. "Amanda is busy with Seth. They're getting the dude ranch ready for the weekly dance. It's kind of a special treat for the guests and Daisy hasn't ever brought the triplets to the center."

Cassie knew his family better than he did. That troubled him for a second before he stepped back. Everything was working the way he'd set it in motion. Perhaps he was suffering from a simple case of be-careful-what-you-wish-for-because-it-might-come-true syndrome. He'd distanced himself for so long, it was now his reality.

"Doesn't hurt to check." He blinked at how he sounded almost positive, like the glass was half full, instead of always empty.

Was Cassie's optimism rubbing off on him?

She glanced down at her clothes and groaned. "I'll just tell Penny and Easton we'll miss this month. Judy and Doc Jenkins will understand."

"I'll take them," Jase offered before he could consider the words.

"That would be such a relief." Her expression already seemed brighter, and her eyes gleamed once more. "I'll feel better knowing they're with you."

Before he departed for the seniors' center, he'd call the sheriff and verify that they would double up the patrol while he was gone. Between extra surveillance and the new security system, if Cassie was meeting with Yablonsky, he'd find out about it.

She accompanied him to the farmhouse. Easton was delighted with the arrangement, although Penny seemed crestfallen. Cassie pulled Jase aside and gave him permission to take the pair for ice cream after the outing.

With that treat in mind, he drove the pair to town. Easton chatted the whole way while Penny stayed silent. Jase had wrenched confessions out of hardened criminals, but he suspected Penny would prove tougher than any of them.

Once again, the seniors' center had a packed parking lot, and they had to wait for a space to become available. Finally, he escorted Penny and Easton inside.

Doc Jenkins hailed Easton, placing his arm around the kindergartner. "Back for another game of checkers?"

"I've been practicing with Patches and haven't lost a game yet!" Easton said.

Doc Jenkins met Jase's gaze, and they both withheld a laugh at Easton's winning streak against the calico cat.

"I had to fight off some competition for our

usual table, but the board's already set up." Doc Jenkins spirited Easton away while Penny glanced around the large room.

The setup seemed clear. Young kids were matched with someone older. Some seniors sat on sofas with children reading aloud while others played board games.

"Are you looking for someone in particular?" Jase asked. "Judy?"

Penny shuffled her boots and shrugged. "I don't see her. It doesn't matter."

Her voice gave away how much she cared. Jase's heart went out to the young girl at the absence of someone important in her life. "What do you normally do here?"

"Sometimes Miss Judy and I bake cookies in the kitchen, or we play go fish or something like that," Penny mumbled and played with the ends of her hair.

"I can bake cookies." If they had the proper ingredients and equipment, that was.

Penny scuffed the beige carpet with the tip of her sneaker. "Nah. I'll watch Doc Jenkins beat Easton at checkers."

"We can give the baked cookies to today's participants and take the rest home to your mom?"

At that, Penny's eyes lit up. "Mommy loves pumpkin spice raisin cookies." Then she stared at him with suspicion. "Do you know how to make them?"

Jase pulled out his phone and searched for a recipe. *Thank you, internet.* "We've got this. Show me the kitchen."

To his surprise, the kitchen was stocked with everything they needed. One of the center's employees asked them to mark down what they used so the items could be restocked.

"Someone always bakes on Adopt a Grandparent Day," Penny explained as she measured flour, taking care not to spill any on the counter.

Within minutes, they had the first baking sheet in the oven. "Guess we'll need to taste test them before we share them with Easton and Doc Jenkins. A hard job, but someone has to do it." Jase patted his flat stomach.

Penny turned toward him, frowning. "You think they're gonna turn out bad?"

That wasn't his intent at all. He'd merely been joking and trying to gain her trust, but once again, he'd taken the wrong approach. Winning over Penny was a Herculean task bordering on the impossible. Jase caught his breath.

"None of my grandchildren are bad bakers."

The voice from behind warmed Jase's heart, the same as it had ever since he could walk. Smiling, he turned and found Grandma Bridget at the archway, both hands grasping the handle of her cane. "Grandma!"

She opened her arms, and he flew into them. He stood several inches taller than her, unlike his childhood days, so it was she who nestled her head against his shoulder before they broke contact.

Grandma Bridget pressed her soft hand against his cheek before making her way over to his co-baker. "Are you Penny O'Neal?" she asked.

The young girl nodded, her gaze never leaving the cookies. "Yes, ma'am. My brother, Easton, is playing checkers with Doc Jenkins."

"Judy texted me and asked if I'd fill in for her today." Grandma Bridget smiled and then pointed at Jase. "Glad to see you here. You, out of all of your siblings, loved baking the most. How wonderful."

The tremble in her voice brought him a wave of guilt. By initiating a sort of separation after the police academy and his move to Denver, he'd distanced himself from the person who'd taught him so much about relationships, responsibility...and so much more. Thanks to Grandma Bridget, he could sew his own buttons *and* win a lasso competition. All this time, he thought he'd been doing her a service by keeping away. Maybe, though, he'd been doing a disservice to them both.

"I'll let you in on a little secret. I liked spending time with you and eating the results." Jase laughed.

Grandma Bridget shuffled alongside him and hugged his arm. "I don't want to let you go. You need to visit more often."

Jase shrugged. "Seems like my siblings keep having weddings that bring me back." He'd attended Daisy and Ben's recent ceremony and would return for Seth and Amanda's soon enough.

"Is there anyone special in your life? Martin and I would love to meet her."

Cassie popped into his mind, and he flinched. Why was he thinking about her? Just because she was everyone's friend and rather attractive was no reason to take his focus off his mission.

"I'm not dating anyone." Come to think of it, he hadn't had anyone special in his life in a long while. The last time he'd been in a relationship that crossed the six-month mark, she'd ended it before they could celebrate their seven-month anniversary, claiming he had more devotion for his work than her. She wasn't wrong.

That was over a year ago. Maybe even two.

The timer rang, and he was thankful for the distraction. He donned the oven mitt and removed the cookies. Something wasn't right. They still looked like dough globs.

Disappointment lurked in Penny's hazel eyes. She sighed and faced his grandmother, who stared at the cookies and arched her eyebrow.

"Seems like I came just in time. Someone has forgotten everything I taught him, namely, to make sure the oven is turned on before putting the cookie sheet in the oven."

Penny giggled, but Jase felt relief wash over him. Who'd have guessed that his mistake would break the ice between them? Penny grinned at Jase, her cuteness factor increased tenfold by her missing bottom tooth. Perhaps there was hope she'd accept his presence.

He couldn't wait to tell Cassie about this potential breakthrough. Then again, was he so distracted by Cassie that he was forgetting the most basic life skills?

This was getting out of hand. He needed to know if she was involved in this case or if she was innocent. He had to go to Thistle Brook Farm.

One look at Grandma Bridget, and he smiled. He couldn't have planned this more perfectly.

He removed his apron and placed it on his grandmother. "I forgot something at the farm. By the time I get back, I'm sure you and Penny will have done a much better job. I'll let Doc Jenkins know where I'm going… He can watch over Easton."

Jase pecked his grandmother's cheek, the lines deeper and more finely etched than the last time he saw her in person.

She raised her chin and pointed to the door. "The cookies will taste better once they bake in a preheated oven. We'll be fine."

He turned to leave but heard Penny's soft voice. "Thanks for trying… Jase."

He paused and nodded and gave a quick smile.

Not long after, Jase was talking to the police officer currently keeping an eye on the farm. Officer Nguyen had nothing new to report, so Jase traveled along the road to the farmhouse but stopped short of where he would normally park. He decided stealth would be his friend. Adrenaline pumped through him as he buckled on his duty belt. It was the moment of truth.

Was Yablonsky here? Or was Cassie innocent?

With caution, Jase approached the house, but a quick tour proved fruitless. Where was she? Not only had Officer Nguyen seen no one arrive, but he'd also seen no one leave, and Cassie didn't have a working vehicle. That meant she was somewhere on the farm, but was she alone?

He only had two hundred acres to cover, but a farm this size could still provide ways for someone to slip in unnoticed. Yablonsky could already be on the property.

Suddenly it became that much more imperative that Jase found Cassie.

He'd start where he'd left her this morning. As he approached the greenhouse, he heard pop music. That was one mystery solved. He entered and bit back a laugh.

Cassie was dancing and singing while holding a potted plant in her hands.

He covered his mouth, but his laughter gave him away.

Cassie turned and gasped. Two bright red patches covered her cheeks, and she looked all the more endearing for it.

"Jase! What are you doing back so soon?" The color faded from her face as she looked beyond him. "Are Easton and Penny okay?"

In his haste to return to Thistle Brook, not once had he considered what excuse he'd give Cassie if

Yablonsky wasn't here. "Yes, absolutely. They're fine." He quickly came up with a reasonable explanation for his presence. "My grandmother filled in for Judy, and I thought of you handling everything by yourself. I came back to help. After all, four hands work faster than two."

A huge smile showed off a dimple in her right cheek. Her enthusiasm made him believe in people again. "That's the nicest thing you've done since yesterday." She wrinkled her nose and turned off the music. "I hear plants prefer classical anyway."

"I'm sure they don't mind since you're a good singer." Jase caught her gaze, and suddenly he was entranced by those hazel eyes. The green flecks were almost mesmerizing. "I won't tell anyone you sing to your plants."

"The plant singer and the hen whisperer. I can't imagine why we don't want to shout our talents from the rooftops." She winked at him. "I guess it will be our little secret."

He gave a shudder. *Secrets.* His job was to ferret them out, and yet the minute he stepped foot in Violet Ridge, they came back to haunt him. Even innocent ones like this added extra weight to his shoulders.

His phone pealed, and he excused himself. After a short conversation with Grandma Bridget, he returned to Cassie, a pair of garden shears in hand, the pop music at a lower volume. She pointed to his phone. "Did they find Keith?"

"It wasn't Shields. It was my grandmother inviting us to dinner." It would be easier to refuse Captain Shields, which never happened, than to say no to his grandmother. "She wants to know if you're okay with my grandfather driving Penny and Easton to Lazy River?"

"Of course." Then Cassie frowned. "I'm sure they're just inviting us to be polite. They can drop Penny and Easton here while you go have dinner with them, if you'd prefer?" A glimmer of her earlier smile returned. "You have an amazing family. Spend time with them while you can."

If Cassie and her children were there, he'd not only get to enjoy their company but frankly also have an excuse to put off his conversation with his siblings and grandparents to a future date. With that in mind, he passed on the message from his grandmother. "Grandma Bridget predicted you'd say something like that, and she ensured me the invitation is for all of us."

Whether it was to alleviate any tension or raise her matchmaking game, Jase wasn't sure, but he did intend to pull his grandmother aside and assure her he wouldn't be dating during his short stay in Violet Ridge. Work demanded his full attention. And even if he took the easy way out and didn't tell his family about that fateful night his parents crashed, he still wouldn't be interested in seeing anyone romantically. Because if he were going to date while he was in town, Cassie would be the only person he'd want to ask out. That notion floored him.

"What time is dinner?" Cassie looked at the rows of plants. "I have another hour of pruning and watering that I have to get done today."

"Count me in." He rolled up his sleeves and prepared to get dirty.

"You've already done so much..." But she let the protest fade away and pointed to the hose. "Can you water that row of tomatoes?"

Jase nodded and turned on the hose, sneaking a peek at Cassie as he watered the vegetables.

She talked to each plant before setting the pruning shears to them. The farmer was sincere and kind, and so far had done nothing to contradict his perception of her. Every time he searched for some sign that she wasn't as she appeared to be, she proved him wrong. In fact, he only found more about her to admire.

No wonder Grandma Bridget was eager to set Cassie up with him. But he resided in Denver, and by this time next year, he'd be the youngest captain ever in his department.

But at least they'd have dinner together tonight.

CASSIE EMERGED FROM Jase's sedan at the Lazy River Dude Ranch and glanced over at him. There was something different about him, something that troubled her. It wasn't to do with his physical appearance. If anything, he looked more striking with his blue Oxford shirt and a pair of black dress pants. The stubble on his face only added to his appeal. Then it hit her.

His eyes. They didn't hold the same intensity she'd come to expect from him. Tonight, they seemed dull.

Was he dreading tonight? If so, why? She was the outsider, although she had spent more time here since she and Amanda had become friends. When she met Amanda at Blue Skies Coffee House several months ago, they'd found many common interests. Since then, their friendship had cemented to the point where Amanda was practically an aunt to Penny and Easton. Amanda's sister, Sami, was also a favorite of Penny's. Both Amanda and Sami offered Cassie an open-ended invitation to drop in at the Lazy River any time, and Cassie took advantage of that whenever she had the chance. That was less often over the past few months, with the corn maze preparation.

Still, whenever she visited, Jase's grandparents always greeted her and treated her children with the utmost kindness. That was what confused her about Jase. He had nothing to fear being here, and yet he was acting like he had something to hide. It seemed as though he was counting the minutes until he could return to Thistle Brook Farm. Was he that worried about her brother turning up at any moment?

Maybe she was reading too much into his expression. So far, Jase had shown he was a master at shielding his feelings from everyone else. She supposed he had to, considering he was a detective. Interrogating others without giving anything away was probably a standard part of his job, as was protecting the public. His intensity was probably his most effective trait in those interviews. After all, his forceful personality made a big impact on her.

It struck her how fortunate she was that Jase had been assigned this detail. Other officers in his place might have judged her and assumed she was guilty because of her connection to Keith.

After he'd been found guilty, she threw herself into every activity that would have her, lending a hand to anyone who asked her. What started as a way to gain favor had quickly turned into something more special and meaningful, an opportunity to feel needed. She loved the community garden and anticipated tasting Judy and Penny's cookies and always enjoyed seeing Doc Jenkins play Easton at checkers. One of these days Easton would beat Doc Jenkins fair and square.

Jase met her at the passenger's door, and his hand brushed her back. The shock from his gentle touch went straight to her heart.

He startled as if a rattlesnake had darted in front of him. "Sorry about that."

Her nerve endings went on full alert, and she blinked away the warm sensation. She had to stay focused. He was assigned to protect her and her kids. That was all. As soon as Keith was apprehended, Jase would return to Denver, and she'd remain at Thistle Brook Farm.

Unfortunately, one look at his strong profile

ruined her determination to put everything into perspective. It wasn't his actual touch that was causing these feelings of attraction. It was his loyalty and protectiveness that was causing her to react to him like this. Who wouldn't respond to his heroic nature during a stressful time?

Add in how he was going above and beyond his official duties by helping her with farmwork, and she couldn't blame herself for feeling this way. Still, she steeled herself against falling into the same behavior that had caused her so much heartache in the past.

"No harm done." Still, something was bothering the detective, and she intended to use her people skills to ferret the truth out of him. She laid her hand on his arm.

This time, it was her turn to feel startled, the contact with his firm muscles more powerful than she'd expected. "Now, I'm jittery. Is there something wrong? It's almost like you don't want to go inside."

He scrubbed his face and glanced at the dude ranch's main lodge, looking conflicted. "I should have stayed in Denver. Sometimes there's too much water under the bridge."

As much as she wanted to see Penny and Easton and hear how Adopt a Grandparent Day went, she longed to spend more time with Jase first. After all, his mere presence reassured her, so maybe she could return the favor.

The sound of horses nickering in the distance called to her.

"It's a beautiful night. Can we take a minute to compose ourselves before we head inside?" She crooked her arm and held it out to him. "Want to take a stroll and visit the horses? We'll only be a few minutes."

He hesitated before pointing toward the meadow and accepting her arm. "I'd like to see Wilma and Betty again. They're the oldest horses on the ranch."

"I love that your grandparents gave them a permanent home." They walked arm in arm toward the meadow. "You know what I love about horses? They're resilient and remember people who are meaningful to them."

A comfortable silence fell between them, and she gazed out at the sight of mustangs running and grazing. Jase pointed to a pair of horses standing near each other, both of whom had blankets on their backs. "There they are. Wilma and Betty. Wherever one is, the other's not far behind."

Wilma spotted them and whinnied. She trotted over and nudged Jase's hand until he reached into his pocket and produced a sugar cube. Wilma ate it out of his hand and then let him stroke her muzzle.

"She remembers you," Cassie observed.

Once again, the detective was full of surprises, keeping a sugar cube for Wilma in his pocket. Her heart thumped even harder.

Wilma soon had enough and departed. Jase

leaned on the post of the fence and faced Cassie. "I remember you from high school. You were hard to miss, especially since you were on every committee."

His notice was news to her. "I never realized you knew I was alive."

He shrugged and transferred his gaze back to the horses but not before something passed between them—a flicker, a spark. No matter the past, he knew she existed now.

"I never dated in high school since I was counting the days until I entered the police academy."

More shocking information from Jase. "There are stations here in Violet Ridge. Why didn't you end up settling nearby?" Cassie glanced at the craggy, snowcapped mountains and the mustangs in the meadow. This was almost perfection as far as she was concerned.

"There was an incident at the academy. A minor car accident. No major injuries." He paused, and she murmured a note of concern. "After that I needed a change, and Denver was big enough to suit me."

How a person could prefer any place to Violet Ridge was beyond her. "Is Denver everything you hoped it would be?"

He faced her, his expression strange, and she caught her breath. Jase Virtue was showing emotion.

"Seems you can run from yourself but never

hide." He jammed his hands into his pockets. "Are you cold? Ready to go inside?"

Not when she was this close to finding out something personal about the detective. "I'm not cold." Her jacket was fleece lined and oh-so-deliciously warm. "What are you running from?"

She should have been the one running, straight to Florida and her mom's caring embrace, but she'd never leave her home.

"Right now, my nerves. My grandmother is a force to be reckoned with, and I'm sure I'm in for an evening of questions." No doubt he preferred to be on the other side of the interrogation table.

"Seems like I should be the one who's nervous." Not that she had anything to hide. After Keith, she prided herself on being as transparent as possible when it came to how she lived her life. "Your family has the reputation of living up to your last name, and well…"

Her maiden name wasn't regarded highly in Violet Ridge. But she worked hard every day to prove she was nothing like her brother.

"Has it been that difficult since Keith's conviction?"

"Let's just say I discovered who my friends are." She wouldn't name names or bad-mouth anyone. "Your family has always been kind."

"Your farmstand customers seem loyal," he said.

It was her turn to stare out at the meadow and take comfort from the mustangs' rambling. "It's taken a long time for some people to see me for who I really am."

"Do we ever see people as they really are?" The weariness in his voice struck her. Did that mean he was ready for a change? Perhaps a career change to a quieter hamlet? Maybe he needed this time in Violet Ridge more than he realized.

"I think so. In spite of everything, I know the people who've supported me and focus on them rather than the naysayers."

For the first time since they arrived, he smiled a genuine smile, the same one that had always caught her attention in the high school hallways. "Thank you for supporting me. You've already made this evening easier." His shoulders relaxed, and he seemed ready to take on the world again.

"Any time." His strength bolstered her resolve as well. "Tonight when we get back to the farm, I'm going to tell Penny and Easton about Keith."

He nodded his approval. Then he clenched his jaw as if her reminder about her half brother had closed off any possibility of a lasting connection with her.

She couldn't blame him. The last thing he needed for the good of his career was to become involved with anyone related to an escaped convict. Her stomach grumbled, and she tried to put aside the new tension. "Guess it's time to face the music."

As they entered the main lodge, she couldn't help but wonder what it would have been like if he hadn't visited Violet Ridge until it was Seth and Amanda's wedding. If she and Jase had become reacquainted then…would she have allowed this flicker of attraction for him to roar to life?

No, she wouldn't have acted on it then, either. He was firmly entrenched in Denver. He belonged there, same as she belonged here.

At least, he was in Violet Ridge for now. She couldn't think of a better person to guard her family against the possibility of any harm from Keith.

A BETTER PERSON would know how to respond to the look on Penny's face right now, Jase thought. Glancing at the plump pillows on Cassie's couch in her living room, he wondered why Penny and Easton couldn't have fallen asleep on the way home from dinner at the dude ranch.

The meal had been delicious. Ingrid, their beloved cook and longtime friend, had outdone herself for the celebration of Jase's return. Tonight revolved around family togetherness rather than a time for revelations and possibly their hurtful consequences. Grandma had made the right call asking Cassie and her children to accompany him. Not only did it give Jase a solid reason to postpone the difficult conversation, but their company provided him with a chance to linger on the periphery and observe his family. It was easy to register the concern on Grandpa Martin's face whenever he sent a loving look toward his wife, a reminder of the stroke's impact on them. And another reason to cherish the invitation.

Before Jase and the O'Neal family had headed back to Thistle Brook Farm, his grandparents surprised him with the news they were transporting Highlander, a spirited mustang, for him to ride at Thistle Brook while he was in town.

He didn't often have a chance to ride in Denver, and he intended to get in some quality time before the precinct claimed him once more. Another advantage to having Highlander at the farm would be the convenience of going anywhere on the farm, searching for any places Yablonsky might have hidden his stash.

But now, here Jase was, sitting in Cassie's living room with Penny and Easton staring straight at him. Cassie had asked for him to be present when she told the children about her half brother's past, and he'd agreed.

He never imagined Penny would blame him. Jase's heart ached at Penny taking her anger at Yablonsky out on him. Her eyes, so much like Cassie's, burned with a fierceness that he wouldn't ever forget.

"You probably don't even like our farm. You're going to leave us, just like my daddy."

So that was what was bothering her. This wasn't about Yablonsky; this wasn't about him. She was really angry at Brayden for abandoning her and Easton.

"I don't get it. You rebuilt the coop." Easton

looked confused, and Cassie repeated the story of how Jase came to be there. Easton rattled Jase's hand. "You're not Mommy's helper?" The trust in Easton's eyes faded like the last rays of sunlight on a summer day.

Cassie shifted, and her children turned their attention toward her. Easton let out a cry and ran toward her, his sniffles almost breaking Jase's heart.

"Penny, Easton." Cassie hugged them, her nurturing side roaring to life once more. "Jase is the good guy here. He didn't have to help with the henhouse roof or drive us around or give us a hand with other things, but he did anyway because he's an upstanding man. He's here to make sure you're safe. I trust him, and so should you."

Cassie's words splintered Jase's heart. She trusted him. And he was hiding a whopper of a secret from her—that Shields was still convinced she was aiding and abetting Yablonsky. Even though Jase had found no evidence of that.

Penny shuffled her feet. "Can I go to sleep now?"

Cassie sighed and nodded. "I'll get the eggs tomorrow morning."

Penny opened her mouth as if to argue. Then she walked away as if recognizing the value in Cassie's offer. She left the room with Easton still looking as if he was trying to make up his mind about Jase.

Jase tried to convince himself it didn't matter, yet the opinion of the O'Neal children meant a great deal to him. Jase glanced at Cassie, trust coming out of those deep hazel eyes. That it could be misguided or premature struck him like an arrow.

Tonight, family had certainly been on his mind. He realized what he'd been missing by cutting himself off from others, from having someone special in his life. Daisy and Seth had found happiness with Ben and Amanda, and he reveled in seeing them in love. Even Crosby seemed more present than usual, a far cry from his absent-minded self, always occupied with some random historical detail. He supposed that was how he and Crosby were alike, determined to get to the heart of something. Except in Crosby's case, no one was likely to get hurt.

Jase wanted to know how Crosby's story would play out. All of his siblings' stories, actually. And yet he'd given up that privilege of his own accord a long time ago. It was only fitting that he felt so alone now. Or before he'd come to Thistle Brook Farm.

It wasn't time to confront anything else yet, not when Easton needed him present in this moment. Easton tugged on Cassie's shirt and motioned for her ear. He whispered something to her.

Cassie hugged him and replied out loud, "Sometimes doing the right thing means standing on your own two feet. Penny will come around and see Jase is a good guy."

"I can't help if you keep me in the dark." Jase wanted Easton to trust him.

Easton turned to his mother, who nodded and sent him a look of pure encouragement. "Jase has three siblings. He might have insight that I don't."

Inching closer toward Jase, Easton gulped. With his face scrunched up, he said, "I love Penny, so can I like you and still be a good brother?"

Jase met Cassie's gaze, her nod subtle but clear, giving him the go-ahead to answer Easton. Jase scrubbed his face, the stubble more pronounced this late in the day.

"I have a sister and two brothers, and believe me, we don't always agree. But that's okay. Thinking differently about something doesn't mean we don't care about each other. Even though I don't agree with Seth and Daisy and Crosby all the time, I still love them, and they love me."

Easton seemed satisfied. A big yawn came over him, and Cassie sent him upstairs to get ready for bed.

"Thank you. You handled that like a true friend." She came forward but then steered away from Jase with a nervous chuckle. "Sorry about that. I was about to hug you for such a terrific answer, but I'd best make sure Easton brushes his teeth. See you tomorrow."

Jase watched Cassie follow Easton up the stairs, regret coursing through him at missing out on her hug. The peace he'd sought for so long never felt more out of reach.

He pushed those thoughts aside. If Captain Shields found out he was developing feelings for a possible suspect, he'd be removed from the case in a fast second. The next detective might not be convinced Cassie was innocent. Worse yet, the detective might slip up, and harm could befall Penny, Easton or Cassie.

Jase wouldn't let that happen.

CHAPTER FIVE

JASE WAITED AT the bus stop for Penny and Easton. Another two days had passed, and still no verified sightings of Yablonsky. Captain Shields and the department were stymied about how one man could escape notice so well. Yablonsky must be working with someone, but whom? Cassie was under twenty-four-hour surveillance, and everything pointed to her innocence in both the robbery and the escape.

But if she wasn't aiding Yablonsky, who was?

Everything was getting too complicated for his liking, especially given he'd never been so personally attached to someone involved in one of his undercover assignments before. He was, dare he even think it, happy at seeing Cassie first thing in the morning. It wasn't just her beautiful smile, either, but the beautiful person she was on the inside. Her kindness, her smartness and her humor. She was downright gleeful when she discussed the benefits of organic farming. He craved listening to the advantages of avoiding synthetic pesticides and improving biodiversity, which was a sure sign he should pack up and be on his way back to Denver.

The school bus screeched to a halt in front of the mailbox. The door swung open, and Easton ran to greet Jase with a hug. It was too easy to imagine becoming a part of this family, at breaking his hard and fast rule not to become involved, but one look at Penny, mistrust written all over her face, brought Jase crashing back to earth.

Easton chattered all the way to the farmhouse while Penny kept her distance, trailing behind and kicking at the gravel path.

As soon as Easton was out of breath, Jase asked Penny, "How was your day?"

Penny jutted out her lower lip and shrugged. "My music teacher chose someone else for the solo, and they ran out of peaches at lunch. I had to have boring raisins instead." She glanced around Jase. "Where's Mommy?"

"She's harvesting the turnips in the upper field."

In his peripheral vision, Jase caught sight of movement near the root cellar. A loud thump startled them, then the door thudded against the frame. It couldn't be Cassie since he had just left her a few minutes ago. His senses went on high alert. The children's safety was his top priority.

"Penny, take Easton into the farmhouse. Lock your bedroom door behind you." Penny stood with her mouth wide open as if to argue with him. "Now."

Penny must have sensed his urgency for she

grabbed Easton's hand. Jase watched the back door close behind them before he proceeded to the root cellar. With caution, he passed the old pickle barrel and approached the wooden door with his weapon drawn. He'd already been inside the cellar once, the stairs leading to a dank, dark room lined with shelves, the icy temperature perfect for storing vegetables.

He could only make out one set of boot prints in the dry, brown dirt. There hadn't been any rain for a couple of days. They looked on the small side. Could Cassie be down there after all?

As quietly as possible, he opened the door, the hinges rusty and creaking. So much for stealth mode.

A calico streak ran past him, yowling as it bolted from the root cellar where Cassie stored harvested vegetables and flat cardboard boxes.

He holstered his weapon. A quick examination of the room proved the culprit had indeed been Patches the cat. That was the second time Patches had caused Jase's heart rate to skyrocket. Holding his flashlight aloft, Jase spotted a rock on the third step. Cassie must have used the rock as a doorstop, only for Patches to dislodge it and get trapped in the cellar.

Penny and Easton! They must be scared.

Jase hurried to the house and found the back door locked. Using his key and resetting the security system, Jase entered the mudroom when he caught sight of a baseball bat aimed at his head.

Jase raised his arms. "Cassie, it's just me."

Cassie lowered the bat and laid her hand on his arm. "Jase! Are you okay?"

The softness of her skin on his bare arm registered as he regained his composure. "What are you doing here?" He sounded too breathless for his liking.

"Penny sent me an alert on my phone." She reached into her jacket pocket and brought out her cell along with a clump of dirt that fell to the clean floor.

They went upstairs and tried Penny's bedroom door. Locked. Hushed singing greeted Jase's ears before Cassie knocked and identified herself and Jase.

The murmurs stopped, and he heard something scrape across the floor before Penny opened the door.

Smart and protective. That was Penny. Just like her mother.

"It was Patches, not Yablonsky," Jase wasted no time explaining to the young children. "Your cat almost trapped herself down there."

Penny rushed over and hugged him. "You were so brave."

Jase registered Penny's remorse. A rush of emotion overwhelmed him. It took all of his training to reign in his feelings. He was a detective and had to keep his joy at her acceptance from clouding his suspicions and doing his duty. Getting too involved was a recipe for disaster. It would lead to heartbreak for all of them, if not something worse. His gaze went to Penny's bookbag on the floor. "Do you have any homework?"

Cassie let out a nervous laugh. "For once, I think that can wait until after dinner. I'm just grateful everyone is safe. Thank you, Jase."

He didn't like being the center of attention, especially when he was just doing his job. "Yablonsky is still on the loose, and we have to be vigilant."

"Point taken." Cassie glanced at Penny and Easton. "Highlander arrived while you were at school. How about we all go to the stable and say hello?"

"I'm gonna change into my favorite boots right now." Easton's enthusiasm was boundless. He approached Jase and paused. His already-endearing grin brought Jase a sense of pure joy. "I knew you wouldn't let anything bad happen to us."

The boy threw himself around Jase's midsection, and all the emotion he'd tried to hide burst forth in spite of Jase's best efforts. This family was piercing his resolve, no matter how strongly he wanted to keep them at bay.

Easton reminded Jase so much of himself when he was five, the year before the car crash that claimed his parents' lives. Jase had basked in his mother's love and his father's attention. Now, his memories of them were fleeting. A whiff of jasmine would remind him of his mother. Musky aftershave would bring a flash of his father's face before it was gone. He still missed them.

Jase faced Easton, his resolve intact once more. "I'm not infallible."

"Huh? I don't know what that means, but you're really nice, and you're protecting us." Easton smiled at him. "And now your horse is here, and he'll become best friends with my horse. Yes!"

Penny and Easton grabbed their boots and hurried downstairs, leaving him behind with Cassie. Somehow this pretty farmer was the one he needed to guard his heart against the most.

"It's not every day that I allow homework to slide." The twinkle in her eyes was almost his undoing. "But Highlander's beautiful, and it's still early in the day. They can finish after dinner."

"Discipline..." Jase let the words fade away and nodded. "I'll be downstairs in a minute. Wait for me?"

"Of course." She hesitated and then threw her arms around him, the smell of apples and sweetness and goodness enveloping him. Every day it was getting harder to think of Cassie as anything other than a beautiful mom who captivated a community rather than someone who might be a hardened criminal. "Thank you for protecting them."

Cassie let go of him and went to join her children downstairs, leaving him by himself. Soon enough, he'd be back at his apartment, alone, the quiet different from the perpetual noise at the farm with either the hens, the children or Cassie herself always in motion.

For now, it was enough that he was protecting this family.

It had to be enough.

IN THE STABLE, Cassie stared at the saddles with longing. After the scare with the root cellar and Patches, a long ride sounded perfect. The four horses came over to the railing as if agreeing with her. They could use the exercise.

She had an idea and pulled Jase aside. "You're here to look for the money that might be hidden somewhere on the property. Who better to help us than Penny and Easton? Kids are great at treasure hunts. They see things with a different perspective."

He seemed to be weighing her words with the same care and caution he gave every situation. There wasn't anyone else she'd want here at the farm guarding her and her children for that exact reason.

"You have a point."

"And you can count on the Violet Ridge officer patrolling the area. He'll let you know if he sees Keith." She rubbed her hands together at the prospect of a long ride.

"But if we come upon Yablonsky, I can't protect all of you." His jaw clenched, and he shook his head. "I won't risk that."

"If we find the money, Keith will have no reason to invade my space." It was bad enough her half brother had put her on edge; she wouldn't let him disrupt everything for a moment longer than necessary.

Jase glanced in Highlander's direction, and he relaxed his shoulders. If Cassie wasn't mistaken, her detective even possessed a slight smile on his lips.

"Grandma Bridget told me Highlander lives for the trail," he said, and she knew they were about to saddle the horses.

"And this is the prettiest land around." Her insides celebrated at the thought of an early evening horseback excursion and sharing more time with him.

"Do you see the good in everything?"

Now it was her turn to sigh. "For years, I couldn't see the good in people when they were looking at me as if I were responsible for my brother. Then I woke up and decided I couldn't control the past, but I sure could control my future."

With that being said, she enlisted her children to prepare the horses for the ride. In no time, they were on the trail. Pride filled her at the way Penny and Easton had taken to horseback riding from a very early age. As soon as they knew their right from their left, she'd had them on Hickory and Honeybee.

Jase pulled up on Highlander, and the rest of them halted. He kept his gaze on Penny and Easton, although it was clear he was also laser-focused on his surroundings.

"If you had something you wanted to hide from

your sibling, where would you go first?" Jase asked the kids.

Ha! Jase was taking her advice to heart.

Penny shrugged, and Easton looked pensive. "Penny doesn't play with my cars or any of my stuff, so why would I want to hide them from her?"

Penny rolled her eyes and huffed. "He means like allowance or when Grandma Theresa sends us money for our birthdays." Her gaze landed on a spot in the distance, and she nodded. "I know a good place."

Her daughter took the lead, skirting around the back of the corn maze. Hazel trotted along the path while Cassie did some fast calculations. Even with all the delays, she was on schedule for the corn maze grand opening but barely. The construction company would finish the last-minute touches next week. She still needed to prepare the concession stand price board.

And that was on top of her other farm chores. With the first frost expected any day now, she needed to finish harvesting the last of the fall crops and sort them into the subscription boxes for her customers.

Perhaps she had spread herself too thin. She had to start saying no to some of her new ideas.

Still, the next few days were jam-packed, and she did have a determined helper, so she'd best savor every moment of this ride.

Soon, they arrived at a peaceful landing where

Thistle Brook, an offshoot of Lazy River, cut a natural boundary between her property and the rocky terrain of her neighbor's ranch. This was a favorite family location for summer picnics, flat rocks providing a tabletop and aspens delivering cool shade.

Cassie dismounted and helped Easton off Honeybee. There were signs that elk and deer had visited recently, and Cassie kept an eye out for any unwelcome visitors.

Jase secured Highlander to a nearby aspen and turned to help Penny with her horse. "If you had to hide something here, where would it be?"

Penny tapped her chin and squinted. "Not too near the water. Sometimes the creek rises, and I wouldn't want my money getting wet."

"Smart and insightful. You'd make a good detective." Jase's praise sat well with her daughter, who beamed.

Easton came over and pulled on Jase's coat. "I know where I'd hide it." He pointed to a nearby grove of scrub oaks. "In a tree."

"Another detective in the making." Jase searched the area and motioned at the pair, who followed him to the grove. His gaze made quick work of the scene. "I don't know about hiding treasure in these trees. Hmm, none of them have knots to indicate there'd be holes big enough to hide that much money."

Easton's face fell, and Cassie reassured him. "That was some good thinking, though. Both of you. You're right that the banks sometimes flood, and your gift from Grandma would be a soggy mess. It's getting late, and we should head back for dinner. Besides, you have school tomorrow."

Easton groaned. "Can't we stay here a couple more minutes?" He picked a pebble off the ground and tossed it in the air before catching it. "Can I skip some stones first?"

"Stay where I can see you." Cassie watched as Penny joined her brother at the creek bed, each taking turns trying to skim stones over the water's surface.

Jase remained behind.

Cassie could see the wheels in his mind turning. "Do you really think Keith hid the money here at Thistle Brook Farm? Could this be the place?"

"Until recently, our intel was that he hadn't traveled this far after the robbery, but new information confirmed he did." Jase scoped out the area with a critical eye.

"If Keith hid the money here, I'm glad you're the one looking for it. It's easier working with someone with ties to Violet Ridge, someone who knew me growing up. Otherwise, I'd probably be suspect number one."

That tic in his jaw throbbed once more, and she wondered if he wasn't telling her everything. Of course, he couldn't. He was conveying what she needed to know and, most important, what would keep her family safe.

Did she need to pull back where Jase was concerned? It would be too easy to mistake her gratitude for personal feelings, too easy for her to imagine something that wasn't there. Likely, Keith would be in custody before long, and Jase would be back in Denver. Then she'd sort out these emotions she had, whatever they were.

She stepped back and called for Penny and Easton. They still had homework and dinner and some playtime to get through before bed, and the sun was starting to set. They'd all best return to the farmhouse before any of those unwanted visitors came upon them.

CHAPTER SIX

WITH THE NOONDAY sun shining bright, Cassie knelt at the last row of turnips, digging them out by hand. The day was slipping away fast, and she had a mere couple of hours before she'd meet Penny and Easton at the bus stop.

On the other side of the field, Jase was doing the same. Since the ride to the creek two days ago, he'd become glued to Cassie's side. While she bristled at having to account to him for every minute spent, Jase was a sweetheart under his tough detective persona. Seeing him last night at the dining room table patiently listening to Penny recite her multiplication tables and then reading with Easton? It would take a harder heart than hers to resist that man.

Other detectives would have probably kept their distance, but Jase blended into her family so well.

Almost too well. For the umpteenth time, she reminded herself he didn't live in Violet Ridge. Good thing, too, or once this was over and Keith was in prison again, she might do something that would go against everything she'd worked for these past few years. Like putting her heart on the line and telling him about her growing feelings for him.

Then what? Like a detective would want to get involved with the half sister of a convicted bank robber, even if she did have the two most adorable children in the world. Like someone as intense as Jase would want to get involved with someone like her with her soft heart who said yes to every cause and commitment around.

Besides, she had told Brayden she loved him, and he still left for Alaska.

Even if she did tell Jase, there was a promotion waiting for him in Denver. How could she compete with that?

Cassie stood and stretched in an attempt to get the kinks out of her back. She leaned one way, then the other before brushing the dirt off her jeans. She reached for the basket of turnips and found Jase beat her to it. "You don't have to carry them for me."

"Grandma Bridget would give me a tongue lashing if I didn't."

She saw through his excuse. Modest, humble and a hard worker, he was a gentleman, through and through. Unlike her former husband, who never helped her if he could manage it. Brayden always claimed his job exhausted him, and eventually it was easier to just do everything herself. She never should have let him get away with that.

"I have ginger scones and pumpkin butter waiting at the farmstand. Whatever we don't finish,

Penny and Easton will polish off when they arrive home." Cassie had kept some snacks separate from the ones she'd sold to this morning's customers.

"Homemade scones?" Jase licked his lips. "I can't guarantee there'll be anything left over."

She smiled, appreciating the compliment about her baking. Together, they walked to the farmstand. While slathering a fair amount of pumpkin butter on her scone, she caught sight of the farmhouse and hoophouses. Sometimes it was hard to believe this was the same farm her mother signed over to her when she left to retire in Florida in return for a share of the profits.

Cassie loved her father, but he was a much better farmer than businessman. He taught her plenty about organic pesticides and crop rotation, but she learned everything about promoting the agritourism aspects of her farm from the seniors at the center. Many shared worthwhile advice with her whenever she brought Penny and Easton to the Adopt a Grandparent Days.

She listened to Glenn Bayne discuss the ins and outs of smart accounting. Former mayor Zelda Baker had brought up the idea of seasonal subscription boxes, which had been a huge hit with her customers.

Cassie savored the last bite of the scone as much as the first, then washed her hands thoroughly at the sink. There was no sense wasting the few minutes until Penny and Easton were due to arrive, so she reached under the table for the cardboard boxes to fill with autumn vegetables for her subscription customers. Zelda's promotional idea had been an absolute godsend.

She wiggled her fingers into fresh latex gloves and offered Jase a pair before she stopped in her tracks. "What am I thinking? You're a guest. Finish your scone."

Jase scrunched his face before he popped the last bite into his mouth. He accepted the gloves and began negotiating them on. "It was delicious, thank you. But I'm your hired hand, remember? I told Penny and Easton when I arrived that I intended to help you. I keep my word."

Unlike some people in her life, namely Keith and her former husband. What was more, Jase's actions of the past week were more than enough for her to take his statement as fact. He'd already made a believer of Blossom and Patches. Now, whenever she threw out chicken feed, Cassie thought Blossom was waiting for Jase to arrive and take over for her.

"Well, thank you for your help then. Some customers will start picking these up tomorrow. I've hired a neighbor to deliver the rest." Last year, she'd had them prepped a week in advance, but the corn maze construction and Jase's arrival had messed with her schedule.

Jase sent a perplexed look her way. "What are these boxes for anyway? Isn't it first come, first served?"

"Not with my sign-ups." Her gaze went to the

produce she'd hauled in before harvesting the rest of the turnips. "After one of the Adopt a Grandparent Days, Zelda Baker suggested I join a local group of farmers and ranchers who offer subscription services. Customers pay ahead of time for a box of produce or whatever every month. You remember the former mayor, don't you?"

"Anyone who's lived in Violet Ridge knows Zelda." Zelda and her identical twin sister had entrenched themselves in every facet of town life, and in the very best way. However, since the former mayor maintained a pixie cut in an attractive shade of green, while Nelda always wore fluorescent clothing, there was no mixing up the siblings.

"She sold me on the idea of these boxes," Cassie explained. "Each season, folks put a down payment on getting boxes of fresh produce every week. In summer, I provide red-leaf lettuce, eggplant and cherry tomatoes as well as other vegetables. I make them special by including produce that's not available at my stand. It was slow going at first, but I now have a waitlist to join. Tomorrow is the first of the fall boxes." She motioned to the different types of vegetables on the worktable. "This box will have sweet potatoes, spinach, squash, lettuce, onions and peppers. The extra item is a pumpkin pie. Each time there's a little variety."

Jase looked at the bounty and boxes, plus other supplies at the farmstand. "By having the customer come to you, they also get a look at whatever else you're selling in terms of pickled veggies, jam and baked goods."

Cassie tapped her finger against the side of her forehead. "Exactly. Zelda's a genius. Her encouragement has meant to world to me." She pointed to the farmhouse. "Best of all, the farm is self-sufficient because of it and then some. I've installed a new roof and updated the siding just in time. If I'd waited any longer, the termite infestation would have caused serious problems."

"Termites?" Jase wrinkled his nose.

She nodded. "My ex-husband, Brayden, hired his friend as our exterminator. Turns out his company wasn't very good." Cassie blew out a sigh. "I went with a different exterminator after Brayden left. The team did a great job and ultimately saved me thousands."

Cassie instructed Jase on the fastest way to fill the hundred boxes, and they both set to work. Silence reigned until Jase stopped for a sip of water. "That's only the second time you've mentioned your ex-husband. The first was in passing when you needed a security code Penny and Easton could remember."

Was it? Cassie reflected on the time since Jase had arrived, and he was right. "They get upset when his name is mentioned, especially Penny."

"I noticed her initial reluctance to accept me revolved around him."

As much as Cassie poked Brayden to return

more often, he insisted everyone would be happier if he remained in Alaska. If he could only see Penny's face whenever Cassie made excuses for him…

"Penny's more sensitive because she sees her friends' fathers and feels like she's missing out." Cassie stopped and wiped a strand of sweaty hair off her forehead.

"I remember what that was like at her age." Jase took another drink of his water. "At least I had my grandparents. They made the difference."

Cassie had almost forgotten how young he was when his parents passed away. "You were six, weren't you, when the accident happened?"

He nodded.

Her heart sank. "I must have seemed insensitive. After all, your parents died."

A shadow flitted across his face, then he placed his water on the worktable. "The three of you are so close, and Penny seems well-adjusted. When I first arrived, you talked about sending them to your mother in Florida, but you didn't suggest Brayden. Why?"

Was Jase asking as a detective or a friend? The answer would be the same either way, but it was easier talking to him as a friend than in his official capacity. "Shortly after I confirmed I was pregnant with Easton, Brayden figured out fatherhood wasn't for him. He's now a bush pilot in Alaska. Every so often, he'll text me updates, but those texts are getting fewer and farther between."

She located her reusable water bottle with its built-in filtration system. Finding it empty, she refilled it from the sink.

Jase's gaze didn't leave her the entire time. It was hard enough that he was here because her brother had escaped prison. Now he also knew about her failing at marriage. Brayden's departure from not just the farm but Violet Ridge, and their subsequent divorce had taken its toll on her, but it was nothing compared to Penny's hurt. Occasionally, she still asked if her daddy was coming home. That made Brayden's decisions to stay away so much worse.

Jase approached Cassie. His soft brown eyes showed incredible tenderness as he lifted her chin with his fingers. "He lost the best part of his life when he left this town," he said, his voice husky.

Cassie gulped as the air between them became charged. Did she want this? Now? It had taken her a lot to pick up the pieces after Brayden while raising two children. But there had been a long recovery period, and her heart had finally healed. Now she was at the point where she relished her independence and friends.

One glance at Jase with his inner strength and goodness told her it would take her forever to mend her heart if she ever let herself fall for him and it didn't work out in the end. Despite that and the other things that could keep them apart, she was still drawn to him. There was something about

Jase, something unique buried deep inside him. Vulnerability? Self-doubt?

He drew nearer, the full impact of his words finally reaching her core. For the first time in a long time, she found herself looking at a man's lips. Would Jase's still taste like pumpkin butter with a faint trace of ginger from the scones?

Despite everything in her life swirling around her like a whirling dervish, she wanted to kiss him. To know him in that way. She wanted to throw caution aside and dive.

Licking her lips, she wondered if one kiss would satisfy her. Could they then resume their normal lives on the farm and in Denver? No one else ever needed to know about the kiss.

His body tensed, and she realized it wasn't as simple as that. Jase was too honorable to keep it only between the two of them. If he told his superior about the kiss, at the very least, he'd be off the case. Penny and Easton would be devastated. So would she. At worst, Jase could be reprimanded or even demoted.

"What was that?" he asked.

He had to ask what an almost-kiss was, one that promised to be earth-shattering and wonderful? She raised her eyebrow. "How..."

He held up his hand. "Shh. Do you hear that?"

It was too early to be the school bus, yet it sounded like the dull roar of a truck motor. Was the mechanic delivering her truck to her farm? No, he'd have no way of getting back to Violet

Ridge unless someone else was following in a separate vehicle. "Maybe someone got their days mixed up and is coming here to pick up their box today."

Whatever was out there backfired, and Jase went on full alert, his eyes dark and stern, a far cry from the languid liquid steel of a minute ago. "Or it could be trouble."

A shiver went down her spine at the approach of possible danger. She blinked. Penny and Easton! If this was Keith, she had to get word to them to stay away from the farmhouse while the police apprehended him.

And then Jase would return to Denver. Perhaps she'd actually been saved from the secondary danger of kissing him.

"What about the extra patrol? Could it be the squad car that circles the property every other hour?" Cassie tried to latch on to any chance that it wasn't Keith. Should she phone the school, try to intercept the kids?

Jase went for the walkie-talkie at his belt and confirmed it wasn't the Violet Ridge police. He signed off with the responding officer before turning toward her. "We need to vary the pattern with Penny and Easton, so they're not predictable."

If only Jase was predictable and staid and boring, she wouldn't feel the attraction between them growing stronger.

"I'll escort you to the farmhouse and then notify the bus driver to take Penny and Easton back to school. Ben can pick them up. He won't let anything happen to them."

Cassie glanced at the boxes of vegetables when a faint sound attracted her attention. She looked at Jase, who stiffened even more if that was possible.

The whine of an animal, most likely a dog, gave everything away.

"It's not Keith." Cassie rushed toward the mailbox and blew out a breath at the sight of a messy medium-size retriever mix tied to the post with a rope. Someone had abandoned another dog on her property.

"Cassie!" Jase caught up with her.

"Unfortunately, this happens too frequently out here in the country." Her heart went out to the dog, whose gaze connected with hers. There was an old soul resting in those depths, too much like the man whose presence was starting to pervade her every thought. She expected the dog to make a fuss or bark or something, but he continued sitting there as if he'd been waiting for her all along.

Approaching him, she held out her hand so he could sniff her. She checked and found her supposition to be correct. The dog was a he. "Hi, sweet fellow."

Jase stood beside her, his body on edge. "Have you ever seen this dog before?"

The dog gave one tail thump before resting on his haunches beside the mailbox as if he'd lived here his entire life. That was unusual. It usually took her a week or longer to gain the trust of most dogs abandoned on her property. She always found them good homes. "No, but this happens six or seven times a year. Enough so I have a bag of dog food and treats in my mudroom. I've also found kittens on my doorstep. Patches was one of them. Another time a pair of hamsters." Toddler Penny insisted on keeping the duo, who became a part of the family for two years. "They stayed, but I put my foot down about the iguana, who now lives with your brother."

Cassie went to untie the dog when Jase placed his hand on her arm. "I'll call animal control."

"No, you won't. This guy is a sight more docile than most." Cassie inserted herself between Jase and the dog. "People around here know I relocate any animal dropped off here. I won't violate their trust."

"But he could hurt you." Jase stood his ground and reached for his phone. "You don't know if he's current on his rabies shots or anything about him."

Cassie found herself defending the dog, who continued sitting there patiently, his gaze never leaving her. She straightened her own spine. "I'll take him to the vet and have her check to see if he's microchipped after Penny and Easton arrive home. Perhaps she'll know who he is and have his vaccination records."

Something attached to the dog's neck caught her eye. She untied the rope from the mailbox and reached for the note. Just as she thought, a missive explaining someone couldn't keep the dog.

Her hackles rose at someone abandoning a loving animal like this. She crumpled the note and jammed it into her coat pocket. Expecting him to run for the road, perhaps even to try to track his former owner, she carefully loosened the rope attached to the dog's neck. Here went nothing. She untied him and waited.

The dog rose from his position and eyed her with trepidation before sniffing her hand. She held her breath, waiting for his reaction with Jase nearby, acting as if he was ready to pounce.

The dog licked her fingers and stood next to her as if he'd be her friend and defender forever more. How would Cassie say goodbye to him, unlike the other animals who'd come to the farm? After mere minutes, the dog had already bonded with her.

A little like the man who was standing guard beside her.

ON THE PATH to the farmhouse, Jase cringed. There was no way Cassie had just met that dog. Already in sync with her footsteps, the retriever mix stared at her with a devotion that needed time and energy to nurture.

Whatever was written in that note she slipped into her pocket was the key to the entire episode. He forced back the groan. The note was probably from Yablonsky. He needed to retrieve the slip of paper. Better yet, he'd have to treat it as evidence and take care that none of his fingerprints obscured Yablonsky's.

Before the dog alerted them to his presence, Jase had come close to kissing Cassie, which would have gone against everything he'd ever been taught. Believed in. Worse yet, before the dog arrived, he wouldn't have thought that was a bad tradeoff. A potential lifetime with Cassie? What had Brayden been thinking, leaving for the wilds of Alaska when he could have had a family with two great kids and a loving wife?

Now? How naive Jase had been. One hard-luck story, and he'd been ready to throw away his career by kissing Cassie.

If the note was from Yablonsky, it would confirm Captain Shields's theory that Cassie was the accomplice. He should have known Shields was right. After all, they had cleared the bank manager, Clara Abbott, a woman on the verge of retirement, who died a year after the robbery of cancer, shortly after testifying against Yablonsky. All the other employees, none of whom had initials starting with *C*, had also been ruled out.

Cassie's phone rang, and Jase went on high alert. Although Cassie had agreed to have a tracker placed on her phone, it could still be a new ally, hiding and helping Yablonsky.

Cassie held the phone to her chest. "It's the mechanic. Can you take me and Penny and Easton into Violet Ridge after dinner? My truck is fixed." She glanced at the dog who wouldn't leave her side. “You could drop us off at the clinic. The vet has extended hours tonight.”

The house would be unoccupied, raising his suspicions even more. He wouldn’t be fooled again. What was more, he’d make sure the local sheriff authorized double coverage so Yablonsky couldn’t sneak onto the property unnoticed. “Sounds good. I have another errand, anyway.”

Cassie sent him a smile of relief and lifted the phone back to her ear, confirming the details with the mechanic. They had arrived at Cassie’s back deck when she received another call. “Hold on, Mr. Mescal.” She pressed her phone against her chest once more and faced Jase, pointing to her bracelet with the fixed clasp. “Can you claim my watch while you’re downtown? I’ll pay you back.”

He agreed, curiosity about the note still tugging at his mind.

The dog followed them inside, and Cassie headed to the mudroom. The dog sat beside her like he’d done so a million times before. Jase had been around too many animals. This type of obedience didn’t happen without training.

Except it had with him and Blossom.

Jase ignored that thought and focused his attention on Cassie. Somehow, he had to get that note.

She pulled down a large plastic container and moved to the kitchen, the dog and Jase on her heels. She extracted a couple of harnesses from the container and compared sizes before picking one for her new best friend, along with a leash.

Jase tapped his foot. “A walk? Isn’t the bus supposed to arrive soon?”

“You remembered!” Cassie beamed and drew near, her arms reaching for him almost as if she was about to hug him. She took one look at him and stepped back, a hurt expression on her face. “We’ll have to hurry. After the kids arrive, I still have to finish sorting the vegetables. Maybe we should wait until tomorrow to go to town?”

“I can see the mailbox from the farmstand, and it won’t be any problem to finish sorting the vegetables into boxes while you get Penny and Easton settled.” Besides, Jase had every assurance Yablonsky wouldn’t try anything now that he’d communicated with Cassie.

“That would be a huge relief.” That shadow left Cassie’s face, and she looked like her normal self once more. “Come on, Rusty.”

Rusty followed her back to the mudroom, and Jase kept himself from gasping. If he had any doubt that the dog and Cassie had a history, it was dispelled at her calling him by name and the dog responding to her.

Cassie stopped at the trash can and threw away the note.

Surprised at how easy she made it, Jase lagged behind and excused himself, claiming a need to use the bathroom. In the kitchen, he found a plastic baggie and a pair of tongs. Necessity and urgency called for quick action.

His heart sank when he read the note written in

block letters with pencil. This only confirmed his worst fears about Cassie's involvement.

I CAN'T STAND BEING COOPED UP ALL DAY. I NEED A CHANGE. I TRUST YOU!! MAKE EVERYTHING BETTER. THERE'S NO ONE IN VIOLET RIDGE WHO IS BETTER FOR ME. PLEASE HELP ME.

Jase felt nauseous, a frown forming on his lips. Having her role as Yablonsky's accomplice spelled out in black-and-white like this felt like a punch to the gut.

With no time to spare, he made it to the farmstand. After a call to the Violet Ridge police department alerting them that he'd be bringing by a key piece of evidence by for analysis, he finished sorting the vegetables.

The next thing he saw was the school bus trundling past the farm. Easton ran toward Jase, the grin one of a kind. "Hey! Did you meet that great dog? I've always wanted a dog, but Mommy always finds homes for the ones who visit. Can you talk Mommy into letting us keep him? Please?"

Easton's words gave Jase pause. "I thought he was your dog."

Easton shook his head, his attention drawn to the leftover scones. "Can I have one? Mommy's are the best, and I'm so hungry. I ate lunch so-o-o long ago."

Penny and Cassie caught up with them, Rusty

not leaving Cassie's side. What if Easton was telling the truth, and the dog had never seen Cassie before? Could Jase be jumping to the wrong conclusion?

Maybe, but that note sealed his renewed belief in Cassie's guilt.

She examined the completed vegetable subscription boxes and smiled. "Thank you, Jase. Everything's exactly where it should be. If you ever get tired of working as a detective, you have a future in farming." She laughed and nodded at Easton's request for another scone.

It was such a family moment. For a split second, Jase had the faintest glimpse of his mother holding out a fresh tray of her excellent molasses cookies to him and Seth. Before he could latch on to the rest of the memory, it was gone. He didn't have many flashes of his mother anymore. His throat grew as dry as an empty creek bed at her loss.

Jase pushed away the memory. It had been his choice to leave Violet Ridge, and it was Cassie's choices that would bring her time with her family to an abrupt end for quite a while.

He kept that thought in mind throughout dinner and while accompanying the trio to the vet's office.

Rusty was quite intent about staying outside, digging his paws in at the threshold of the vet. Jase couldn't blame the poor fellow. This had to be a traumatic day for him. Still, he'd ended up with a great family. There was something to be said for Rusty's good taste that he bonded with Cassie so fast.

Jase clenched his jaw. Cassie turned him topsy-turvy if he believed that she'd never set eyes on Rusty before today. And still he felt a huge twinge of guilt deep inside that he wanted to belong to this family, too.

He needed some distance so he could compose himself. Become the tough and observant detective once more. "You'll be safe at the vet's. I'll collect the watches and meet you here after I run my errands."

Ignoring their protests, Jase hustled in the other direction before doubling back to his sedan. He collected the evidence and delivered it to the police precinct. The officer promised that the captain would receive the analysis as soon as possible but stopped short of a specific date or time. As always, Jase found himself at the mercy of the lab technicians.

For good measure, Jase hurried to Mescal's Repair Shop. With minutes to spare before closing time, he entered and recognized one of two people at the display counter. The man met Jase's gaze.

"Jase!" His younger brother, Crosby, immediately headed his way, enveloping him in a hug. He'd never quite adjusted to Crosby growing taller than him. "Sami, it's Jason, my long-lost brother."

The woman smiled and offered a quick wave. She looked as though she'd stepped out of the pages of a fashion magazine. Unlike Crosby's bedraggled appearance with a sweater that seemed like it was plucked out of their parents' closet, this woman wore clothes that spoke of style and careful choice. Her long blond hair was immaculately styled, not a strand out of place, and her makeup was elegant and understated.

"So I'm finally meeting you, Jase! I've heard so much about you, you rascal." Her smile grew wider, if that was even possible. "I'm Amanda's sister, Sami."

As if that was all the introduction they needed, she launched herself at him, giving him a big hug before returning to Crosby's side.

"What are you doing here?" Jase wanted to take back the words instantly, or at least the harshness in his tone.

Sami hooked her arm through Crosby's. "Your brother acts too old for his age, Jase. As his best friend, I've taken it upon myself to make sure he does something new and fun, and youngish every week."

Crosby's expression betrayed him. Jase didn't have to draw on his detective skills to see how enamored his brother was of Sami—who had just stated the two were best friends. His heart went out to Crosby for falling for someone who didn't feel the same way about him, at least as far as he could tell.

Then the world spun full circle. Had Jase fallen for the one woman with whom he had no future?

Confused and heartbroken, he tried to focus on the pair before him for distraction.

"What's the challenge this week?" Jase asked.

"Shopping." Crosby removed his arm from Sami's and went back to the glass display case. "Sami has never owned a watch, so we're here to buy her one."

She shrugged and waved her phone around. "Who needs a watch nowadays?" Her attention seemed to flit from one corner of the repair shop to the next. "I will admit some of these things are romantic. I especially like that grandfather clock over there."

Crosby turned and pushed his black glasses back to their usual position. "I'm surprised. Normally you don't like anything you can't fit in your car."

"Not for me. I was thinking of that as a wedding present for Amanda and Seth. It's so romantic that they're getting married on Valentine's Day, the same day as your grandparents' anniversary." Sami laughed and nudged Crosby's side. "Then we'll officially become family."

Crosby folded his arms, looking unhappy. "But just because Amanda and Seth are married, that won't make us related."

"But you'll be stuck with me forever after." Sami winked at Jase and then entwined her arm again in one of Crosby's. "I promise to send you a postcard from each and every one of my many international destinations."

A shadow fell across Crosby's face before he separated from her and peered at the watches.

So Jase wasn't the only brother who needed a distraction tonight. Still, Jase thought of one more question for the pair. "If you're buying your first watch, Sami, what was Crosby's challenge?"

"I talked him into going with me to karaoke night." Sami flipped her long hair to her back. "I have my song already picked out, and I'm trying to convince him to give it a go."

At that moment, Mr. Mescal appeared from behind the curtain. "I thought I heard voices." He nodded in Jase's direction. "I have Cassie's watch."

Jase paid for it and started making his excuses to his brother, who was having none of it.

"We can head to Brewer Brothers for a drink before the karaoke starts." Crosby whipped out his phone. "It's early enough. I can see if Seth and Amanda can join us."

"That would be so much fun," Sami agreed and stood on her tiptoes in an attempt to see over Crosby's shoulders. "Find out if Ben can watch the triplets so Daisy can come. It'll be a family reunion."

Jase's breath caught. The less of those while he was in town, the better. He shook his head and placed his hand over Crosby's phone. "I drove Cassie and her children into town. They're taking her dog to the vet."

"Cassie didn't have a dog the last time I visited her." Sami frowned and stopped looking over Crosby's shoulder. "Did someone drop another animal off at her place? Speaking of which, how's your iguana?"

"Sundance is fine." Crosby pocketed his phone and met Jase's gaze. "You need to come to the next weekly dance at the dude ranch before you head back to Denver. It would mean the world to Grandma Bridget if you danced with her."

Jase considered Crosby's offer. He'd never intentionally do anything to hurt his grandmother, but sometimes things happened that changed everything in an instant. No matter how much you might want to shield someone, sometimes that choice was wrested away from you. He'd waited too long for a discussion that was way overdue. His grandmother's stroke had given him pause; she deserved to know everything about the night her son died.

The irony that he might lose his family while gaining some semblance of peace by finally revealing the truth wasn't lost on him.

Crosby and Sami surrounded him like a shark circled its prey.

Jase was ready to bolt, but his heart still wanted one more dance with his grandma Bridget. One more fun night with his family before he finally shared his burden, one that could tear them apart. This time for keeps.Jase nodded and accepted the watch from Mr. Mescal. "I'll try."

Sami hugged him again and then smiled at Crosby. "Bring Cassie and Penny and Easton. They'll love it. The dances are every Saturday night until the dude ranch closes for winter."

Jase remained noncommittal and hurried to the door. “Rusty’s probably done by now.”

Sami laughed. “She named the dog? Oh, he must be special. I predict she’ll take one more wounded soul into her fold.”

With that, Jase escaped.

Wait a minute. Was Cassie only being nice to him because she sensed he was a wounded soul? Did he emit some kind of vibe? Was that the reason she almost kissed him today? Or had he come close to kissing her? It didn’t matter who instigated it; it would have been a catastrophe. But not for the most obvious reason: crossing a professional line.

No. Afterward, he might never want to leave Violet Ridge…and Cassie.

CHAPTER SEVEN

JASE ENTERED THE Violet Ridge Police Department, a low sandstone brick building. Solid and resolute. This was what he needed right now—a reminder of what he did for the community and why Cassie was off-limits to him.

His stomach grew queasy at the thought of finding out the fingerprint analysis of the note, and just the day after the dog's arrival. He still found it hard to reconcile the warmest, sweetest woman he'd ever met with a cold-blooded bank robber.

Another officer escorted him to Police Chief Zander Gutierrez's office. He shook hands with the chief and acknowledged Captain Shields on the laptop screen. Wasting no time, the chief explained two sets of prints were found on the note attached to the dog's collar. One belonged to Cassie since she had touched the note, but neither set of prints was in the system.

"That confirms the author wasn't Keith Yablonsky. As much as I'd like to track down the dog's previous owner for charges of animal cruelty, tying a dog to a mailbox like that, I have no leads on the actual person who abandoned the dog," Chief Gutierrez explained.

"Thank you for expediting the analysis and meeting with us this early in the morning." Jase was about to take his leave when Captain Shields asked for more of Jase's time.

Chief Gutierrez excused himself, keeping the blinds and door open while giving Jase privacy to confer with his superior.

"Hold on, Lieutenant Hayes. I'll be right there." Shields went offscreen and talked to his number two before returning. "Are there any substantial leads that Yablonsky is in the area?"

Jase searched his mind and came up with nothing. "There's been no sign of him at the farm. So far, all the searches haven't yielded any traces of the bank stash, either. I've checked the house from the attic to the mudroom. I've looked in every building from the maintenance shed to the chicken coop. The accomplice could have cashed the bonds from the safety deposit box and spent the cash by now."

"But the farm is in good financial shape, and there have been renovations to the farmhouse and outbuildings?" Shields leaned back in his office chair and tapped a pencil against his desk. "That might be enough to get a warrant for O'Neal's bank statements."

Jase wanted to shout no but clutched the edge of the desk, his knuckles turning white under the tan he'd acquired while working on the farm. "Cassie explained all that to me." He outlined the subscription service and the long line of loyal customers waiting every morning of the three days a week Cassie operated the farmstand. "Some people drive hours for her pumpkin butter, and others regularly ship her jams and muffin mixes as gifts. She's turned around the farm through hard work and dedication."

Shields dropped the pencil, his expression stern. "Then in fact we *don't* have enough for a warrant to comb through her financials. Lieutenant, wait a moment." His gaze averted to his assistant once more before returning to Jase. "That's a wrap then. Return to Denver, and you can take over the leads coming in from the tip hotline. So far, the only verifiable sighting belonged to that one truck driver. After that, it's as if Yablonsky disappeared in thin air."

Jase felt his control slip away. Without being nearby, who'd protect Cassie and Penny and Easton when Yablonsky made himself known?

Cassie would. She'd protect Penny and Easton with her entire being, just as she devoted herself to everything she did with courage and honesty. Somehow, Jase would have to get used to solitary breakfasts and runs once more.

The thought made his heart ache.

"Requesting permission to wait until Monday. My family has a dude ranch here, and I'd like to spend time with them."

For so long, he'd denied himself those moments,

letting the guilt of being the lone survivor set in and deciding what was best without trusting them with the whole story. But now his resolve to talk to them was firm. And he wanted to form some final memories that might have to last him a lifetime. After his confession to them, he'd return to Denver and take a note from Cassie's book and try to pick up the pieces.

Shields grabbed a pencil and started scribbling. "The sooner the better, Virtue. See you next Tuesday."

Shields clicked off the video call on his end, and Jase stared at the chief's screensaver. His time in Violet Ridge was drawing to a close, and nothing was resolved. Yablonsky was still at large, he hadn't confided the truth to his grandparents, and Cassie…

His insides were a jumbled mess about the dedicated single mother. He'd spoken her praises to Shields while staying as honest to his professional self as possible. Perhaps the return to Denver was for the best. Otherwise, he might compromise his search for justice.

But what if Cassie was innocent in all of this? He loosened his grip on Gutierrez's desk and considered the evidence.

The only link between her and the robbery was the cellmate's confirmation there was an accomplice whose name started with *C* and was an attractive brunette. Shields was convinced on the basis of Cassie's first name that the money was hidden at the farm. Yet Cassie had lived in Violet Ridge at the time of the robbery, and no link had ever been found connecting her to Clara Abbott, the bank manager whose key had been used. From what Cassie had told him, she'd only visited her half brother once, which the prison records confirmed.

Turning to Yablonsky's escape, he examined the facts. With Cassie's schedule and alibi, there was no way she could have helped Yablonsky at the prison or made contact with him to aid his plans. His communication at the prison was limited and monitored. And Jase wasn't even sure Cassie found the time to sleep.

Gutierrez returned to his office, and Jase thanked him for his time. As the chief escorted Jase to the entrance of the building, Jase found himself admiring the different vibe here. He liked the small-town ambience, even though the goals were the same with his unit in Denver.

Growing up, he'd never aspired to work in this type of department. For the first time, he wondered what it would be like to report to Gutierrez instead of Shields.

He pushed that out of his mind and returned to the farm. He'd have to tell Cassie he was leaving next Monday.

CASSIE LOADED THE last two subscription boxes into the rear of Mrs. Olsen's SUV before lowering the liftgate. Another satisfied customer brought her this much closer to a fun evening at the Harvest Festival with Penny and Easton.

Should she invite Jase to go with them? Before Rusty arrived yesterday, there had been a moment when she thought something was changing between them. After they discovered the abandoned dog, however, it was as if a switch had been flipped with Jase acting distant and occupied.

No, she'd take Penny and Easton by herself. Jase was committed to his job, and she needed to draw a line before Easton became too attached to the affable detective.

She trekked back to the vegetable stand where the delivery driver approached her, dragging a cart full of boxes. "Hey, Cassie." Travis Longfellow tipped his baseball hat toward her. "Someone knocked over the rain barrels near your root cellar. Wasn't me. I sure do appreciate your business."

Cassie thanked him and rushed in that direction. Sure enough, every barrel was on its side, and she muttered under her breath. *Who did this?*

Keith's image popped into her mind, filling her stomach with dread. Should she inform Jase of this development?

Then again, last night's whistling wind might be the culprit, not to mention any one of the customers who had been coming and going all morning. Besides, a friend or neighbor would have noticed her half brother. His picture was plastered all over billboards and the front page of the local newspaper.

Cassie headed to the barn for a set of heavy-duty work gloves. The latex ones she'd been using were too flimsy. Grabbing a pair, she exited the barn and found Jase leaving the stables.

Her stomach did a funny flip at the sight of his confident stride, already so familiar. She did a double take; he'd traded his suit for jeans, a flannel shirt and boots. "Are you going for a ride on Highlander?"

Jase shrugged and looked sheepish. "No, I was sneaking him an apple. Didn't want your horses to feel left out, so I gave them a treat, too."

This was what she'd come to expect of him. Conscientious Jase with a hint of mystery. Once again, she cautioned herself that he wasn't here to stay, although she could get used to his presence in a hurry if he was. "Thanks." She pointed in the direction of the root cellar. "Duty calls."

"I can help."

She hesitated and then decided to tell him about the pickle barrels. "Come with me."

As soon as he saw the barrels, the smile faded from his face. "Have you touched anything?"

She held up her hands, now encased in heavy-duty gloves. "I was concerned about splinters."

"Stay here."

Cassie started to protest when that feeling of dread took root once more. There was no doubt Jase believed Keith was responsible for this. Despite her thick jacket, chills tingled along her arms.

Jase returned with a fingerprint kit, and her nerves finally came under control.

Jase donned latex gloves and took photographs with his phone. "How long have the barrels been like this?"

"I don't know. Since there was no rain in the forecast, I kept the boxes scheduled for in-person pickup at the farmstand, so I didn't have any reason to come to the root cellar this morning. Travis told me about the barrels."

Jase inspected the area. "Too muddy for any identifiable tracks."

"That's because of the collected rainwater that spilled everywhere. Perhaps the wind knocked them over, or one of my customers."

He shook his head. "This barrel weighs about seventy-five pounds when empty. Judging from these puddles, there was a fair amount of rainwater in them, making them even heavier."

"How could he have been here without anyone seeing him?" Jase was concentrating on his task, but she could tell from his expression he was wondering the same question. "And how can you tell if any of the fingerprints are his?"

He turned toward her. "I did a quick preliminary check. There aren't any fingerprints on the barrel."

That should have made her feel better, but it didn't. "Penny and Easton will be home soon." She shook her head. While she was done letting Keith dictate her life, her children's safety was paramount. She'd have to cancel their outing.

"Didn't they mention the Harvest Festival this morning?" Jase asked.

With Jase by their side, her family would be safe. "They've been looking forward to this event for so long." She gritted her teeth. "Are you busy tonight? Can you come with us?"

For a second, she thought he was going to refuse, but then he nodded. "It's been years since I've eaten a corn dog. Sounds good right about now. Thank you for the invite."

They walked back to the farmhouse together where Rusty greeted them. Last night, Cassie had given up the pretense of finding another home for the dog since he seemed part of the family. Next week he had a follow-up vet appointment for a microchip. After giving him a friendly pat, she excused herself to freshen up.

Even with Jase accompanying them, she intended to keep a close eye on Penny and Easton this evening.

THIS YEAR'S HARVEST Festival wasn't the tiny school fair of Jase's childhood; this was a bustling enterprise on the grounds of the Irwin Arena, home to concerts and the local rodeo. Strains of country music played over loudspeakers while residents and tourists roamed the area. They passed the game booths where shouts of joy heralded the winners.

Easton reached for Jase and yanked him along

the path, distancing them from Cassie and Penny. "Hurry up. My stomach's so empty."

Cassie caught up with them. "Easton! You're being impolite."

"Sorry, Mom." He stopped and let go of Jase's hand, rubbing his belly. "He talked about corn dogs all the way here."

"I don't want to get between a boy and his corn dog," Jase said, interceding on Easton's behalf.

Cassie chuckled. "Or a man and his corn dog, either."

In no time, they were clutching their dinners of corn dogs and fries and claiming a picnic table just as another family departed. Jase listened to Easton's story about coming in second in today's school race while paying attention to every shadow and sound. He continued to be on high alert while Penny and Easton started an animated discussion about what to do next.

"I want to see the quilts. I like the pretty designs," Penny said, folding her arms for emphasis.

Easton winced. "I want to ride the bumper cars."

They turned toward their mother, as if each expecting her to take their side in the matter, when Jase's grandparents approached their table.

"Grandma Bridget! Grandpa Martin!" Jase slid out of his seat and hugged them both, surprised but pleased to see them.

His grandmother returned her hands to the crook of her cane. "What a wonderful evening. A blue ribbon for my quilt and seeing my grandson enjoying himself with a lovely family."

Easton clambered out of the booth. "Where's your blue ribbon? Can I see it?"

Grandma Bridget chuckled. "It's on my quilt."

Jase didn't know who looked more proud about her achievement: her or Grandpa Martin.

Easton clapped and turned toward Cassie. "Can we see the quilts, please? Then we can go on the bumper cars, and I can crash into Penny." Easton slammed his hands together to show what he had planned.

Grandpa Martin whispered something to his wife, and she nodded. "Cassie, can we take them to the exhibition hall?" Grandma Bridget asked. "Then you and Jase can have some time to do whatever you young folk want to do."

Cassie blushed, and Jase realized his grandmother was playing matchmaker. Penny and Easton surrounded Cassie until she relented.

After they arranged to meet at the Ferris wheel later, Jase watched the quartet leave. "I see that worry on your brow, but my grandparents will spoil them and protect them at the same time."

"They raised you, and they're good people. I trust them."

Jase let out a slow breath. It was time he did the same and revealed the circumstances of that fateful night with his parents, namely the details about his scream and his subsequent guilt. "I do, too."

She ate the last bite of her corn dog. "What would you like to do?"

"I'm game for the Ferris wheel now if you are."

"It's my favorite, so let's go."

They finished their food and threw away the dinner plates. She seemed lighter tonight than any other time since he'd arrived in Violet Ridge. He didn't want to ruin the happy mood by relaying his conversation with Shields about the barrels.

While Jase was convinced they hadn't fallen by themselves, Shields wrote off the incident as a prank. Jase had pressed his superior that the lack of fingerprints meant someone wiped the surface clean, but Shields had an answer for that: the rainwater that had escaped washed away any prints. Shields continued to insist Jase return to the precinct on Monday.

Tonight was a festive occasion, and Jase wanted to live for today. There would be time to tell Cassie about his departure tomorrow.

He had doubted her innocence. And now he felt like he'd betrayed her by doing so. He didn't deserve that radiant smile she was bestowing on him, the one where the clouds parted and sunshine warmed his inner core.

They waited in line, excitement registering on Cassie's face. "I haven't been on a Ferris wheel in years."

"It's my grandmother's favorite." Jase remembered the time his grandparents had taken the family to an amusement park. He'd been so focused on the guilt from the accident that he'd also shut out the positive memories of the past. That wasn't fair to them. Or himself.

"Your grandparents are sweet to take Penny and Easton for a while."

"In case I didn't tell you yet, you remind me of my grandma Bridget."

Her smile grew even broader, and she reached out for his hand, covering his with her warmth. "That's one of the nicest compliments I've ever received." She moved closer to the front of the line. "She's one of the most patient, wise people in Violet Ridge, and I'm hardly that."

Add modesty to the long list of character traits that was drawing him to her.

"You have a way about you, and you make farming seem idyllic, even easy." They were next, and he braced himself for sitting close to Cassie and the feelings she was sparking in him. "Growing up on a working dude ranch, I know what you do is anything but, yet it seems like a fun adventure to you."

Just being in her presence, especially here at the festival, brought about joy he hadn't felt in years.

Cassie's laugh was like another ray of sunshine. "Penny and Easton would hardly agree with you when I wake them up early on holidays so we can gather the eggs and feed the horses." She gazed in wonder at the ride as the wind ruffled her hair and the Ferris wheel rotated. The wheel slowed to a stop, and the attendant ushered them into a gondola. Jase waited for Cassie to go first, and then he sat next to her. The wheel moved and stopped again so riders behind them could board. They weren't high enough yet to see the town at its finest. His gaze landed on her. "Have you thought about adding another permanent employee on the farm?"

"You're asking me why I do this by myself."

"Yes. Tell me, please." He found himself caring very much about everything she told him.

"Thistle Brook Farm has been family run for three generations." She gazed to the mountains and beyond. "But times change, that's just what they do, and I've had to adapt. I've done my best, but I didn't want to risk hiring someone only to let them go a week later if finances got tough. The farm hasn't always done as well as it is now. Someday I'd like to hire more employees, but that takes money and a willingness to cede control. It's taken me a while to let people help with the farm. It took a lot on Amanda's part, for instance, to convince me to change the farm's logo, but she's good at marketing, and I trust her."

Trust. That quality never came easily to him. Whether it was due to his job or his innate nature, he'd never know.

"You're a smart businesswoman, besides being a good farmer." He stopped talking as the gondola moved once more. They were almost to the top.

"Jase Virtue, take a look around you." Cassie

extended her arms. "We're almost at the top of the world. Enough talk about my farm."

When he was around her, he felt on top of the world. Even in this tight space, there was nowhere else he wanted to be. That compulsion to know everything about her came back. "What better place to find out everything about you?"

She folded her arms across her chest. "Are you using this gondola as an interrogation room?"

He shook his head. "No. I want to know you, Cassie, the real you."

Cassie relaxed and reached for his hand. Hers was almost as cold as a brick of ice, her calluses a reminder of how hard she worked to make her farm a success.

He rubbed them until warmth started coming to the surface. "I like spending time with you."

They stalled, the wheel's rotation halted, but Jase didn't mind. This festival was the night he didn't know he needed. Just like having Cassie in his life was a blessing—the calm in the midst of everything swirling around them.

"Even with circumstances as they are?" she asked.

He liked how she challenged him to go deeper. "It's not ideal, but I have to come to terms with how my future is tied to my past."

"But is that future here in Violet Ridge? When Brayden arrived in town that spring and we went out on our first date, I tried telling myself he wasn't going to stick around Violet Ridge, so don't get attached. But then he seemed to fall in love with the town as much as he said he was falling for me. And I believed him. I was so naive, caught up in my feelings." Cassie met Jase's gaze before the gondola moved once more, stopping at the top. "He was so strong and independent, and I responded to that in the wake of Keith going to jail and the quick decline of Dad's health."

"You're stronger than you think, Cassie O'Neal."

"You're giving me too much credit for being tough. The truth is, I seem to latch on to people when I'm vulnerable. I'm worried I'd—"

"Make the same mistake again? You'd consider me a mistake?" He waited on the edge of the gondola for her to tell him otherwise. To tell him she cared for him.

"I consider you a…" Her hazel eyes were fixed on him, and he met her gaze. She was frightened of her feelings, but they were there. He'd felt the connection between them growing stronger every day. "A friend."

"What if we want more?" She pushed him to want more, to be more, to talk more about what was really going on inside of him.

"Seems we're both guilty of that. You've wiggled your way into all our hearts, and I'm scared."

He'd been running since he was six, so he recognized her fear. Maybe it was time to start heading toward something substantive and beautiful. "But it seems like you're running away from the possibility of us?"

She met his gaze, her long black lashes framing those beautiful, expressive eyes of hers. "Maybe I am, but I don't want to start something that I know will end. Possibly badly."

Cassie deserved a clear path to rainbows and her own happily-ever-after, same as his grandparents who were approaching their sixtieth anniversary.

The thought of letting her go for good, though, left an ache that far outweighed any doubts he had about a future without her and the kids. Maybe she was the key to the peace which had eluded him for so many years. Maybe it was time for him to stop running, too.

"Can we take this one day at a time then?" The words slipped out before he could stop them.

"Starting tonight?" She looked out at the town, nestled and snug in the hollow below, before turning to him. "Have you ever seen such a beautiful sight?"

Not ever. Everything he'd ever wanted was at his fingertips, and they drew nearer. Apples and sunshine tickled his nose, and her lips came close to his. One kiss, and he'd want to stay forever.

"Cassie." He didn't want to leave, but she needed to know that his departure was happening soon. "Captain Shields wants me back on Monday."

Those long lashes fluttered closed for a brief moment as if she was weighing his statement. When she opened them a second later, she seemed to see right through him, to the genuine Jase. And still he could see that she wanted to be just his friend.

Noted and accepted.

"I'm sorry, Jase. Penny and Easton are my world. I'd never do anything to possibly cause them pain."

She shifted away from him, and he wished he could have spared her pain. The gondola started rotating, and he held on to the bar, feeling his world spin around him.

Circumstances out of his control had brought him here, but they'd also driven a wedge between them that seemed too hard to overcome.

CHAPTER EIGHT

Descending the porch steps, Jase couldn't remember the last time he'd overslept. Last night, after they had arrived home from the Harvest Festival, Cassie scooted Penny and Easton off to bed with a reminder they had to be up early for the bus. Jase had trekked toward the barn, searching the property for any signs of Yablonsky but finding none. When he finally entered the code for the security system, everyone else had been asleep for hours.

He said a brief hello to Blossom before heading to the farmstand where customers were inspecting fresh Swiss chard and cauliflower. With only a passing glance at Cassie, Jase donned an apron and set to work where needed.

Once the crowd thinned and the last customer departed, Jase noticed dark circles under Cassie's eyes as if she hadn't slept well. Also, her face was puffy, like she'd been crying. Was this due to her half brother?

Or was Jase the reason?

He moved toward her. "Cassie?"

She sniffed and stuffed a tissue in her pocket.

Perhaps the puffiness was due to something as simple as a cold. "Thanks for all your help." Her voice sounded garbled, and she busied herself with straightening the shelves. "I didn't have time to ask you last night. Are you staying through Sunday night or leaving earlier?"

She didn't look at him, and he bristled that Shields had recalled him to Denver. The O'Neal family needed him here.

He wanted to be here.

Surprise fluttered through him at his intense desire to stay in Violet Ridge. He had some accrued vacation time. Maybe he should use it and remain at the farm. Just until Yablonsky was back behind bars.

"I'd like to stay." If he was still welcome. "What's wrong? If it's about last night..."

She finally looked at him, a wry smile coming through. "No." She extracted the tissue and wiped the corner of her eye. "My mom called. She has bronchitis, and I'm concerned for her. She says she's not sick enough to be admitted to the hospital. I wanted to fly there immediately, but she said I should stay here in Colorado. It's hard not being there, you know?"

Only too well. He remembered that feeling of helplessness when Seth relayed the news about their grandmother's stroke. Jase was running out of time to talk to his family before he returned to Denver, but he was determined to share the truth with them.

Cassie's phone rang, and she broke eye contact with him. She glanced at the screen and frowned. "I have to take this. It might be about my mother."

Her voice gave him pause, so he didn't hesitate. "Would you like to put it on speaker?"

No one had been with him when he had talked to Seth about Grandma Bridget's stroke. Sometimes it helped having someone by your side in moments like these, especially someone who cared about you.

She blinked but nodded. "Hello?"

"Cassie? This is Regina Dunne-Sullivan at Over and Dunne Feed and Seed."

Jase fondly recalled the local supply store that provided for farmers and ranchers alike in the area.

"Cassie, your order's arrived, and it's making a lot of noise. You've got to come pick it up immediately."

Jase raised an eyebrow. "Were you expecting an order?" he mouthed.

Cassie shook her head no.

"Just come as soon as you can," Regina added. "Oh, and I'd advise bringing a truck." Cassie's screen went dark as Regina ended the call.

Cassie's eyes showed her alarm. "I didn't order anything."

"Well, she called you rather than the authorities. It should be safe. Let's take your truck."

"Can you drive, though? I'm shaking." She held up her quivering hands.

He immediately took them in his, then put an

arm around her shoulder, tucking her into his chest.

"First, though, I need to put Rusty inside. I still don't know how much he likes chickens."

There was no time to ask her to elaborate on her meaning about whether the dog got along with the hens or preferred to chase them. With Blossom in the henhouse, Jase wasn't taking any chances, either.

Cassie's priorities, not to mention her sense of humor, were growing on him, but he pushed that aside. For now, he steeled himself for what they were about to discover, thanks to Ms. Dunne-Sullivan.

EASTON O'NEAL WAS grounded until he graduated high school. Cassie shook her head helplessly at Regina. "I didn't order fifty baby chicks." No wonder there was so much noise behind the counter. What had her son been thinking?

"Cash on delivery. That'll be two hundred and fifty dollars for the chicks and an extra fifty for it being on account." Regina grimaced. "You can't cancel this order. It says that on our website, right where the online order info is entered."

What was Cassie going to do with fifty baby chicks? She glanced at Jase, who looked as though he was struggling to contain his laughter. His smile, she realized, made her heart flutter.

"I don't suppose you have a yard in Denver?"

Cassie asked. "Could I interest you in some chicks?"

"No, I can't take them with me." Jase suddenly got out his phone and headed for the exit.

Cassie faced Regina and pled her case. "Easton's five. I don't know what he was thinking, but fifty chicks? In the middle of harvest season? All tablet privileges have been revoked from now until—"

"Sorry, no exceptions." Regina pointed to a sign behind her although Cassie didn't have to read it. "Once I receive a special order, it's yours."

Of course it was. Cassie blew out a breath and looked to Jase for comfort. Only, he wasn't where he was standing a minute ago. She missed him already.

It had been nice sharing her life with him these past few weeks: laughing at the breakfast table, swooning over the way he and Blossom interacted and enjoying late afternoon horse rides before dinner. She should have known not to let her heart get involved. He was gone on Monday. He'd said he'd be leaving right from the beginning.

His announcement on the Ferris wheel, though, was as abrupt as Brayden's when her ex-husband told her he couldn't live with her any longer; that fatherhood wasn't for him; that he was quitting them, quitting his crop-dusting business to become a bush pilot in the wilds of Alaska. The last frontier.

In one fell swoop, she'd become a single mother with a toddler and a baby on the way. There had been nights she'd fallen into bed with every muscle screaming at her for not accepting her mother's offer to move to Florida. But then she'd wake up and see the sun rise over the Rockies and the green fields. Then she'd start afresh, taking comfort from Easton's gummy smiles and Penny's wet kisses. And the supportive community that had rallied round them.

Cassie turned her attention back to Regina, tall, midfifties, with long red braids standing out against her blue plaid flannel shirt. "Do you know anyone who would like some free chicks? I'll pay for them, and please spread the word that I'll throw in a month's supply of corn."

Regina nodded. "I suspect my husband, Barry, will take a few off your hands. The ranch's goats and donkey could probably use a little company."

Cassie beamed and gave Regina a fist bump. "That's a great start."

"And Seth will take a dozen for the dude ranch." Jase's voice came from behind her.

He'd been arranging homes for some of the chicks? Cassie's heart went pitter-patter. She turned and there he was, their pillar of protection. She threw her arms around him. "Thank him so much!" His flannel shirt was soft, a distinct difference from his muscular frame. Realizing what she was doing, she stepped back from him. "Sorry about getting carried away. I thought you'd left."

"I called Seth and texted Ben. He's checking with his sister, Lizzie Harper, to see if her ranch can use any extra chicks. Seems when Daisy married Ben, his family embraced my sister with open arms." Now it was Jase's turn to look uncomfortable, and he tugged at the black T-shirt he wore under his flannel. "It's hot in here."

"If you two can stop making goo-goo eyes at each other long enough, Cassie can bring her truck around, and we can load the chicks." Regina tapped the cash register as if to get their attention.

It was Cassie's turn to feel warm and flustered.

"You can stop at the Lazy River Dude Ranch before you head back to Thistle Brook Farm," Regina added.

Where Easton would have a lot of explaining to do. "Since I'm here, I need to pick up a few supplies." Especially for the baby chicks. "Wood pellets, warming lamps, organic chick feed, plus extra hay for Highlander and some fertilizer for the hoophouse tomatoes."

Regina stared at the chicks. Then the store owner smiled and picked one up. "Right. A few more minutes won't hurt anything. Take your time." She rubbed her finger gently on the fluff. "They are rather cute, loud or not. Barry will have fun with this one and its friend."

Cassie hid her grin that Regina was already enamored. She faced Jase, who was tugging at his collar, a move most unlike him. Jase was a seasoned detective, trained not to give away his emotions. Then it hit her.

He was uncomfortable with her public display

of emotion. But the hug was just a harmless reaction, relief that he'd once again brought a solution to her table, so to speak.

She tried to sound reassuring. "It shouldn't take me that long to buy the supplies."

"Then I have enough time to go somewhere fast." Jase plucked up one of the chattering birds and sighed. "I wonder how Blossom will react to the newcomers in a couple of weeks."

Too bad Jase wouldn't be around when she introduced the chicks to the rest of the brood. She watched him walk away and concluded her business with Regina.

WITH CARE, CASSIE closed her tailgate at the back of the Over and Dunne Feed and Seed and checked on the crates that held the chicks. So far, so good. She located her phone and frowned at the late time. What was keeping Jase? She had to get home and let Rusty outside before she met the bus at the mailbox.

Cassie usually looked forward to the moment when Penny and Easton descended the school bus steps. Today, however, she'd have to talk to Easton about his purchase and why he couldn't do anything like this ever again.

Thank goodness Regina agreed that ten of the chicks could go to the Silver Horseshoe where her husband, nephew-in-law and his wife would take good care of the tiny animals. Amanda was coming over to pick up another ten for the dude ranch along with supplies. That left thirty, ten of whom could stay on permanently while the other twenty needed good homes. For now, they'd be kept warm in a closed-off area of the barn with high walls, heat lamps and pine shavings. Patches wouldn't let anything happen to them, and Easton would probably want to camp out in the barn with his chicks.

Her stomach rumbled, and she hoped she had enough time to make a sandwich before the bus arrived. She started to text Jase only to find him sprinting toward her. He held up food bags, and she nearly swooned. He bought her lunch! If he lived in Violet Ridge, her heart would be in trouble.

She suspected it already was.

"Thank you." She stopped herself from pouncing on the bag he held out to her.

"You don't even know what I've bought." He pretended to peek into each bag. "Liver and onions work for you?"

"Ick, but I'm hungry enough that I'd eat it." She scrunched her nose, then shook her head. "I don't think you'd be that cruel, so how about this? I mix up the bags, and you choose which one you want. *You* might end up with the liver and onions."

"Be my guest. I'll gladly take my chances." He seemed to be calling her bluff, instantly holding out both bags. "But no peeking."

It was hard, but she trusted him. She turned around, switched the bags so many times that even she didn't know which was which and faced him once more. "Your choice."

He picked one and checked the contents. "I hit the jackpot." He popped a French fry in his mouth. "Burger and fries. Hope you enjoy your liver and onions."

She winced and gulped. "You really bought that?"

"Nope." He laughed. "Both bags have the same order."

She was so happy she almost hugged him but remembered that the last embrace hadn't gone over so well. "Come on. Get in the cab." She waited until he was inside the truck before releasing the nervous laughter bubbling in her chest. He didn't know how close she'd come to kissing him. He'd best never find out about her growing feelings for him, either.

Collecting herself, she hopped into the driver seat, shut the door and devoured a couple of fries. "Thanks for lunch."

"There's no place like the Smokehouse." He bit into his hamburger and moaned with delight. "I'll miss this place when I'm back in Denver."

If she didn't ask, she'd always wonder if she should have, so here went nothing. "Then why are you going back? I understand why my mom moved back to Florida—her sister lives there, and she's always wanted to work in fashion—but your whole family is here."

He placed the remainder of his hamburger in the to-go box. "It's easier to be a lone wolf."

"Is it? Because when I look at you, I don't see a lone wolf. You worked hard to gain Penny's trust, you're not clamoring to go to the bar every night, and you're besotted with one of my hens."

Now, Brayden had been a true lone wolf. Which should have been her first clue that he never intended to stick around Violet Ridge even though he said otherwise.

"I like a microbrew every once in a while, but I haven't indulged in Violet Ridge's after-hours scene since I'm always on duty." Jase selected a French fry and then emptied a packet of ketchup into a corner of the box. His gaze returned to her. "You weren't talking about me, though, were you?"

Sometimes she was so at ease around him, she forgot he was a detective. "Once Penny was born, Brayden found excuses to work longer hours and network to expand his business. His preferred place for that was the Blazing Buffalo Bar on the outskirts of town."

"And then he decided to leave for Alaska, right?" Jase let out a breath. "You're doing an incredible job raising Penny and Easton."

They ate in the privacy of the cab. She polished off her hamburger and then started the truck.

She was a few miles out of town when he broke the silence. "Has he visited at all?"

"He claims his bush pilot business has taken

off. No pun intended." Heat rose up her face, and she kept her attention on the road. "He barely remembers to send them cards for their birthdays or holidays." Her stomach clenched but not because of the meal. No, unlike with Brayden, she'd miss Jase. Pure and simple.

"No wonder Penny acted the way she did," Jase said.

Penny was sensitive, but when she put her heart into something, she was all in. Cassie worried how that would play out in the future, but she had to focus on right now.

"Are you going to say goodbye to them before you leave?" Had Jase been around long enough to create that big an impact on them? Of course, he made an impact. That was his nature.

"I'd like to, but only if you think it's best."

Keeping her gaze on the road was for the best. Otherwise, she might take one look at him and start gushing about her feelings. She clutched the steering wheel. "Yeah, you should tell them you're going back to Denver."

She was about to ask if he intended to visit his family at the ranch and how often, when her mailbox came into view, and she turned into the drive. Something wasn't right. Rusty was outside.

Cassie slammed on the brakes. Before she could even say anything, Jase was out of the cab. "Stay in the truck," he ordered, but she was frozen and couldn't have moved if she'd wanted to.

Everything was a blur. It was like she was being

dragged into a deep pit of quicksand, her limbs heavy.

Rusty let out a single bark, and that was what she needed to focus again. She disregarded Jase's order and rushed to Rusty's side. It was the first time she'd ever heard him bark, and he thumped his tail upon her approach. Then he moved in front of her as if he was guarding her.

"Good dog." The fact he didn't run away when he'd had the chance caught her as much by surprise as his presence outside of the house.

Jase left the farmhouse, his eyebrow arched when he saw she'd gotten out of the truck. "I thought I told you to stay put."

"I was worried about Rusty and the chickens." And about Jase as well. She swallowed so that her heart was no longer lodged in her throat.

"Come with me. You need to see this but don't touch anything." Jase's warning came through loud and clear, and she braced herself.

She entered her home, and her head spun. The living room looked as though a tornado had demolished it. Ripped sofa cushions were scattered around the room. Someone had opened all the drawers of the desk and sideboard, contents spilled all over the hardwood floor. Curtains were ripped off their rods. Papers, games and toys had been tossed everywhere.

Cassie felt violated and raw. She longed to right something. But Jase said she couldn't touch a thing. "Did Keith do this?"

"There'll be a crime scene analysis." Jase's icy tone sent chills through her. It was as if the friendly Jase who'd become a part of her household, almost a part of her family, had disappeared. "But yes, my gut says it was him. And there's more."

He motioned for her to follow him, and Rusty stayed close by her side.

The dining room was also a mess with damaged chairs on their sides and the display cabinet's doors ajar. At least he hadn't smashed their grandmother's porcelain dishes. As it was, her heart was breaking with all the other damage, as well as Jase's impending departure.

Jase pointed to the top of the table, and Cassie went over to it. Her breath caught when she saw the note.

Where's my money? It's mine, not yours. I'll be back.

She gasped. Keith was here. How? Why? Well, the why was obvious, but she didn't know where the money was.

Penny! Easton! School was about to end, and they would board the bus for home.

"I can't let them see this. I have to protect them." She noticed Jase's jaw clench, but she continued, "This is their home. I can't send them to Florida with my mom being sick, and I can't send them to Alaska because I don't know where Brayden is."

Her thoughts swirled, but she tried to keep calm.

Anything to make this helpless feeling stop. It brought back a flood of memories of her father and Keith arguing. Whenever things were bad at home, she'd stay busy and commit to every activity. Every waking moment was scheduled with something to fill the empty void.

And now?

She couldn't run from her feelings. She had to face this so she could be sure Penny and Easton were safe. She met Jase's gaze and saw conflict there.

The full meaning of the note crashed into her. He couldn't believe she was in on this…

"I don't know where the money is." She hurried to protest her innocence. Of all the people in Violet Ridge, she'd come to value Jase's opinion the most. "I'd have turned it in immediately."

His eyes searched hers, and his shoulders relaxed. "I believe you." He took a deep breath. "Ben was in the military. He'll keep them safe. Do you want him to pick them up from school?"

Jase's endorsement of Ben was enough for her. If he trusted Ben that much, so did she.

She sagged as everything in the past month caught up with her. Jase provided his strong arm until she was steady once more. *Overwhelming* didn't even begin to describe her inner turmoil. Having Jase trust her, be there for her… A lone wolf taking charge for a pack that wasn't his own? She could face everything knowing he believed in her.

"Thank you, and yes," she whispered, but she felt her determination growing.

"I'll do my best to protect them, too," he said.

His touch sent a spark through her, something she'd never felt before. It would be easy to just write off whatever was happening between them as something related to stress and the moment, nothing more. To walk away and let this fade into the night.

Yet, once again, she thought of her son, pushing the boundaries even if it meant trouble down the road. Forget down the road. Trouble was now. "Are you protecting them only because it's your job?"

She tried to stare at the carpet, the open display cabinet, even Rusty, but she couldn't look anywhere else except into his dark eyes, compelling and real.

"A week ago, I'd have said yes in an instant. Now? The O'Neal family and their safety are important to me personally, not just professionally." He reached for her and cupped her face with his hands, his strength everything she needed in this instant. "But, Cassie, I'm not the man you think I am."

"No, you're so much more than you think you are. You might see yourself as a lone wolf, but Blossom and everyone on my farm knows you belong here. Part of our family."

With that, his lips quieted hers while also sparking them to life. He tasted sweet and salty, and his stubble tickled her cheek, but she couldn't get enough of him.

This kiss should have been about protection, safety, yet she sensed commitment and more. He was her shelter in the storm, but she could be that for him, just as much. She returned the kiss, hoping it conveyed her belief in him.

Rusty started barking, and Jase broke away from her, his eyes even darker as he added distance between them. She wanted that kiss as much as he did, but he was shutting her out now.

Could she blame him? Her brother just made his presence known, and Jase's career and promotion meant everything to him. There were so many reasons why their kiss shouldn't have happened. But no matter what, she would never regret it.Rusty's whines became plaintive, and Jase clenched his jaw. "Police sirens. I called them, but they must have already been on their way. He probably triggered the alarm. We must have missed him by minutes, maybe even seconds."

"I need to call the school." The real world came crashing into her life once more.

She hurried outside, Rusty on her heels, not letting her out of his sight. He sat on his haunches at her side, on full alert. Cassie didn't need to look behind her to know Jase was on the porch, waiting to lead the investigation.

This was a job to him, but this was her farm, her life, her children. Relying on him was too risky when he'd said more than once he wouldn't be staying in Violet Ridge.

When life was at its darkest, it was up to her how to respond. She could either be upset and resentful that Jase would return to Denver, or she could treasure that kiss and this time with him.

Cassie touched her lips and knew she had to trust everything would turn out for the best. Looking for the light in the darkness was the only way she had held on to her inner self for all these years. That hadn't failed her yet.

Still, her heart ached at the thought of having Jase and happiness in her grasp, only for both to slip through her fingers.

Reaching down, she patted Rusty. "Thanks for sticking around, boy. One heartache a day is enough."

CHAPTER NINE

WITH DAWN ON THE HORIZON, Jase found himself on the front porch of Thistle Brook Farm rather than on the steps leading up to his Denver condo. After he reported the break-in to Shields—more extensive than at first sight; Yablonsky also damaged the corn maze and tipped over additional barrels—Jase's stay in Violet Ridge was extended until the convict was captured or too much time elapsed for Jase to do any more good here.

His night had been spent at the local police station reviewing evidence and pursuing leads. He reached for the doorknob of the farmhouse and hesitated.

There'd been no moment alone with Cassie after their kiss. It would be easy to commit to her. Yet he still had doubts, actually, a secret that could ruin the idea she had of him. And there were other things, too, like his career and the promotion that beckoned. How could he give up everything he'd worked for the past nine years? It didn't make sense, not even for Cassie, whose idealism and trust in the good in people remained intact. That was rare and unique, beyond special.

Unlike him, Cassie hadn't run away from Violet Ridge. She'd overcome her past with the help of her family and community. And then she and her children had accepted him just as he was.

For a long while, he'd believed he didn't deserve to be part of something bigger than himself. Because of that, he'd distanced himself from the best siblings anyone could ever ask for: Seth with his take-charge attitude that went along with being the oldest; Daisy with her maternal instincts who always took care of everyone; and Crosby, who was uniquely Crosby to the core.

As much as Jase would like to stay in Violet Ridge and become an integral member of that group and see if this chemistry with Cassie could go somewhere, he didn't belong here. Even he could see the irony in Shields assigning him to stake out Thistle Brook Farm as an insider when Jase was anything but that.

Had he been his own worst enemy? Jase itched to set everything right. Talk to his family and see if maybe, just maybe, open communication could pave the way to an honest, authentic future with real happiness.

But if he revealed his growing feelings about Cassie, or if anyone caught wind of them, Shields would pull him off this case, and Jase wouldn't be here to protect her or Penny or Easton.

As it was, he'd had a hard time convincing Captain Shields that Cassie shouldn't be arrested. While Jase argued the recent note from Keith was circumstantial at best, Shields was more convinced than ever of Cassie's guilt. He insisted the siblings had a spat after Yablonsky's escape and the convicted felon was angry about taking the fall for the entire rap and was now back to claim the remaining money.

Jase had countered with the extensive damage to the corn maze. Cassie would never have allowed that. She'd been counting down the days to the grand opening. Shields had an answer for that, too. Yablonsky was sending her a message that she shouldn't mess with him anymore. No matter what Jase said, Shields went on the defensive.

It was time to examine the cold hard facts.

If Cassie had been involved, why not leave Violet Ridge with the stash and her children?

This case posed so many questions and too few answers, something Jase especially didn't like in his profession. And yet, here he was with his hand on the doorknob, anyway. The sooner he found Yablonsky, the faster he'd return to Denver, far away from the O'Neal family. Whether he'd be leaving his heart behind at Thistle Brook Farm intertwined with Cassie's was a notion for another day.

"No one's in there." A voice came from behind, and Jase was frustrated with himself at failing to detect Cassie's presence.

He turned, her sweet apple scent flooding him.

He was more tired than he'd realized. All night, he'd been reviewing evidence and every page of the old case files at the station and communicating with Shields.

"Good morning, Cassie." He kept his voice modulated, anything so she wouldn't see the impact she was having on him."Thank you for arranging for Penny and Easton to stay with Daisy and Ben and the triplets. It was hard but for the best." Conflict broke out on Cassie's expressive face while Rusty caught up to her, standing guard at her side. "I miss them, but it's reassuring to know they're safe."

"I talked to Daisy last night. Easton is following my nephew, Aspen, everywhere, and my nieces have brought Penny under their wing." That reminded Jase of something else Daisy asked of him. Jase was hesitant, though, to bring up the dude ranch dance. He'd give anything to ask Cassie to the dance as his date rather than as her bodyguard, but he couldn't.

Instead, he'd have to relish the little time he had left with her.

"That's exactly what I needed to hear." Cassie swung a basket of eggs from side to side. "I couldn't sleep, so I went to the corn maze to see the mess for myself before starting my chores."

He drew in a crisp breath. The mountain air grew chillier with every passing day, a reminder autumn could become winter at any time here in Colorado. "By yourself?"

"And the two police officers watching over the place." She pointed toward the road. "I tended the baby chicks, who seemed happy to see me, and the horses. Then I called the contractors who built the corn maze. After the police clear the scene, they'll be here to repair the damage."

"I'll try to expedite it, but we have to be thorough." Jase shivered at the thought of Yablonsky's increased threat.

She gave a wistful smile. "I only walked the perimeter, but I'll have to delay the opening by a week until the crew can do their repairs. I just hope people don't stay away because I've had to push back the grand opening. I posted about the new dates on Facebook. I also texted Zelda Baker and Doc Jenkins and asked them to spread the word. The former mayor knows everyone in town, so word should spread quickly."

Somehow he found the strength to keep from taking her in his arms and hugging her at her crestfallen expression. This was her livelihood. Now that he was convinced of her innocence, his desire to apprehend Yablonsky had spiked. Cassie and her family should be safe and her customers should be able to return even if it meant the end of his own time here.

"The delay's only temporary." The sun had crested over the mountaintops, and a soft light was filling the farmyard. The day was officially starting.

Jase caught his breath. Once again, Cassie's subtle positive influence was beginning to color his perception of everything.

It was time to stop running and start grasping his future with both hands.

Rusty huffed. Cassie set the basket down and reassured the dog with a friendly rub around his ears. "Like your time at the farm?" she reminded Jase. "Are you back to pack your bags and head to the big city?"

With everything that had happened, he hadn't told her about his extension. He relayed the information and gauged her reaction, hoping for any sign she welcomed the news. For a split second, her eyes lit up before she guarded her gaze once more. Yet that one second was all he needed. She felt something for him. Maybe when this was over, he could ask again if there was any hope for them.

After yesterday, they both needed to regain their bearings.

"Can you spare some time this morning for another search of your acres? Maybe there's a spot we've missed? I know it's unlikely but..."

Cassie worried her lip. "There is another possibility, but it's only accessible by horseback. I'll spare the time. Until Keith's caught, my life can't return to normal. But you have to grab some shuteye first." She held up her hand as if to wave off any argument. "It's obvious you've been up all night."

Talk about making the best of a bad situation. He'd get to ride Highlander, and they might find the cash yet. His stomach chose that moment to let out a loud grumble. "If you throw in breakfast first, I'll sleep better."

"That hungry, huh?" Her smile lit up her face.

"I'm just wondering if Blossom left me a gift this morning."

Their mutual laughter broke the tension that hung in the air.

"You're in luck. I collected quite a few eggs after I checked on the chicks." She passed by him, swinging the basket once more and jabbed her finger into his chest.

He stepped aside and pushed open the door, hoping against hope it wasn't for the last time.

Knowing the extent of Yablonsky's destruction yesterday, Jase couldn't believe this was the same place. Cassie must have stayed up late setting everything back to rights. There wasn't a dish, sock or stuffed animal out of place. "This had to have taken you hours to sort out."

"Amanda and Seth came over and lent a hand." She turned, and her smile grew wider. "They're such a wonderful couple."

There'd be no argument from him on that account.

He followed her into the kitchen, and they fell into a comfortable rhythm making breakfast together. Even better was the shared laughter as they swapped stories and exchanged bites of each other's meal.

While he went to grab some shuteye before resuming the investigation, he took one long lingering look at Cassie. It was too tempting to imagine what it would be like to live here, be a part of this family, kiss Cassie on a regular basis.

Instead, he steeled himself that he was here to protect her and get to the root of the problem, not become part of it.

CASSIE PULLED ON Hazel's reins. They'd made it to near the fence that separated her farm from the Valley T Ranch. After dismounting, she secured Hazel to the sole Joshua tree while Jase tethered Highlander to a nearby aspen. He raised his hand to shade his eyes.

"This is the end of our property," Cassie said. "The Trujillo family owns the Valley T. It's craggier and more barren than my acreage, but it works for them. They raise about forty head of cattle. Keith and I would come out here and sneak onto their ranch and hike up the mountainside."

The craggy red rocks gave rise to a mountain path, and Jase squinted as if considering every angle. "Gabriel Trujillo inherited the Valley T Ranch, didn't he?"

"Yes. About three years ago, along with his sisters Elena and Renata." Cassie plucked her water bottle from the saddlebag, taking a long swig. "They're silent partners."

Jase examined the barbed wire fence marking the boundary. "Looks new."

"Some of his cattle escaped and ate my crops.

Gabriel worked nonstop for a couple of weeks installing it. Wouldn't accept any help with it, financial or labor." She frowned. "He keeps to himself more than his dad did, but he's been a good neighbor."

"I remember him. We graduated in the same class." Jase knelt beside a post and rubbed the earth in his fingertips. He switched his attention to the aspen and made a beeline for the tree. After a quick search, he shook his head. "Trujillo would have found the money when he replaced the fence, and there are no knots in the tree, let alone any hiding places to keep a box safe from predators. Can you think of any other spots Yablonsky favored?"

Cassie searched her mind and came up empty. "Keith never loved farming or the outdoors, except for the occasional hike. When I was in high school, he'd head to the bar or somewhere else in town the minute he was done with a day's work."

Jase ran his hand through his hair and exhaled. "We might as well go back. I'll search the house again. I must have missed something."

Exasperation ran through her. She'd had enough. "I've lived in that house my entire life." She threw up her hands. "The money's not there. Somehow, everyone's convinced that it is, but it's not."

She plunked herself under the Joshua tree and closed her eyes. When she opened them, Jase held out two pumpkin scones. "I swiped these from your kitchen."

"Why, Detective Virtue…" Cassie let whimsy guide her words "…that's positively scandalous."

"I know the baker. I figured I'd appeal to her softer side." Jase grinned before the smile faded. "How do you do it?"

She knew he wasn't asking for her recipe, so she led him to a flat outcropping at the base of an immense red rock where they'd be more comfortable. "Some might consider me too soft." Unlike Jase. His hard edges suited his profession, and his sense of duty and honor drew her to him like a nematode to her carrots. However, she also saw how tender he could be. "I stay because I love it here. Would you ever consider moving back to Violet Ridge?"

Dare she hope that, for the first time, she might actually find someone who'd stand by her and not let her down?

He stared into the distance, and she felt the thread of hope unraveling. "It's not that simple."

"You have a knack for adding degrees of complexity to everything. Maybe you need someone who can take you back to basics." She had a bite of the scone, the pumpkin flavors enhanced by nutmeg and cinnamon.

He demolished his scone in a few bites, then wiped the crumbs off his jeans. "That sounds fine, but I see all kinds of humanity in my profession. I have to get into the minds of people in all walks of life."

"And yet you acknowledge that humanity. That's a rare gift."

His gaze met hers once more, and a genuine smile emerged on his face. "I owe that to my grandmother Bridget. She and my grandfather took all four of us in after my parents' deaths. My mother's brother wanted to split us up, but my grandparents wouldn't hear of it."

"The four of you are close in age, aren't you?" She polished off the rest of her scone.

"Seth's the oldest. He has the habit of being right all the time, quite infuriating really. But he cares for the ranch and does what's best for it. Daisy's too sweet for her own good, yet she has a will of steel. Good thing, too, as the mother of triplets and Ben's equal. Then there's Crosby." He stopped and laughed. "He's younger than I am and quite absent-minded. His head's often in the clouds, thinking about the past, but he's made us all proud by becoming Dr. Virtue, PhD."

She heard the love in Jase's voice as he talked about his family and their achievements. It all the more confounding about why he lived in Denver. Jase obviously cared about them and this area. Why not come home for good? Another mystery to go along with the ones regarding Keith's whereabouts and the missing money.

"And your family's expanding. Seth and Amanda are getting married next Valentine's Day. She's already like a sister to me, and now I know Daisy and Ben better, too." Cassie couldn't get over the kindness they'd extended toward her. "I'm in their debt for taking such good care of Penny and Easton. You have a great family."

"The Lazy River Dude Ranch molded us into who we are today." A shadow came over his features, almost as if that same land was the reason he'd moved elsewhere.

She scoffed. Now she was seeing things that weren't there. Didn't she have enough to deal with without overcomplicating matters? She brushed away the scone crumbs and that line of thought. "It must have been fun growing up on a dude ranch."

"Most of the time." Jase nodded and tilted his face toward the sun. "Seth's personality suits the place. It's better with him as the new controlling owner since he lives and breathes the ranch, same as my grandparents."

"That sounds like my father and me. I inherited my love of farming from him." There was something satisfying about planting a seed and waiting for the results. "There's no place like Thistle Brook Farm as far as I'm concerned."

"Did your father leave you the farm outright? Did he leave anything to your half brother?" Jase sipped from his water bottle.

"Dad left the ranch to Mom and me since he'd already had his falling out with Keith. Dad and the family attorney made sure Keith couldn't get his hands on the farmland. That's another reason why I was so shocked when Keith broke into my house."

"Shocked?" Jase's brow furrowed, and she could tell he was in full detective mode.

Cassie let out a sigh. "I would have thought Keith would have hidden the money anywhere else. Somewhere he felt comfortable."

"Or maybe he hid it here because he knew you weren't going anywhere," Jase pointed out.

It was something she'd never considered. "That's true. I have to think long-term when it comes to the farm. I rotate the fallow fields, but I've used each of them since he's been in prison. I'd have found the money and bonds if he buried them." Cassie tapped her fingers on the hard rock, the surface firm and constant. "It can't be hidden in the barn, either. A couple of years ago, right around Christmastime, there was a blizzard that damaged the barn roof, but come spring, I replaced it and the floor. There was nowhere he could have hidden the money."

"But what about a map?"

Cassie let out a whistle at Jase's question.

"The way the house was ransacked made me wonder if he could have hidden a map for where he buried the money. Maybe it's in the mountains bordering the farms. That's why I suggested another ride."

That was yet another aspect she hadn't considered. "Then it could be anywhere?"

"It's probably not in the house or the corn maze. Then again, the security system or Rusty might have prevented him from having enough time to get the money. The next time I'm in town, I'll go to the deeds and records department at city hall and examine the blueprints for the farmhouse and farm and see if we've missed anything." Jase stood and headed for the horses.

She noticed he didn't include her in his plans. "I want to see them, too," she shot back, unwilling to cede her ground here. "This concerns me and my family."

"I'm more than capable of taking care of it." He rubbed his hand against his jaw, and she refused to think about how good he looked with a layer of stubble.

"You're one of the most capable people I've ever met, but this is my farm and my house, so I should be there." She was done letting others forge a path that impacted her own. "I know every inch of this farm, and I can tell you what the blueprints can't."

He extended his hand for the rope that bound Highlander to the tree but never took his gaze off of her. His chest rose and fell, and he dropped the rope and strode over to her. He cupped her face as if he was memorizing every detail, every facet of her for when he returned to Denver.

"Every time I think I know you, you surprise me..." He paused, and she could see what this was costing him. "But we both know the stakes here. Your reputation. My career. I can't fail."

She leaned into his touch, the way he made her feel alive. Of all the people to cause this type of joy, it would be from the one man who didn't intend to stick around and whose time here would impact her family's destiny. "You won't." She smiled. "Hello, Detective Virtue."

Cassie stared at him, almost daring him to walk away. A long second passed, and she didn't flinch or move. Instead, she let the same patience that had guided her through so much in the past seep into her now.

They were so close she could see every black fleck in his deep brown eyes. "Hello, Ms. O'Neal."

His lips met hers, and she savored the taste of him. Everything she loved about autumn was in this kiss. Pumpkin spice, warmth and authenticity merged together for something exquisite and raw. The kiss deepened, and she stopped thinking of the past that had brought them together and the future that could only tear them apart. She was grounded in this moment and embraced her feelings, refusing to run away from them anymore.

Only the nickers of the horses interrupted what was a perfect minute. He released her and stepped back. If anything, this second kiss was more incredible than the first. Instead of the shock of finding her house in tatters and knowing the kiss was for comfort, she'd kissed him here solely because he was Jase. Thoughtful, brave and generous.

The problem was, she cared about the complex Jase, the man who reminded her to live in the moment when life could go haywire in an instant. However, he was the last person she should be kissing. After Brayden, she'd made it a point to only consider dating men who had strong ties to Violet Ridge. Though Jase had the strongest of ties to their town, he didn't live here.

Penny and Easton deserved someone in their future who would stick around. She deserved the same.

As hard as it was to stop these swirling emotions for him, she had to. For her children, yes, but most of all for herself. She stepped back, too.

"We can't let that happen again." Though she'd hold the memory of it close.

He nodded and turned away, and she let out the breath she hadn't realized she'd been holding. Not ten seconds passed before he faced her again. "My grandparents and Seth are hosting the weekly dance at the dude ranch tomorrow night. They want me to attend."

"Why are you telling me this?" Then it hit her. "Oh. You won't be at dinner tomorrow night. Don't worry. Keith won't try anything with the increased police presence."

He ran a hand through his short black hair and sounded frustrated as he said, "I want you and Penny and Easton to come with me."

"That's not necessary. The police will deter Keith."

He closed the distance between them once more. "Cassie, I want you and Penny and Easton there. I want to show you my favorite places at Lazy River just like you've done for me here." He started to reach for her hands and stopped. "I also have to do something that's difficult. Having you nearby..." He let his words fade into oblivion.

Cassie could tell how much that admission was costing him. Even more, she wanted time with him. Soon, he'd be gone, and whatever connected them would be a bittersweet memory. That kiss proved good things came when she lived for the present. That was all she had right now, so she'd go along with it.

"Thank you, and we accept." She noticed he'd mentioned the kids, so it wasn't as if this were a date. Although, she would have accepted an invitation to one of those with him in a heartbeat. "Penny and Easton will be very excited. We've heard wonderful stories about the weekly dance, but we've never attended one."

Jase looked as though he was about to add something. Instead, he gave a curt nod and rushed to Highlander, mounting the mustang in one graceful motion. Cassie did the same with Hazel. The she watched as Jase flicked his horse's reins, sending Highlander into a full gallop.

Alone now, she gave into temptation and licked her lips, wondering if she'd just made the biggest mistake of her life.

Or her best decision yet.

CHAPTER TEN

JASE QUELLED THE nerves in his stomach as he approached the Lazy River Dude Ranch. Or better yet, *home*. After all these years and miles, this place was still his refuge and shield. He'd run a good long time and ended up right back where he started.

The time had finally come to tell his family. Before he left the ranch tonight, he'd share his story about that fateful night when his scream and thrashing out had caused his father to veer off the road and hit the tree.

Everyone assumed he'd been asleep at the moment of impact. So had he, until another automobile accident during his police academy days brought everything into focus. It had only been in the past few years, when the survivor guilt combined with not telling his family the truth right away, had eaten at him. Since then, he'd found excuse after excuse for keeping the secret to himself.

His grandparents might kick him out, and where would he go? His family was better off without him. They would stop loving him. They would hate him.

He clenched his jaw. He'd heard every excuse in the book when perpetrators in the interrogation room tried to justify their actions. Now, it was his turn to face his grandparents. He'd go along with whatever they decided about his fate with the family.

At least the truth would prevail. That was important to him, just as it was to all of them.

A lone bark drew him out of his reverie. Jase noticed Cassie's truck heading his way, Rusty's head sticking out of the rear passenger window. She pulled into the open spot next to him in the ranch's gravel lot. Penny and Easton ran over to Jase with Rusty alongside them.

"Jase, you don't gotta dance if you don't wanna." Easton yanked on his hand, a huge grin lighting up his face. "Rosie told me all about it. There's gonna be lots of food, enough for everyone. Aspen says to make sure to eat the little cakes. He said they're so yummy." Then he wrinkled his nose. "Why do they call them petty-fours? Why not petty-threes or petty-fives?"

"I don't know, but my grandmother Bridget will." Jase was sure of that. Grandma Bridget was a fount of information growing up on the ranch. No one knew more than her about the best type of lures for fly-fishing or how to baste a hem.

Penny tapped her toes. "Rosie says there's a real band here. I want to learn to play the guitar." She pretended to strum an air guitar with her fingers, and her eyes widened. "Or maybe the violin or tuba. My friend Naomi plays the piano every day, and she can play two whole songs."

"Grandma Bridget encouraged each of us to play an instrument. Seth is the guitar player of the family." Each Virtue sibling had chosen something different. "Crosby is our fiddler, and Daisy plucks a banjo."

Cassie approached, and his breath escaped him. On her farm, she was pretty in her jeans and flannel shirts, but tonight? Her brown hair fell in waves over her shoulders. Her coppery orange wrap dress hugged her curves, the flare skirt designed for dancing, her brown boots embossed with flowers and curlicues. She was beautiful.

Cassie made herself clear yesterday when she said they couldn't kiss again, and he was a man of his word. Somehow, he'd have to keep his distance from her tonight. It shouldn't be too hard with the way she looked—everyone would want a turn with her on the dance floor.

A twinge of jealousy rose through him before he stifled it. He had made his choice to go back to Denver.

"What about you, Jase?" Cassie asked.

A second went by before he finally found his voice again. "Mouth organ." His voice warbled in a way it hadn't since he turned sixteen and started shaving every day. He cleared his throat and then mimed as if he was playing his instrument, which was tucked into his top drawer in his Denver condo. "More commonly known as the harmonica."

"Will you have a chance to demonstrate your prowess tonight?" And then Cassie blushed a bright red. It seemed as though they were both dancing around the sensitive topic of how to address this attraction humming between them. She coughed and waved a hand in front of her face. "I just meant…"

"I don't play the harmonica in public, much to everyone's appreciation." Despite himself, Jase found himself reaching for her hand. "You look beautiful."

Easton pulled on Jase's suit jacket. "Come on. I've never had a petty-four before. They might run out if we don't hurry."

Jase looked at Cassie over Easton's head. "I can't argue with that kind of logic."

Together they went toward the barn where the dance would take place. Although he'd been here a few times since he arrived back in Violet Ridge, this was the first chance Jase had to take note of the changes Seth had made in the past few months. New paint, updated color schemes, enhanced curb appeal… More proof that Seth was the correct Virtue to maintain the legacy of the dude ranch.

Not that Jase had ever doubted that. Besides, ranch management was never what Jase had wanted to pursue. Putting pieces together and righting wrongs were always more his speed. There wasn't a better career for him than detective.

Inside the decorated barn, Penny gasped her approval. Jase had to admit she was right. He'd never seen it look more appealing. Glittering fairy lights intertwined with green garland decorated the archway leading into the barn. Suspended from the ceiling like a chandelier was a spectacular wreath of fall mums. Orange and burgundy bunting on every wall enhanced the festive look.

On either side of the doors were hay bales with pumpkins and gourds on top. Farther on, tables with white linens and mason jars of orange and yellow marigolds occupied one side of the space with a raised stage for the band and the makeshift dance floor on the other. At the back was the main banquet table, loaded with desserts, including Easton's petits fours.

The dance was already in full swing with a country band performing. Before Jase could even gain his bearings, Doc Jenkins came up to Cassie and asked her to two-step. With a twinge of jealousy rocketing around his insides, even though Doc had a good forty years on the both of them, Jase reassured Cassie he'd look after Easton and Penny while she danced. After all, that was part of the reason he was here in the first place.

Reminding himself about duty and commitment had steadied him in the past, but watching Cassie stand alongside the retired veterinarian, guiding him through the steps and laughing over their mistakes? The world seemed to spin off its axis. Returning to Denver, he wouldn't see her every day or hear her laughter or see what animal she'd rescue next.

Was he only another rescue to her?

That was ridiculous. He didn't need rescuing. He was a detective for one of the finest police departments around. He lived alone by choice and kept to himself for the same reason.

Yet, staring at Cassie on the dance floor, he couldn't help but wonder if he did need rescuing after all.

Someone pulled at his jacket, and Jase glanced down at Easton. "Do you know what a petty-three looks like?"

"Petits fours," Jase corrected Easton, and nodded. "Yep, and Ingrid, the cook here at the Lazy River, is a skilled baker. Come on."

He escorted Easton and Penny to the dessert table but not before glancing once more at Cassie. She was still laughing and dancing with Doc Jenkins. That could have been him.

Seth and Amanda were also dancing, and his brother seemed to sense Jase was hesitant. A second later, Jase's instinct was confirmed when his brother whispered something to Amanda, and the pair fanned themselves before heading his way.

"Penny! Easton!" Amanda reached for a plate. "Will you help me decide what to eat? Everything looks so good."

Easton paused with half a petit four in his hand,

crumbs surrounding his lips. "You have to have a petty-five. They're little cakes!" At least that was what Jase thought he said since Easton's mouth was full.

Seth came over to Jase's side. "Have you seen the pond with all the ducks since you've been back? Remember the time Crosby walked into it fully clothed when he veered off the path while reading a book?" They laughed at the memory. "You won't recognize it with all the new landscaping."

It didn't take a detective to realize Seth wanted to talk to him alone. Ben's warning came back to him, and Jase grabbed a cup of punch, wishing it was fortified with something stronger for whatever his brother wanted to tell him.

On their way out of the barn, Seth occasionally stopped and chatted with dude ranch guests about their week while Jase waited for him. Seth was a natural at this.

"Sorry about that." Seth grabbed his jacket as they headed out of the barn. "Less than a month left of this season, then there's the thank-you week for the employees. This year, we're opening for Christmas for a trial run."

Positive changes like this only proved that Seth knew what he was doing with the business, especially with Amanda at his side guiding him. They reached the pond, and Jase noted the improvements. Less undergrowth and more polish while keeping true to the feel of the dude ranch. Jase had a feeling Amanda had played a part in this. From what he'd seen, the two of them complemented each other with Amanda's sunniness bringing out the best in his methodical brother.

With a barnful of guests and a lively band, Jase figured Seth didn't have time to waste, so he got straight to the point. "What's on your mind, Seth? You and Amanda were smooth, but it's obvious you have something to say."

"Grandma and Grandpa aren't getting any younger." Seth jammed his hands in his pockets and tilted his head as if to invite Jase to walk with him along the circular path. Seth always preferred to be in motion while sorting through his thoughts. Must be a Virtue family trait. "They'd like to see you more than once in a blue moon."

Jase picked up a smooth stone and skipped it over the pond's glassy surface, the moonlight reflecting off the ripples. "Hard to get away whenever I'm in the middle of a case."

Seth stopped and found a pebble of his own, flicking it with ease. It bounced five times before sinking to the bottom. "You aren't even coming home between cases or on vacations. When was the last time you took time off, anyway?"

"Last year." A high fever and a visit to the doctor kept him out for two weeks. Seth's raised eyebrow led Jase to explain, "Bad bout of the flu."

"You should relax more often."

Now it was Jase's turn to raise his eyebrow at his brother's statement. Seth? The ultimate workaholic was advising Jase to rest more? "Wouldn't that mean more coming from Crosby?" Jase met his brother's gaze and they both laughed.

Seth grew serious once more. "Crosby has a stronger work ethic than he lets on. It's not that the books he's reading or working on put him to sleep at the Miners' Cottage…" Jase recognized the name of the oldest surviving building in Violet Ridge. It now served as the historical museum where Crosby worked. "…it's that he stays up so late, he just falls asleep there."

Seth had a point. Perhaps all of the Virtue siblings worked a little too hard.

"Still, you must be burning the candle at both ends with all the changes around here," Jase countered before taking a look at the barn, still visible from this side of the pond.

"Amanda helped me realize the dude ranch is a family effort, and all the employees are part of the Lazy River team. We're working together." Seth skipped another stone and then sat on a bench.

With some reluctance, Jase settled beside him. There wouldn't be another chance to dance with Cassie. That thought alone created an empty ache inside him. Silence stretched out, and Jase emptied the rest of his punch. "Amanda will be a great addition to the family. I'm glad you had the good sense not to screw that up."

"I'm happy Amanda had the good sense not to give up on me." Seth nudged Jase until Jase had no choice but to look at him. "We haven't given up on you, Jase. Any time you want to come back, you're always welcome."

Jase traced the rim of his glass as if it was suddenly the most fascinating thing in the world. "I've worked hard to get where I am. I'm the top candidate to replace Captain Shields when he retires. I'll be the youngest captain in the history of the department."

"And I'm proud of you." Seth poked him, and Jase let Seth's acknowledgment rest deep inside him. "I've sensed a change, though, since you've been here. More than that, I've seen a change. You actually smiled and laughed tonight. You're happy."

Jase blinked, and he found to his surprise that Seth was once again right. He *was* happy, just for the sheer joy of what and who surrounded him. It was a good thing Captain Shields couldn't see him, or he'd be off the Yablonsky case in a heartbeat. Most likely relegated to desk duty for the rest of his career, too.

"Just because you and Amanda have something special doesn't mean that everyone else is falling in love." Jase caught his breath and hoped Seth didn't pick up on his words.

"I didn't say anything about love," Seth said, dashing Jase's expectations. He arched his eyebrows. "Cassie has had a rough time of it the past few years, and she deserves someone who's going to stick around and be by her side."

That couldn't be Jase. "Denver is three hours away, and I can't move here."

Seth rose and zipped his jacket. "Let me just say that while I've always considered you one of the most perceptive people I've ever known, I might have to reconsider that if you let what's between you and Cassie slip away."

His brother stopped talking and drew him in for a firm, brotherly embrace. For a second, Jase kept his hands by his sides before he reciprocated.

Would Seth feel the same way when Jase told him his part in their parents' death? Jase pushed that away and cherished this time with his older brother. Even if Seth was wrong about Jase and Cassie.

Or was he?

Of course, Seth was wrong. Big brothers weren't infallible.

They started walking back to the barn when a familiar figure approached. "Two of my favorite boys."

Jase held back a laugh at Grandma Bridget's pronouncement. Only their grandmother would still refer to him and Seth as boys.

"One of my favorite girls," Jase returned her greeting and enveloped her in a big hug.

No one in Denver hugged like Grandma Bridget.

Except Cassie. Being in one of her embraces made him feel exceptional, just like her.

Grandma Bridget patted Jase's cheek and leaned on her cane once more. Physical therapy and sheer determination helped her recover most of her movement after her stroke years ago, but there were still traces of the traumatic event in the downward turn of her lips and the shakiness in her grip.

"I suspect two of your new favorites are in the barn, and yes, I'm talking about Cassie and Penny O'Neal. Not to mention that sweet boy, Easton." Grandma Bridget's eyes twinkled, and she winked at Jase. "It would be nice to see three of my grandchildren partnered up and content."

"Your wish is granted." Jase raised three fingers and ticked each one as he said, "Seth, Daisy and Crosby."

"I'm not talking about Crosby, and you know it." Grandma Bridget tapped her cane in the dirt. "I love my youngest grandson, but he still has to claim his happiness."

Did everyone see the sparks between Jase and Cassie? Maybe it was time to take himself off the case. If he was too involved, he might hesitate when it mattered, and Cassie's livelihood, and possibly her life, was at stake.

Telling his family what he had to and then going back to Denver would probably be the best way to keep Cassie and her kids safe.

Jase's gaze traveled to the barn where Cassie was dancing with Easton, the pair laughing and having a good time. He wanted to be a part of that family.

Taking his time, he waited until he'd composed

himself before glancing at his grandmother. She had the same satisfied look on her face that he'd seen on many a Christmas morning when Grandpa Martin would kiss her and proclaim her the most beautiful woman in all of Colorado.

"I have a job that is really satisfying and a condo that's paid for. What more could I want?" Jase asked.

"If you have to ask that, I didn't teach you enough about life." She thumped her cane, her lips drawing into a thin line.

This time, Jase reached out for her. "You taught all of us plenty about life."

"Relationships are a part of life, Jason." His grandmother only used his first name on occasions when she was irked with him. "There's nothing wrong with making yourself vulnerable for someone else's love, friendship and companionship."

His gaze went to Cassie again and then back to his grandmother. Perhaps this was the time to broach the sensitive subject. "Grandma, there's something I have to tell you."

"No, there's something you need to tell Cassie O'Neal." She kept her gaze on him. "More to the point, ask her to dance."

"This is important, and I might lose my nerve later." Jase wanted this off his chest once and for all.

Grandma Bridget laid her hand on his. "Cassie is important."

At that moment, his grandfather made an appearance, his eyes lighting up when he saw his wife. "Bridge, I've been looking all over for you. I'd be honored if the most beautiful woman here danced with me."

Grandma Bridget gave Jase a stern look before turning toward her husband of almost sixty years. "You're a charmer just like your grandsons."

"I should have known I'd find Bridge wherever you are." Grandpa Martin clapped Jase on the back, and then pulled him into a firm embrace. "You'd make your grandmother the happiest woman in Violet Ridge if you returned home for good."

Grandpa Martin began to escort Grandma Bridget toward the barn and the dance floor, but then she turned and mouthed something to Jase. It took him a second before he realized she was reminding him to ask Cassie for a dance.

The band was performing a slow ballad. *Perfect.* He'd be able to hold her close and smell the sweet scent of her shampoo. This dance might even be the highlight of his trip.

CASSIE LISTENED AS Easton raved about the petits fours while standing on her boots and swaying to the music. How he could dance and talk with that much energy was a mystery.

Speaking of mysteries, it was good to get away from the farmhouse and have an evening where she could savor her surroundings without worrying about Keith invading her space.

Jase came over and tapped on Easton's shoulder. "May I cut in?"

Easton frowned. "Did ya bring scissors?"

Cassie kept from laughing as Jase shook his head. "It's an expression," Jase said. "I'm asking if I can dance with your mother in your place."

At that moment, Penny rushed over and tugged on Easton's sleeve. "Daisy said she'll take us to the stable so we can look at the horses." Then she turned to Cassie. "Can we go, Mom? Ben's going and Rosie and Lily and Aspen."

Both children gazed at her with stars in their eyes. They'd be safe with Ben and Daisy and have more fun with the triplets, who were close to their age. Cassie nodded. "Listen to Ben and Daisy."

They were out of the barn with Rusty on their heels before she finished her sentence. That left her alone with Jase. Well, alone as someone could be at a country dance.

Jase stepped in front of her, his arms outstretched. "May I have this kiss? Er, dance." His cheeks flamed a bright red. "May I have this dance?"

She was only too aware of the slow tempo of the song. With some trepidation and a heart ready to jump out of her chest, Cassie agreed.

He drew her into his arms. They moved in time to the music. It took all of her effort not to rest her head against his charcoal gray suit jacket. Every other man here was dressed casually in jeans with bright gold belt buckles and bolo ties. Not Jase.

He matched his impeccable suit with a red silk tie in a Windsor knot, although he did have a slight concession to the night by wearing brown cowboy boots.

Then again, Jase would stand out wherever he went. How did he blend into the environment as a detective when she was so aware of him at every turn?

Somehow she'd done a poor job of guarding her heart against men who'd leave at a moment's notice. In spite of her misgivings, though, she moved closer to Jase, losing herself to the slow tempo of the song and the twinkling lights. For too long, momentous challenges had decided her life's trajectory. Just this once, she wanted something sweet and positive to be the cause of change.

Cassie gave into her impulse to lay her head against Jase's shoulder while the soft music swirled around them. It was her nature to trust, and Jase had proven himself more than worthy of that trust. She knew he was leaving soon, but she could still grasp this moment and cherish it.She just didn't expect the song to end a minute after Jase cut in. Those few seconds weren't enough.

The singer paused, spoke to the band and then stepped up to the microphone. Cassie braced herself for what might come next. The singer began clapping. "Are you ready to parrrrrrty? Let's kick this up a notch. Line up and let the music guide your feet."

The crowd hooted and hollered and clapped

along as the band segued into a song with more attitude and a faster tempo. Guests formed into lines and began stepping from side to side.

Jase huffed and looked at his feet with a grimace. "Line dancing. Why does it always have to be line dancing?"

She laughed at his frustrated tone. "Aha! So you have a weakness. I was getting worried you were perfectly perfect." She shimmied and rolled her shoulders. "Come on. It'll be fun."

He shrugged, found a spot in the line and started sliding with the rest. Seeing Jase Virtue line dancing? The night had just gotten that much better.

CHAPTER ELEVEN

There was nothing like twelve hours to bring about a total change in circumstances, Cassie reflected. Last night, she'd been line dancing with Jase at the Lazy River Dude Ranch, her dress swirling around her legs while he looked elegant in his charcoal gray suit. Right now, she was pausing to rest under her broken tractor in the barn on this dreary drizzly morning. Instead of makeup and heels, her face was bare while she was clad in her oldest jeans and flannel shirt with the sleeves rolled up. A long black streak of grease graced her left arm.

In the corner, the chicks were chirping under the full benefit of the heat lamp, growing bigger every day. Rusty was standing watch over them while Patches had taken up residence in the stable, upset that her domain had been invaded like this.

At least the chicks were having a good morning. Her relatively new tractor wouldn't start, and so far she couldn't pinpoint the problem.

"Cassie?" Jase's voice echoed off the rafters.

Backing out from under the tractor, she bumped her head.

"Ouch!" She rubbed the spot of impact and glanced at Jase, who showed no signs of staying out late on a Saturday night although something seemed off about him. "Did you need me for something?"

He pointed to the fence. "Did you forget to latch the gate after you collected the eggs this morning? The chickens escaped. Blossom came straight for me, and then a couple of her friends followed, but I counted, and three are missing."

Cassie bumped her head with her hand and winced as she made contact with the sore spot. How could she be so forgetful this morning? One look at Jase provided the answer. Her mind had wandered to the slow dance while she was gathering the eggs.

"They'll be home for dinner tonight," Cassie said. This wasn't the first time some of them escaped. Penny had left the gate open a couple of times, and the hens always returned for their next meal.

One look at Rusty gave her pause. She didn't want any predators getting to the chickens or any of them getting hurt by the extra patrol vehicles. "On the other hand, I'll have a look around for them. I don't want anything bad happening to them. Then I'll finish fixing the tractor."

Cassie passed two of the stragglers and retrieved the bucket of chicken feed hanging on the peg on a fence post. Blossom demanded Jase's attention, and Jase cuddled the hen, who preened proudly. Cassie loved seeing the pair but started spreading out feed on the ground and clucking her tongue, hoping the errant hens weren't too far away.

Within minutes, all but one of the three was back inside the henhouse with the lone straggler in sight, still enjoying her freedom.

Cassie held her breath as Rusty approached. The red retriever seemed more interested in making a new friend than eating the hen, much to Cassie's relief. Rusty settled on his haunches and watched the hen peck at the ground before herding her back inside the fence.

"Seems Rusty found a new friend."

Jase was so close that when Cassie turned around, she bumped into him, spilling most of the chicken feed to the great delight of the remaining hens.

This close, everything about him was magnified, leaving her breathless. His hair was slightly damp from a recent shower, his freshly shaven face as appealing as when he wore a layer of stubble.

"You can never have too many friends," she said quickly. "Take you and Blossom. She now considers you part of the family. And your family is bringing me into their fold on your behalf. I don't even know how to thank Ben and Daisy for letting Penny and Easton stay with them and hang out with the triplets these last few weeks. It's not every mayor that would personally escort two of his constituents to and from school. Penny and Easton are thrilled about the behind-the-scenes tour of the dude ranch from Amanda and Seth today. Your family is really coming together to support you, and I'm the true benefactor."

Jase held up his hand and shook his head. "Don't you know?"

"Know what?" She was eager for whatever he was about to explain.

"It's not me. They're helping you because you do so much for other people, Cass." He reached out his hand, and his palm started to caress her cheek before he pulled back and grabbed the bucket. "Here, let me refill that for you."

She stood there, unsure what to unravel first: that his family might be doing this for her, or the effect of his sweet touch that she hadn't wanted to end.

Before she could process her emotions, a loud rip followed by a sharp cry of pain startled her. She turned and saw Jase grab his leg, obviously in pain.

Rushing over, she discovered the source of the problem: a nail sticking out of a post. "You snagged your pants on that nail." Those looked like nice work pants, too, but now they were torn badly. Worse yet, she saw a long streak of red on his leg. While getting rid of that nail was now a priority for her, especially given how Easton was a whiz at finding ways to get into new scrapes on the farm, she needed to tend to that leg first. "I have a first aid kit in the farmhouse."

Jase looked down and shook his head. "It's nothing. I don't even need stitches. I can help you finish fixing that tractor."

"When was your last tetanus shot?" She might have to take him into town.

"Last year for my job. I'll be fine."

She wouldn't take no for an answer and insisted he accompany her inside, where she fetched towels and warm water. "Another set of eyes never hurt." She waited until he hiked up his pants to the knees. With a delicate finger, she traced an old scar that went from his knee to the middle of his calf. "Is this from your job?"

A reminder of how he put his life on the line in his profession. Of course, who'd have guessed his latest injury would come thanks to a chicken coop?

"It's not recent. It's from childhood." He winced as she washed the blood off his leg. "After the accident, I had surgery to reset the bones."

Searching the bathroom cabinet, she retrieved the first aid box and rifled through the contents until she found the antibiotic ointment. Then she moved him into the living room where there was more natural light. "That must have been hard. Losing your parents and needing surgery at the same time."

He kept a stoic face during her ministrations. "The surgery was the least of it."

She applied the ointment, the cut not deep

enough to require stitches, just as he'd predicted. "You don't talk about the accident very often, if ever, do you?"

"How did you know?" He looked at her with wonder.

"Just a feeling." She unwrapped a length of gauze and cut it off the roll. "You might want to consider talking to your grandparents."

"You don't know how often I've thought about just that." His voice was drier than the desert.

"My mom and I still talk about Dad. Just a couple of months ago, we even went over his final moments. It helped both of us." She applied the gauze to his leg. "It was even cathartic. The accident was a long time ago, but sometimes talking to someone who lived through a crisis with you can be healing."

"I've never thought about it like that, but there's more underneath the surface."

"I wasn't there, so I don't know the details, but I know you. You're deliberative when sometimes you just have to let emotions guide you." She taped the gauze in place and finished wrapping his leg. "Sometimes it helps to just remind someone you love them. Knowing your grandparents, that's all the thanks they'd ever want for getting you through those surgeries."

"I'd hardly think they'd want my thanks after..." He rolled down his pants leg. "Thanks for the bandage. It feels fine."

He started to head back outside, and she reached out her hand to stop him. "After what?"

"Nothing. I'll change into jeans and help you fix that tractor." He escaped her grip and stepped back into the wall.

"After what?" she repeated her question, and he stopped where he was.

"You won't let this go, will you?" He closed his eyes for a long beat before looking at her, agony welling in those dark depths. "I did something they might find unforgiveable. I've distanced myself by my choice, and I don't know what I'd do if I couldn't ever come home again."

"Whatever it was, you were six when it happened. Your grandparents won't hold anything you did at that age against you." She stood firm. "And I know your grandparents. They will never stop loving you."

If anyone should know about a family ripped apart by an individual's actions, it was she. Keith was an adult when he'd stolen from her father and then from the bank. And Jase's heart was made of gold. He could never purposefully do anything to hurt someone.

"You don't know the details." Jase flexed his muscles. "The tractor..."

"Can wait another minute." She replaced what she'd taken out of the first aid kit. "You need to talk to them today. Leaning on someone is actually a good thing, Jase."

He searched her face. "Who's there for you, Cassie?"

"Amanda, Doc Jenkins, Zelda Baker." Not only had Zelda helped Cassie formulate the subscription boxes, she also dropped off a casserole after Easton was born. The following day, Zelda's identical twin Nelda brought a baby blanket and a strawberry pie. "Come to think of it, everyone at the seniors' center. Possibly even the whole town."

Rusty came over and nudged her hand. The farm cats and other animals had also given her so much love.

One look at Jase showed he was mulling over her words. That was a start to defrosting that icy exterior of his and possibly accepting the help he deserved.

He pulled out his phone and sent a text. A minute later, he nodded. "Tonight. Crosby drove out of town this morning, and it's the earliest he'll be back." Then he blew out a breath. "I'd prefer to keep busy until then. I'll change and meet you at the barn."

She let him off the hook for now. A short time later, she was tending the baby chicks when Patches sauntered inside and climbed into the loft.

Cassie chuckled at the cat. "Couldn't stay away for long, could you?"

"Of course not." Jase entered, and her heart thumped. If only he meant those words. "Grandma Bridget taught me everything she knows about tractors."

"It's most likely the gas filter," she said. "I need to go into town and buy a new one."

"How about we have another look at the tractor together? Then we'll go into town if it's the gas filter." Jase lifted the hood.

"I thought my trouble with tractors was over when I saved enough to buy this beauty, but it's as temperamental as the last one."

"Hand me that wrench, will you?" His muffled voice reached her, and she did so.

He accepted the tool and focused on the machinery once more. She went to the other side and tightened the spark plugs. She'd just replaced those last month, so that shouldn't be the problem. It had to be the gas filter.

A minute later, Jase knocked on the hood. Standing, he reached for a rag and wiped his hands. "Try it now."

She rolled her eyes. Nothing about this temperamental tractor could be that simple, and he'd see that soon enough. Though sometimes you needed to see something for yourself, so she settled behind the wheel and turned the ignition.

The tractor purred to life.

"It was a loose wire," Jase said. "That might have been the trouble all along. It shouldn't be bothering you anymore. What's next?"

"Thanks." She shut off the tractor. One good turn deserved another. "I need some supplies for tonight's grandparent visit at the seniors' center.

With half the town there, I'll be safe while you're talking to your own grandparents."

He arched his eyebrows but brought out his keys from his pocket. "I'm ready for town if you are?"

She plucked at her shirt and pointed to the streak of grease on her arm. "I'll change into fresh clothes and clean up. See you soon."

At least that would be true for a little longer. She couldn't deny there was a connection between them, but for once she'd listen to the voice in her head that urged caution and patience.

JASE NODDED TO KELLY, the diligent receptionist at the Lazy River Dude Ranch check-in desk. Then he climbed the stairs to his grandparents' suite on the third floor of the lodge. By the time he'd finished line dancing with Cassie last night, his grandmother had said she needed her sleep, so he hadn't been able to talk to his family until now.

Cassie was safe thanks to an off-duty police officer who was on patrol, and a horde of loyal people who'd stay by her side.

Standing in his grandparents' living quarters, he bypassed the coffee maker and headed to the bar where he fixed himself a whiskey and soda. Glass in hand, he settled on the couch, his nerves keeping him from being anything but settled, in fact.

Grandpa Martin and Grandma Bridget greeted him, their laughter only adding to Jase's nervousness. For so long, the distance between them was his doing. His heart had warned him to stay away.

Why dredge up the past when it was behind him? Why not stay with the status quo?

Until he spoke the truth, though, he wouldn't know peace in the future.

They sat on the sofa opposite him. Grandma Bridget held out a plate with a piece of triple berry pie.

"I know it's your favorite." His grandmother smiled at him, and he stored that expression in his heart. "Your brothers and sister are on their way."

He nodded and placed the plate on the coffee table in front of him, his hands trembling. Joking and teasing could be overheard before his three siblings piled into the room. Jase stayed where he was and gulped his drink, the whiskey burning his throat.

"I'm to blame." The words tumbled out before he could think about them. So much for easing into the conversation.

Grandpa Martin shifted on the sofa. "For staying away so long? I agree. What are you going to do about it?" He placed his hand on his wife's knee and gave it a squeeze. "Daisy's married, and Seth is getting hitched soon. Are you finally moving back where you belong?"

Daisy echoed their grandfather's sentiments while Grandma Bridget wiped a tear from her eye.

"It's about time you acknowledge what we've known for years." His grandmother's voice was raspy but firm.

Guilt twisted his stomach. It wasn't what he'd

come here to say, but should he go along with it? Hurting them more seemed intolerable to him. "You don't understand. I have to explain why I've kept my distance. This is harder than I thought it would be, yet all of you dropped everything when I asked to meet you here tonight."

"Of course we did. It's because of unconditional love." His grandmother looked at her husband and smiled. "Your grandfather still tests that concept from time to time. Why it was just earlier this year I found out he'd kept the new mortgage a secret from me."

"For your health. The bills needed paying, and you already had so much on your plate with your recovery." His grandfather patted her hand and then kissed it. "And it was all because I love you unconditionally and want you around for much longer. It all turned out well. The dude ranch is earning a profit, thanks mainly to Seth, and we're gaining another granddaughter out of it."

"If you'd just talked to me when it happened, though, it would have been easier on everyone, dear." Grandma Bridget offered a small smile. "He still worries about me after almost sixty years of marriage. Isn't that sweet? But I have to tell you. I'm tougher than I look."

"But what I have to tell you might exacerbate your health," Jase worried aloud.

She leaned over and squeezed his hand. "If it's important to you, we need to hear it. We want to hear it."

As difficult as it was, they deserved to know the truth about that fateful night. "Earlier today, Cassie said something, and I knew today was the day to be honest with you. Finally."

Grandma Bridget's face softened into a wistful smile. "I like Cassie O'Neal. She's smart, and she's come through so much. She deserves a little happiness. What did she say?"

"She asked whether I ever thanked you for all you did after the accident." He took a deep breath and continued, putting everything on the line. "I hope I did. I hope you knew that. But I caused the accident. I screamed and acted out, and then Dad plowed into the tree. If it wasn't for me, they'd be alive today." He placed his head in his hands, his whole body shuddering.

"Jason Virtue."

His grandfather's sharp voice caused Jase to look toward him. Disappointment was written all over his face.

His worst fear was coming true.

He was losing his family all over again.

"I'm so sorry." Jase's voice came out in a whisper, husky and hoarse. What could he say that he hadn't felt over the years? "I'll accept your decision, no matter what, even if you never want to see me again."

Grandma Bridget frowned. "For once, you will listen to me, Jason. It's called an accident for a reason. That crash was simply that. An accident." Her gaze went to her husband. "Tell him, Martin."

Jase transferred his attention to his grandfather, who looked smaller, thinner than ever.

"You've stayed away all these years, ran away from us because you thought you may have caused the crash?" Grandpa Martin gritted his teeth, rose and poured himself a drink before coming back to sit on the sofa.

Jase reached deep into himself and found his voice. "I caused the accident," he repeated, looking away from the people who mattered the most.

Cassie's face came to mind, followed by Penny, then Easton. The three of them had also come to live in his heart.

"That's just not right, son." Grandpa Martin pursed his lips and shook his head before downing his drink. "Weather conditions were terrible. They never should have been on the road at all, but sadly, sometimes bad things happen. You have to understand that. Besides, it wouldn't make sense. Your father and mother had been parents for a good long while, so your fussing, no matter how loud or bothersome, wouldn't have rattled your dad enough to cause him to drive off the road the way he did. I went to the scene. It took hours because of the storm, but I saw it all for myself. It was a tragic accident for our family, but it was simply that. An accident. You didn't cause it. No way, no how, Jason."

Jase searched every face through a veil of tears. "But Dad..."

Grandma Bridget reached for his hand at the

same time his sister leaned over and grasped his other hand. His grandmother repeated the facts and concluded, "It was an accident, Jase. You need to forgive yourself. You did nothing wrong except keep this to yourself for all these years."

Daisy squeezed his hand and then rubbed his cheek. "You've run all this time, thinking we'd hate you. We love you."

Jase noticed his grandfather getting to his feet, his eyes damp with moisture. "I should have known there was a reason you stayed away. If I'd realized…"

Seemed as though this was the night to clear the air. For the first time in twenty-four years, Jase knew he wasn't to blame for the accident. He expected the peace to flow over him, but a different kind of turbulence filled the void. He'd stayed away for so long, thinking he was sparing everyone pain. Instead, he'd brought this torture on himself.

His grandmother released his hand and smiled. "You're a good man. You make a difference in Denver. If you want to stay there and continue fighting for justice, we'll support you, but you don't have to run anymore. You can come home."

As Jase looked at his family, he was filled with the love he'd denied himself for so long. And he wondered if there was another love still open to him.

CHAPTER TWELVE

SOMETHING WAS WRONG. Cassie rolled over and plumped a pillow before realizing Rusty was howling in his crate. She jumped out of bed, her feet finding the slippers she kept nearby as the nights grew colder. With a swift motion, she grabbed her robe off the back of her door.

Jase was at Rusty's crate, releasing the dog who went and scratched on the back door. "I just contacted the officer on guard. No one's been seen coming or going onto your property." Jase opened the door slightly and stopped to look at her. "Please stay inside."

Cassie tightened the belt of her robe and traded her slippers for boots. "What if it's a fox in the henhouse?" She met his gaze and folded her arms. "This is a working farm in Colorado. There are other predators out there besides Keith."

"I'll do a quick perimeter search and then come get you if it's necessary." Jase disappeared into the night.

This was her property. If anyone should be defending her chickens, Patches and the horses, it should be her. She moved toward the door and halted.

In the several weeks since he'd been here, she'd come to trust Jase. He'd arrived under the worst possible circumstances and protected her and her children. More than anything, she wanted Jase to apprehend Keith so Penny and Easton could return home to their own beds. Although, she'd be forever grateful to Daisy and Ben Irwin for allowing them to stay at their house.

As hard as it was to do nothing, she remained in the house with Rusty standing guard.

Moments later, Jase reappeared. "The chickens are fine, but I need you to come with me." His gaze landed on Rusty. "He needs to stay here."

Relief traveled through her, knowing Blossom and the others were still safe in the henhouse. She followed Jase to the corn maze, her boots sinking into the soft ground, a result of the fall rainy season. He nodded at the police officer who was putting crime scene tape around the perimeter of the maze and an overturned barrel.

"What's going on?" Her relief about the hens gave way to panic about yet another delay to the newest attraction. At this rate, Violet Ridge residents would have to travel to Gunnison or beyond if they wanted to participate in a corn maze.

Jase pulled out a plastic evidence bag from his pocket. "I found this inside the maze." The crumpled beer can caught Cassie's eye. "Is it yours?"

She shook her head. A stiff breeze rustled

through the aspen tops, a reminder that the first snowfall was imminent even if it was only the beginning of October. The cold cutting through her, however, had nothing to do with the weather, and everything to do with Keith being here on her property. "It's Keith, isn't it?"

Jase handed the evidence bag to the police officer. "Run a fingerprint analysis on that. Then check with the stores about those receipts we found on the ground, the ones dated yesterday. See if there's security footage so we can find out if it was him and if he was alone. Bag everything else he left behind as well." Jase outlined more details until he seemed to notice her. Cassie was shivering. "You're cold."

"I'm fine." But she wasn't.

How long had Keith been here, invading her privacy and the sanctuary of her home? How had he evaded the police and the new security system? How long until Jase finally had him in custody?

Thanking the police officer for his work, Jase escorted Cassie back to the farmhouse. Rusty wagged his tail, happy to see her once more. By the time the warm air hit her, she was a frozen mess. She flopped into the overstuffed chair.

"I'll make coffee." Jase covered her first with a dark red plush throw from the end of the couch. Rusty curled into a ball at her feet as if protecting her.

Cassie lost herself in the blanket's softness, letting the comfort seep into her. A few minutes later, she wrapped her fingers around the mug of coffee Jase brought her. “Thank you.” The steam tickled her nose, the rich aroma filling her with calm. Her equilibrium was returning, although one glance at Jase almost made her lose it again.

She finally acknowledged the truth. When Jase returned to Denver, he’d be taking her heart with him.

He sat on the Queen Anne chair her mother loved so much, his tall frame making the furniture look small. “From the rest of the evidence in the corn maze, it appears Yablonsky has been casing your house since the corn maze company finished their repairs.”

Her hand began shaking. A splash of coffee landed on her robe, and she set the mug on the table. “I almost can’t believe this is happening. It’s bad enough what happened in the past with my family, but to have Keith and his actions being revisited on us is…” She had to stop and take a breath, the emotions almost too much.

“Why don’t you get some sleep while I search the farm for any other signs of Keith?”

“It’s hard to sleep when he was so close.” Cassie reached for the mug once more and inhaled the rich blend. “I’m assuming this isn’t decaf.”

Jase shrugged. “I just selected the first pod available.”

“It’s just as well. It’s a little after four, and I’d be waking up soon anyway,” Cassie said, sipping the hot brew. "I'll start with checking on the baby chicks in the barn."

While she finished the coffee, she let her mind wander. Was she falling too hard, too fast for Jase in the same way she had when Brayden arrived in Violet Ridge?

This wasn't anything like that. For one thing, she'd known Jase in high school whereas Brayden was a newcomer to town when she fell for him. For another, in terms of character and personality, Jase was nothing like Brayden, who would never have made her coffee or done anything to comfort her in a moment of intense stress.

Jase furrowed his brows. "Some parts of the farm may be off-limits today."

This time Cassie set the mug on the table with enough force that more coffee sloshed over the top. Rusty raised his head at the sudden movement. "I have to feed the horses, get the farmstand ready and finish filling subscription boxes of vegetables. They can't wait."

"They'll have to," Jase insisted and leaned forward. "This is a police investigation."

"And this is my life." Cassie groaned and placed her head in her hands. Would this nightmare never end?

And where would she and Jase be then?

THE PAST TWENTY-FOUR hours were a whirlwind, and Jase wanted to bask in the sun and see blue skies again. Yet here he was in the fields at Cassie's farm, helping her with the harvest and standing guard in case Yablonsky slipped and made his presence known.

How was the convict evading them at every turn? Was Jase slipping? Giving less than his best? Was he letting his personal life get in the way of his career? He had to keep up his guard when it came to this case.

Finally, the last boxes of freshly picked radishes and carrots were assembled and awaiting transfer to the root cellar. Cassie stood up and stretched her back. "I couldn't stomach breakfast this morning, but lunch sounds good. What about you?"

"We should get this stored in the root cellar first." His stomach grumbled loud enough for her to hear, and he gave a wry laugh. "Or eat first."

She grabbed a couple carrots off the pile before they walked together toward the farmhouse, Rusty dashing ahead of them. Rusty was exceptional—that dog was keeping Cassie safe and had alerted them to Keith's presence. It made Jase feel a bit better, knowing that the faithful family pet was on the job.

In the kitchen, Jase and Cassie were mostly quiet while preparing their food, the silence broken only when Cassie explained to him why he was chopping the carrots incorrectly. He just smiled, happy to follow her lead, while she reached into the refrigerator for her homemade vinaigrette and some leftover grilled chicken. Finally, she added pumpkin muffins to a basket, and they settled at the kitchen table for their makeshift meal.

"Let me show you a picture of your nieces and nephew last night at the seniors' center. They really got into the pumpkin decorating contest, same as Penny and Easton." Cassie pulled out her phone and scrolled through the photos. "I think Rosie, Lily and Aspen ended up with more paint on them than the pumpkin. They missed Martin and Bridget. We all did."

Jase had missed Cassie's children but was glad he'd had that heartfelt conversation with his family. Still, the thought of returning to a condo without Easton's million questions and Penny's thoughtfulness made his stomach churn.

Being alone had never bothered him before. His job had always kept him busy, a new case always around the bend.

These last few weeks had shown him how hollow his life was without close friends and family. Sharing this meal with Cassie, even if it was just as her friend, was something that centered him. He wondered if it might be similar to what Cassie felt connecting with the earth and how farming brought her peace.

He had her scroll back to one of the photos and smiled at the row of decorated pumpkins. Little moments like these wouldn't have meant nearly as much to him a few weeks ago, his iceman reputation earned for good reason. But now…

He wanted to stay in Violet Ridge with Cassie

and Penny and Easton and celebrate all these little moments. After last night, he had more reasons than ever to consider relocating.

What had happened to the detective who was counting down the months until Captain Shields retired? No longer did that absolute ambition drive his every decision. Cassie, with her zest for life and all its bounty, proved there was more to experience, and he was beyond grateful.

"Sounds like it was a great night." He sipped his lemonade, the tart sweetness a little like his time here.

"How's your leg feeling today?" Cassie asked.

He bent down and rubbed the injury. "It's better today, but it was a late night for me. I waited too long to do something, and it cost me a great deal." He blotted some lemonade off his chin and then looked at her.

Her gentle persistence had played a major part in his decision to open up to his grandparents. He and Cassie had taken different routes to get to this moment, and he admired her ability to stay and fight. Having a community behind you and sticking it out rather than fleeing and staying isolated was a tough row to hoe, but Cassie was one remarkable woman.

"Penny and Easton missed you." She placed her phone by her plate and forked another bite of kale, julienned carrots and vinaigrette.

He reached for her hand. "You gave me the strength to confront my past."

He spilled out everything that happened last night. She let him talk uninterrupted, her face showing surprise and empathy, concern and joy. Story finished, he leaned back against his chair as winded as if he'd just run a marathon. He was still holding her hand, the contact between them a lifeline and a connection unlike any he'd ever known.

"You're wrong about my influence," she said at last. "It was the right time, and you recognized that."

He rose and faced her, extending both hands, which she took in hers. She stood, too. Time seemed to slow, and he tried to capture in his mind how she looked just then. Her flowing hair, her soft smile, her expressive eyes.

He pushed a stray strand of her hair behind her ear. "You deserve more than just a compliment."

"I could say the same about you." She stepped closer to him. "Where do you want to be, Jase?"

"Right here," he admitted before putting his lips to hers.

She returned the kiss, her skin soft and smooth. Just like that, his entire world changed, and he admitted he couldn't live in Denver again. He belonged in Violet Ridge.

She smiled, her mouth tempting him again. "Maybe we should finish this discussion tonight. There's still a lot of hard work to do around here."

"That's one way to bring me back to earth." He flexed his muscles. "Time to earn my lunch with an afternoon of heavy lifting."

He had a feeling she'd been doing all the heavy lifting at the farm since her mother left, no matter that she had the support of the town behind her. She was still the one doing extensive labor.

Moving to Violet Ridge would benefit everyone on so many levels. Tomorrow he'd talk to Chief Gutierrez about any openings, either here or in the nearest town. He'd work on getting reacquainted with his family all over again and regaining their trust. He'd see Penny and Easton every day.

And there'd be more kisses and lunch conversations with Cassie.

His heart soared at all the possibilities the future held.

With that in mind, he almost floated to the fields where he hefted boxes onto a rolling cart. He wheeled it while they talked about the season changing and how the holidays would be coming up fast, both of them skirting around the issue of their future. Although, for once, he wasn't afraid of broaching the subject.

They reached the root cellar, and Jase noticed the padlock hanging open.

Cassie frowned. "It looks like someone's been here."

Concern gripped him. "Don't touch anything."

He returned to the farmhouse for his fingerprint dusting kit before rushing back to the root cellar. He dusted the padlock only to find there were no prints, which could only mean one thing: Yablonsky wiped the surface clean. He placed the padlock into an evidence bag, taking in the look of alarm on Cassie's face.

He couldn't blame her. He wasn't doing his job if Keith could move around the farm this easily without detection.

"I'll be right back," Jase said. "If you see anyone coming, give a shout."

He descended the steps into the cool interior of the underground cellar. Nothing appeared to be disturbed. He sniffed the air and detected a faint whiff of smoke. Yablonsky had been here. He followed the scent until he spotted something on the ground: several cigarette butts and a fresh half-eaten sandwich. Jase pulled out two more evidence bags and a pair of tweezers. As soon as he plucked up the sandwich, something shiny caught his eye.

There on the ground was a bracelet with the initial *C* on it. The same bracelet he'd seen on Cassie's wrist before. The same one that hadn't been on her wrist at lunch.

CHAPTER THIRTEEN

JASE HADN'T REMEMBERED the walls ever closing in on him in the Denver precinct before, yet here he was, sitting in Captain Shields's office, feeling as if they were. Earlier this morning, Jase had driven from Violet Ridge to the penitentiary where he'd interviewed Yablonsky's former cellmate again, hoping for some new bit of evidence that might put Cassie in a better light. But there was nothing new. Now, with Captain Shields, he was reviewing his notes from that interview.

"Same old, same old," the captain said, typing on his keyboard. "The latest evidence analysis came back. Yablonsky was definitely in the root cellar and the corn maze. His DNA was on all the evidence you collected."

Jase leaned forward, waiting for the boom to drop. Yablonsky had eluded him on his watch. Captain Shields didn't have to rebuke Jase. Jase was doing that on his own.

Captain Shields answered his phone and delivered a few orders before returning his attention back to Jase.

"What about the bracelet?" Jase could still hold out a shred of hope that Cassie was innocent. He'd seen the clasp break once before. Maybe it had again, and she hadn't noticed it. After all, it was her root cellar; she could have been down there at any time.

"Yablonsky's fingerprints were on it."

Jase went numb. He'd been willing to give up the promotion for her. He'd been falling in love with a criminal. Jase searched every angle, trying to come up with some explanation that could clear Cassie. He failed.

"Hmm." Shields's grunt brought Jase back to the room. "That's strange. His fingerprints were on the bracelet, but hers weren't."

"How's that possible?" Jase asked.

Shields leaned back in his chair and steepled his fingers, a sign that he was putting evidence together. "That's less relevant right now. What's important is that we have enough for a search warrant for her financial records. Tomorrow, we bring her in for questioning."

To Jase, it was significant that her fingerprints weren't on the bracelet. On the surface, it looked bad for Cassie, but could Yablonsky have found the bracelet and left it in the root cellar where he knew Cassie would eventually find it? It wasn't as if the convict was going to knock on Cassie's front door to return it.

That was flimsy at best, but Jase had been around Cassie for the past few weeks. He'd seen her body language whenever Yablonsky was mentioned. He'd danced with her. He'd kissed her. She was genuine.

Maybe she was innocent. If so, she needed someone in her corner. If not him, then who?

Jase exhaled and propped his elbows on his thighs, leaning forward. "I've been thinking, going over everything from the start of all this. We're missing something about the bank robbery that will crack this case wide open. I'm sure of it."

Shields's head snapped up, and he frowned. "What we're missing is O'Neal's bank statement." His eyes narrowed, and he picked up the phone, requesting a subpoena and authorizing the accounting forensics unit to start their investigation. He replaced the receiver.

Jase stared at the cluttered bulletin board on the wall and began to wonder aloud. "How did Yablonsky know the bank would have extra funds that day? How did he get into the vault without alerting the authorities? Cassie has no connection to the bank."

"The bank manager, Clara Abbott, was about to retire and had just been diagnosed with cancer. She wanted money for her daughter, Lucy, and passed on the information to Yablonsky and his sister." Shields resumed his thinking pose. "Did you say Cassie instead of O'Neal?"

Jase clenched his jaw. "I've been staying at her farm for over two weeks. It would be a strain to have continued calling her Ms. O'Neal all this time."

"As far as I'm concerned, this development is the icing on the cake." Shields tapped something into the keyboard. "O'Neal and Yablonsky, knowing you were stationed at the farm, had to start thinking fast. She must have been keeping an eye on you and talked to Yablonsky whenever you were elsewhere."

The implication that Cassie played him like that riled Jase. "If she and Yablonsky were working together, she wouldn't have sent Penny and Easton to my sister's." Despite the case against her, Jase was more convinced than ever she was innocent.

"She knew you were watching her closely and agreed to it all so she'd deflect attention from herself. The bracelet seals the deal as far as I'm concerned. We'll question her together in Violet Ridge." Shields faced forward and nodded. "Offer her a plea deal. With two kids, that should induce her to talk."

This was Jase's last chance to prove the evidence was circumstantial, although he knew it looked bad for Cassie. "I'm not sure she's *C*." Jase outlined his doubts. His Cassie would have already left the country if she was involved. His Cassie had earned the money to fix everything through hard labor. His Cassie had an alibi when Yablonsky escaped. All the while as he spoke, images of Cassie at the seniors' center, at her farmstand, at the vet's office flooded his mind. Cassie couldn't be the criminal Shields believed her to be.

Shields listened, his lips becoming more of a straight line the longer Jase talked. "You've never become personally involved in any of your cases like this."

Jase was too aware of his iceman reputation at the department. "The bank robbery happened on the first week of my police patrol, in my district, and the money was never found. That made it personal."

Shields kept his gaze on Jase, but Jase didn't move. "I'm concerned about your objectivity. It sounds like you've developed feelings for O'Neal."

Jase didn't correct his superior. He wouldn't lie. Cassie made it too easy to care about her, while her farm and kids did the rest. "Cassie's been through a lot. Her father died, her husband left her, and she's built up the farm through sweat and determination, not a windfall from her brother's criminal activity."

Even more reasons he'd fallen for the hardworking farmer. She'd kept her farm afloat, choosing to stay and fight for her reputation, rather than running as he had done.

Jase stopped thinking about Cassie and focused on the details of Shields's office: the gouge marks on the desk, the picture of Shields and his wife at their son's wedding, the strong smell of bleach. Anything to keep his mind on this case so Shields wouldn't reassign him, even though Jase had asked him to do just that on two separate occasions.

"You're not helping your cause." Shields stared at Jase, his voice low. "Can you honestly sit there and tell me you're impartial? That you don't have feelings for her?"

This was the first time in his years on the force that anyone had ever questioned Jase's integrity as a detective. He met Shields's gaze head on.

"Violet Ridge is different from Denver in that everyone knows everyone. That's why you chose me for this assignment in the first place." Jase's ire built, and he thought of Cassie. He channeled her calm self along with drawing on years of training and experience to stay levelheaded. "I'm the same detective I've always been, and I'm convinced she's innocent."

Shields tilted back and surveyed Jase, who kept his face steady and neutral. "Clara Abbott, the bank manager, died right after Yablonsky's trial." He drew out a file from the stack and proceeded to look through it. "None of the employees at the jail who came into contact with Yablonsky has a *C* for an initial. Even the cellmate's description of the accomplice's physical features matches O'Neal."

Jase had been over that file so often, he could recite it backward and forward. "I trust Cassie, and you trust me."

Shields's nostrils flared as he continued studying the documents. "I always thought you'd be the one occupying this office when I retire, but now?" The tic on his forehead that always popped out when he was stressed started throbbing. "If O'Neal is involved, this will be a blemish on your record. I should assign you right now to the new narcotics case."

"I want to see this through." It was time to put everything on the line. "If Cassie is Yablonsky's accomplice, you'll have my resignation on your desk before she's arraigned."

Shields agreed. "Go back to Violet Ridge, but if she's arrested, I'll accept your resignation." Then he narrowed his eyes and steepled his fingers again. "Yablonsky is getting more aggressive, which means he's desperate. I'll question O'Neal on the record tomorrow in Violet Ridge, and then tell everyone I recalled you to Denver. But we'll stay behind and see if O'Neal and Yablonsky meet in person."

Jase nodded his acceptance, then moved to leave. As he closed the door behind him, it occurred to him that he might have also just closed the door on his career.

THE FARMSTAND WAS sold out by noon, giving Cassie extra time to spend in her hoophouse. She watered the tomato plants, then shut off the hose. Time to spread compost over her baby lettuce. The strong, earthy smell should have stopped her from thinking about her mother's text, but it didn't.

Cassie had received the message while taking care of her customers. Now recovered from bronchitis, Theresa was intent on flying to Colorado Springs to visit her friend LeeAnne. Mom wanted Cassie and the kids to stay with them for the weekend.

Cassie hadn't seen her mother since her recent illness. While this would give her a chance to see for herself that her mother was on the mend, Cassie couldn't leave the farm for a weekend, not without staff for the animals and crops. Of course, Penny and Easton would love to visit Mom in Colorado Springs for the weekend.

After she finished spreading the compost, Cassie called her mother with a compromise, and together they solidified details. Cassie would drive the children to Colorado Springs after school on Friday but return to the farm. Theresa and her friend would drive them home late Sunday.

With that settled, Cassie headed toward the stable. Along the way, she waved at the deputy who was patrolling the property.

This morning, after Jase had gone to follow up on a lead, Cassie had talked to Officer Nguyen. His wife was expecting a baby next spring. What could she make with the eggs she collected this morning that the deputy could take home to her? Maybe a veggie quiche with her newly harvested spinach or some fresh pumpkin bars.

The bars were Penny's favorite, so Cassie would make those. The yearning to have Penny and Easton back on the farm almost consumed her as she approached Hazel and the other three horses.

Was it for the best that her children remained in Ben and Daisy's care? Their safety was everything, but last night the Violet Ridge police force and K-9s had combed every inch of the farm, eventually giving the all-clear.

Keith wouldn't risk everything by returning here again, would he?

Cassie wavered about whether to bring the kids home as she mucked the stalls and filled the troughs with fresh water. Honeybee and Hickory whinnied at her. It was almost as if they were asking where Penny and Easton were.

"They're safe. That's what matters."

She smiled and mixed some of Honeybee's favorite oats in with the grain. Then she fed each horse half an apple, giggling when their tongues tickled her palm.

She took care of Highlander, trying to calculate how much longer he'd be here at her stable. Highlander was such a joy, and the Virtue family had gone out of their way to provide more than enough feed and other items for the gelding's care. Highlander had even claimed his spot in the meadow, acting as though he belonged there with the other three horses.

Yet this wasn't Highlander's home, and he'd soon return to his actual residence. Same as Jase. Although he had come so far in mending fences with his family, his whole demeanor now exuded a sense of peace that hadn't been there when he'd arrived at Thistle Brook.

She wouldn't lie to herself. Jase would return to Denver, and Highlander would return to Lazy River.

Hazel neighed at Cassie's approach, and Cassie began tacking her for a short ride to the fallow field.

To her surprise, Jase called her cell phone to find out if she was at the farm. "I need to talk to you," he said.

"I was just saddling Hazel, and Highlander is right here."

"I'll be at the stable in ten minutes." Jase's voice held a note of urgency.

Highlander seemed to approve of the idea, giving a loud whinny.

"Make that five minutes," Jase said.

Cassie was pleased with the idea of a short jaunt with Jase, until she considered what he might have to say to her. Perhaps Captain Shields had decided Jase's presence at the farm was no longer necessary. Or, worse, that he believed Jase was at fault for not capturing Keith yet. Jase might be returning to Denver today.

Then it was for the best that they share one last horse ride.

JASE PAUSED AT the entrance to the stable, questioning whether agreeing to this ride was one of his better ideas. After the other night, he no longer wanted to run from the hard conversations. This latest one might be the biggest of them all, namely informing Cassie that her presence was formally requested tomorrow at the Violet Ridge Police Department.

Before he could broach the subject, she faced him. The late afternoon sun streamed through the open doors highlighted the golden streaks in her brown hair. "Highlander is looking forward to being on the trail. He's happiest after a long ride."

Cassie's joy was evident, and Jase quelled the unease in his stomach. "Cassie…"

"I need to check on my fallow field. It's not far, but it has to be done today so I can order supplies," Cassie said, with a little too much enthusiasm. It was almost as if she was forcing herself to sound cheerful while she cinched the saddle on Hazel.

He was in a bind. This was important to Cassie's livelihood. But he had to give Cassie the news as soon as possible, so she could prepare herself for Shields's interrogation.

Highlander was prancing about as if he knew a ride was coming. Until Jase had visited Violet Ridge, outings on Highlander had been few and far between. What would happen if Jase was off the Denver force for good? Maybe Highlander would be the only one happy about that. An image of his family from the other night popped into his head.

Concerned that he was the same Jase as the one who'd always let work get in his way, he carefully placed Highlander's saddle blanket on the horse. What if he was right about Cassie's innocence but decided to stay in Denver? Would he wake up one morning only to find that a year had passed since he'd last visited his grandparents and siblings? Not to mention the amazing woman in front of him.

He'd ride first, then talk. With that issue resolved, Jase reached for Highlander's saddle at the same time Cassie did. Their fingers collided, and he met her gaze, hope and uncertainty reflected there.

It would be so easy to kiss her, but he couldn't. Not until this mess was over. Not until he proved to himself that he'd changed.

Jase pulled away and lifted the saddle off the stand. Together they finished prepping Hazel and Highlander for this brief break from the stress surrounding them both, and within minutes, they were on the trail, the breeze whipping their cheeks.

This was a fall afternoon made for riding, crisp and cool and invigorating. Even the creek seemed to agree. The soft sounds of water flowing next to the path seemed like an extra companion on their ride.

When had he forgotten how to savor the simple moments like these? Perhaps it was the moment he learned how to raise a shield around himself. All along, he thought he was guarding himself from major catastrophes. Now he knew he'd been his own worst enemy, running from problems of his own making.

He glanced at Hazel and Cassie, the sheer happiness on Cassie's face impossible to ignore. She'd been dealt a rough hand as well, yet somehow had retained her zest for these special moments and for the good people of Violet Ridge.

In a short time, she'd shown him how much he'd been missing. It had been his own pride that had made him keep the details of the accident to himself rather than risk the chance his grandparents might comfort him. Thanks to her, his family was now reunited.

Well, he was done with running.

Together they rode to the fallow field where Cassie completed her task in record time. The ride was going by too quickly for his liking. He released a long breath, admiring the tall aspens.

She prepared to mount Hazel once more. "How can you leave Highlander behind?" No sooner had the words left her mouth than her eyes widened. They both knew she really wasn't talking about his horse.

A relationship started with honesty, and he was sitting on two important pieces of information: his idea to move back here and Captain Shields's next step. The latter might end with uprooting her life and could put his idea in jeopardy.

He scuffed the ground, kicking himself for taking this last ride with her instead of being upfront back at the stables. "Cassie, I know what you're getting at and—"

She held up her hand and gave a wistful smile. "I'm halfway to falling in love with you."

He bit back a grin at Cassie O'Neal doing something halfway. They had that in common; he also was too intense to commit to anything with less than his full self.

That was when he knew. He was already deeply in love with Cassie O'Neal, so much so he'd staked everything on her innocence.

"Captain Shields is on his way to Violet Ridge from Denver."

That smile of hers lit up her entire face. "Then you're not going back today? I thought you called me to tell me you needed to leave soon. Is there a new lead? Are you close to finding Keith? I'll be relieved when he's behind bars again." Then she winced and fiddled with the rope. "Even though that means you'll be leaving for good."

Jase stepped closer. "Let me explain about Captain Shields's intent. He thinks you're hiding Yablonsky and the reason he's evading capture. He's prepared to arrest you."

Cassie blinked, and it was almost like he saw her retreating into herself. He wanted to hold her. But if he did, he might never let her go.

He continued, "He's going to question you officially, inform you of your rights. You'll want an attorney present."

She stared at him with a blank expression until she recovered. "You're serious." Her face paled. She untethered Hazel and mounted her. "I don't think my divorce attorney handles criminal matters. I'll ask her for a referral. Better yet, Zelda Baker. There's no time to lose."

It reminded him of the deep roots Cassie had

in this town. Tomorrow, would everyone be upset with him when Cassie was brought in for questioning and possibly arrested?

Or would they understand he was merely doing his job?

CHAPTER FOURTEEN

WITH A DEEP BREATH, Cassie greeted the attorney Zelda had recommended and walked into the police precinct. As the smells of bleach and stale coffee hit her, so too did her nerves at the prospect of facing tough questions she had no answers for. *Would she be arrested?*

Her attorney led her to the room where Captain Shields introduced himself. Cassie tugged at her suit jacket, her gold bracelet, a gift from her father that would provide a boost of encouragement, digging into her wrist. She removed her jacket and looked around for a place to hang it and settled for the back of her chair.

"Interesting bracelet, Ms. O'Neal. Do you have another just like it?" Captain Shields smiled and folded his hands while Police Chief Gutierrez frowned.

Cassie looked at her attorney, who nodded her consent to respond to the question. "No. Just this one." She ran her finger over the engraved *C*. "This one was a high school graduation gift from my parents. I wear it almost all the time."

His brow rose.

To Cassie's surprise, there were more questions about eight years ago than the past few weeks. "Where were you on the day of the robbery?" Captain Shields asked.

Her attorney protested that her information was already in the file, but Cassie would always remember where she was when her father called her with the news of Keith's arrest. "My mother and I had just arrived back from Florida, where we'd been helping my aunt Olive move into a retirement community." She wiped her eyes. "My father was never the same after Keith's arrest. He died a short time later."

"I'm prepared to offer you a plea deal if you admit you were in on the robbery," Shields said.

Her heart thudded, and her attorney reiterated Cassie's position before Cassie could protest her innocence again.

The whole interview was over rather quickly. From what Jase had said, she'd expected it to be as intense as it was. Where was he anyway? It would have helped to have another advocate on her side in the room during the questioning, but that may be why he had to stay away. It was nice to know she could trust him regardless.

Her attorney escorted Cassie out of the room and through the precinct. After a brief talk, Cassie thanked her and hurried back to the farm.

JASE WATCHED CASSIE'S interview from the observation room. Shock was an understatement when she'd taken off her jacket to reveal the bracelet. She had more than one of the same piece of jewelry!

Captain Shields entered the observation room, shaking his head. His superior tapped his chin. "Did you know there were two bracelets?"

Why was Captain Shields so fixated on Cassie being involved? Or was he right about Jase being too personally involved to see the truth?

Jase suddenly understood the revelation; it explained why Cassie's fingerprints weren't on the bracelet found in the root cellar. "More proof she's innocent."

"We'll see for sure when we put the next stage of the operation into effect. Police Chief Gutierrez knows, but no one else can find out about this." Captain Shields sat in a chair and exhaled. "In forty-eight hours, we'll have Yablonsky and O'Neal in custody, preferably with the recovered money, or we'll be in Denver. If the latter, we'll keep monitoring the tip hotline for leads and get updates from Gutierrez as needed."

Jase slid onto a chair. The bracelet protected in the evidence room didn't belong to Cassie, and she had a solid alibi for the bank robbery. There was nothing to connect her to the crime, but he stayed silent about his qualms, sure that any push-back would get him a one-way ticket to Denver immediately. Instead, he rose and nodded at his superior. "I'll tell my grandparents and Cassie I'm going back to Denver right away."

Shields merely grunted and got out his phone.

Jase wasn't sure which conversation was going to be harder. Here he was with all these new feelings for Cassie, and he'd also just begun a new relationship with his grandparents. Lying about taking his leave could ruin his chances with the pretty farmer and stall things with his family before they could get to know each other again.

NEVER BEFORE HAD she been so thankful to be home. Cassie changed out of her suit. She breathed a sigh of relief wearing her faded denims again. Even more so, she was thankful to be where everything was familiar to her.

There was something disconcerting about Captain Shields, almost like he thought she was in on Keith's escape. Nothing would ever be further from the truth. Keith was related to her, but he wasn't family in the way Zelda and Amanda were. Keith had lost her trust over and over again.

Cassie left the farmhouse by the back door and waved to the deputy, hoping his wife liked the pumpkin bars yesterday. She then headed to the henhouse where Blossom and her crew crowded in front of the gate. Everything was so hectic this morning with the police interview, she hadn't gathered the eggs or scattered feed on the ground.

"Scoot back," she told the chickens as she opened the gate and shooed them aside.

In the distance, she saw Jase approaching the deputy. She knew she wanted a life with her detective. She wanted to see him cuddle Blossom and go on long rides with Highlander accompanied by her and Hazel. She didn't want him to return to Denver.

And yet?

Intensity burned within him, a contrast to her calmer self. That fierce drive compelled him to live, eat and breathe his job. As much as she wished he could be content to settle in Violet Ridge and work as law enforcement locally, the slower pace here would hinder his career and ambition.

Her heart shattered. She watched him as he waved goodbye to the deputy and headed her way. She wouldn't, and couldn't, hold him back. Although she loved him and trusted him with every part of her being, he wasn't destined to stay here any more than Brayden was.

Jase entered through the open gate, formal and solemn in his navy suit. Cassie continued scattering feed for the chickens, who pecked the brown earth. Blossom broke away from the brood and strutted over to Jase. The small mahogany hen pressed her beak against Jase's black dress shoe until he picked her up. She promptly snuggled against his chest while Jase's eyes softened with fondness. Cassie melted at the sight.

He set the hen back on the ground and looked around. "Where's Rusty?"

"Taking a nap. It's almost like he knows when Penny and Easton will be getting off the bus today, although they won't be tomorrow. I'm driving them to Colorado Springs. I already let the seniors' center know I won't be answering questions about gardening tomorrow." She finished scattering the feed and reached for the basket so she could gather the eggs. "My mother is feeling better and flew here to visit a friend. She's looking forward to spending a weekend with her grandchildren."

Jase looked at his watch. "Penny and Easton are due in an hour, correct?"

Cassie's heart raced at his formal delivery. She'd gotten used to the other Jase, the one who was a lot more casual and smiled easily around her and the kids. She nodded. "With the K-9 unit proving Keith isn't on my farm, the bus is dropping them off here again."

He loosened his tie and then removed it, sticking it in his pocket. "Cassie, it's time."

It was funny how those three words could have such a different impact than the three she longed to say to him. And to hear them on his lips in return.

But he was on his way out, ready to leave Violet Ridge and everyone in it behind him. No more meals in the kitchen together or sweet kisses in the moonlight. Even though she wouldn't do anything to stop his success, she still ached with longing. A loneliness settled into her bones. She despised the feeling. Had she learned nothing after Brayden's sudden departure? Rather than holding back trust and letting feelings build over time, she'd fallen for Jase fast.

She reached inside the henhouse and felt through the straw, glad she wasn't facing Jase. She needed to collect her emotions. After she placed the last egg in the basket, her tears started falling. How could anyone leave this view, this farm, her kids?

Why did everyone keep leaving her?

"You've been called back to Denver, then?" Despite her efforts to put her best foot forward, her husky voice betrayed her. She wiped her cheeks with her sleeve and then turned toward him.

He scuffed the ground with the sole of his shoe. "It's part of my job, Cassie."

It was more than his job, and they both knew it. Just as she loved this farm, so much that she couldn't move to Florida to be closer to her mother or to Denver to live near him, he loved his career that was more than a career to him. It was his life. "Do you leave right away?"

He didn't meet her gaze. "I wanted to see Penny and Easton for myself and make sure they're okay."

She gripped the handle of the basket as if it were a lifeline and considered his request. There was no easy answer, just as there was no easy solution to their dilemma. His life was in Denver, and hers was here in Violet Ridge. "Perhaps it's for the best if you didn't."

Her heart would never be the same, and she wanted to spare her children the same heartache if she could.

Jase came over and gently released her fingers until the basket was next to her feet and his hand was holding hers. "Cassie?"

She stared at those brown eyes full of emotion.

Dare she hope he was in love with her? His head approached hers, those lips so close to hers, before he pulled away.

She was having none of it though and closed the distance between them. She poured her heart into the kiss. He was everything she wanted and more. He wound his hands through her hair, and she hoped this could be the start of something new and beautiful.

Was it seconds or minutes that passed before he separated from her? She wasn't sure, and she didn't care.

He repeated her name, and she heard the futility in it. There was no use thinking he'd stay here for her. She held her head high and forced a smile to her lips. "We both know big things await you in Denver. Next time I see you, you might even be Captain Virtue."

It looked as though he was about to say something, but he simply sent a long lingering look in her direction, one that spoke volumes. She believed he loved her, but he loved his job and independence more. He nodded and then left.

Blossom rushed to the closed gate and pecked at the fence.

Cassie went over and consoled the little red hen, knowing exactly what she was feeling.

CHAPTER FIFTEEN

JASE WALKED INTO the main building on the Lazy River Dude Ranch and nodded at guests as they passed him. Given how busy the place seemed, Seth and Amanda were doing a great job ensuring the ranch remained at full occupancy. Now that he no longer had the guilt from the accident weighing heavily on his shoulders, Jase was looking forward to creating new memories and having great moments with Seth and all their family.

However, the relationship that touched his heart the most was the one he could have had with Cassie. Everyone in town loved her, and he could see why.

Their kiss had confirmed his suspicions. She was in love with him. He felt the same, but would she be able to forgive him for only pretending to go in order to lure Yablonsky to Thistle Brook Farm? Doing so had been a direct order from Shields, but meanwhile, Jase still had to prove that she hadn't been a part of her brother's crimes.

First, he needed his grandparents' advice, and to tell them that he was returning to Denver.

Jase made his way to the library where he knew Grandma Bridget was set to teach a knitting class before the dinner bell clanged. He entered and found her by herself.

"Ah. Hello, Jase." Grandma Bridget didn't seem too surprised to see him and looked behind him. "Seth said he texted you earlier, inviting you and the O'Neals for dinner. Did you bring Cassie and Penny and Easton with you?"

She tilted her cheek in an obvious plea for a quick peck, and he obliged before settling next to her. "I let Seth know that wouldn't be possible."

Her knitting needles kept moving, and she didn't take her gaze off the yarn. "That's a shame. I like Cassie."

"I do, too, but Captain Shields is assigning me to another case. I leave for Denver immediately."

His grandmother finally focused on him with the same expression she'd used when he would sneak out for a midnight ride and then find her waiting for him in the kitchen. "I don't know what's going on, but I trust you and love you, Jason Virtue." She directed her attention to her blanket. "Once you flush Keith Yablonsky out into the open, and he's back in police custody, I have a present for you."

His ears perked up. "Present?" The word left his tongue just as he realized his grandmother was aware of Shields's real plan. He only hoped Yablonsky wouldn't be as perceptive.

Grandma Bridget laid down her knitting. "All

in good time." She offered a small smile that Jase returned.

"You can't tell anyone, Grandma, what you surmised." His jaw clenched. "Not even Grandpa Martin."

"Your secret is safe with me. I get it. Your safety's on the line." She resumed her knitting, taking care not to drop a stitch. "By the way, I have a message for you from Martin. Your grandfather thinks you're in love with Cassie O'Neal and that you'd be a fool not to act on your feelings."

"What about you?" Jase asked.

"I already *know* you're in love with her."

He gritted his teeth, anything not to go there, and watched her knit as if they were discussing the weather, rather than his heart. "Thank you for keeping this secret. Until one door is closed, there's no way to open another. I trust you won't tell anyone what you pieced together."

She stopped her handiwork and rubbed his arm, her gnarled hands older and wrinkled but still possessing an overwhelming ability to comfort him. "Always. I love you, Jason."

He kissed her cheek again and took his leave, ready to stand watch over Thistle Brook Farm.

CASSIE LED PENNY and Easton into the lobby of the hotel in Colorado Springs. There was nothing like a mom hug, and she needed one. She searched the lobby until she saw her mom, two suitcases by her side, talking to her friend, LeeAnne, whom Cassie hadn't seen in years.

"Grandma!" Penny and Easton yelled in unison, running toward her and enveloping her in a hug.

"My, how you both have grown." Mom wiped away tears that Cassie knew were happy ones. "I've missed you all so much. This is my old friend, LeeAnne."

LeeAnne nudged Mom's side. "Now, now, I'm younger than you." She chuckled and then smiled at Penny and Easton. "I would have recognized you two anywhere. Theresa texts me photos of you both all the time."

Penny and Easton started talking at the same time about their classmates, the farm and Jase. Cassie's heart lurched at the sound of Jase's name and wondered how long it would be until she could hear his name without feeling sadness.

Cassie pointed to Mom's suitcases. "Was your flight delayed? Did you just check in?" Cassie checked the time on her watch. "I was waiting until I knew what room you were in before bringing in our bags, but I can fetch them while you register at the reception desk."

"LeeAnne," Mom said and reached inside her purse to produce several dollar bills, "would you please take Penny and Easton to the hotel café and treat them to whatever they want?"

Penny and Easton cheered as LeeAnne offered each a hand to hold. LeeAnne was a natural around children, and Cassie had fond memories of the retired schoolteacher babysitting her. But why would her mother send the kids off like that? Cassie bumped her forehead. Of course. That was her Mom's signature move when she wanted to talk in private.

"I should have texted you the latest." Cassie wished she had. It would have been simpler and less painful that way. "The latest K-9 sweep came up empty, but Keith still hasn't been apprehended."

Mom shivered. "I hope they catch him soon."

Cassie did, too. "Keith will make a mistake, and then the police will apprehend him." Her shoulders slumped. "Sorry you won't get to meet Jase again after all these years. He's been called back to Denver."

A huge smile came over her mom's face. "Then the guest room is vacant again?"

Cassie nodded. "Yes, but aren't you staying here in Colorado Springs with Penny and Easton for the weekend?"

"LeeAnne had something come up, so I've had to change my plans. If it's all right with you, we can drive to the farm after dinner, and I'll fly home a week from Monday. I can't wait to see the corn maze I've heard so much about and spend time with you and Penny and Easton. Now how about a big hug for your mother?"

Cassie complied with pleasure.

They joined LeeAnne for dinner, opting for a favorite restaurant chain of the kids. Cassie picked at her spaghetti. Food hadn't had much flavor since yesterday's goodbye with Jase. Soon after their meal, they said goodbye to LeeAnne, and the four of them were on the road, Penny and Easton snoozing in the back seat.

Mom glanced over her shoulder at the children, their slight snuffles a sweet sound in the truck's cab. Her mother laughed softly and said, "I've missed them so much. That's my one complaint about living with Olive in a retirement community. There aren't kids running around playing."

"They miss you, too." They weren't the only ones. Sometimes there was no substitute for Mom. "You don't have to whisper. They're good sleepers."

Mom reached into her purse and pulled out a tin of mints. "Want one?"

Cassie accepted one, the garlic from her spaghetti lingering on her breath. "Thanks."

"I'm glad we have time to talk. Once we're at the farm, I know you'll be busy with chores. Waking up before the sun rises is one part of farming I don't miss." Mom selected a mint and crunched it. "I hope it's okay if I start visiting more often."

"Of course, you never even have to ask." Cassie smiled at her mother before focusing again on the road. "Why haven't you visited more often?"

Mom sighed and thumped her heart with her fist. "Your father isn't there."

"I still miss Dad, too, but I'm glad we're so close and make the effort to stay in touch. I can't lose you, too, Mom." Cassie was glad her mother had found a new place she liked so much, although she missed her every day at Thistle Brook. "The farm is as much my home as yours."

"You and your father love that place, and I loved your father." Mom leaned her elbow against the window as the scenery passed by in a blur. "I know it's harder for you to come to Florida than it is for me to travel here since you have to find someone to tend the farm."

"Not to mention Penny and Easton both attend school now."

"I can't wait to hear more about their teachers and friends." Mom's wise eyes settled on Cassie once more, and Cassie tried not to fidget as she was driving. "Especially Jase. He made a big impression on them. I take it this is the same Jase you've mentioned during our conversations?"

Cassie concentrated on the road with an intensity Jase would have envied. "Jase made an impression on everyone at the farm. Even Blossom the hen loves him." She stopped talking, hoping her mother wouldn't pick up on what she'd just said.

"You're in love with him, too."

The fact that her mom's words were a statement and not a question wasn't lost on Cassie. Her mother casually placed the tin of mints back in her purse.

Deep in her heart, Cassie knew she'd always be in love with Jase. Time wouldn't change that feeling. "He has an important career in Denver."

Mom glanced in the back seat again and then faced forward once more. "He'll visit his family. They own the dude ranch, right?"

And his future sister-in-law, Amanda, had become one of Cassie's best friends in recent months. Her stomach clenched at the thought of hearing updates from Amanda about Jase, especially when he settled down with someone else. However, that news would also give Cassie some peace, knowing Jase was safe given that his chosen profession had a greater element of risk than most.

"Yes, but it won't happen often. Jase will be even more busy if he gets a promotion once the current captain retires." There wasn't anyone better for the job with Jase's intelligence and determination.

"Sometimes our priorities change. When I met your father, I was content with my career start in the fashion industry. I never intended to move to Colorado and settle on a farm. If Jase feels the same way as you obviously feel about him, he'll be back." Her mother sipped the take-out coffee they'd bought before reaching the highway. "Ick. Too bitter. Where was I?"

"You were talking about when you met Dad." Cassie always loved hearing stories about how her father had given love a second chance after his first marriage.

"I never regretted marrying him." Mom placed her cup back in the holder. "And now I have some big news. I wanted to tell you and Penny and Easton at the same time, but I can't wait any longer. I applied and was accepted to my local community college. I start this fall so I can finish earning my degree in fashion."

"Congratulations!" Cassie's grin was genuine, and happiness for her mother warmed her chest. "You didn't tell me about applying."

"I wasn't sure they'd accept me." Mom let out an exaggerated sigh of relief. "I expect you and Penny and Easton to be in Florida for my graduation, time and place to be determined."

"Of course we'll come for that. Wild horses won't keep us away." Cassie passed a tractor trailer and then moved back into the right lane. "You'll have to design dresses for Penny and me, just like you did for my homecoming. A Theresa Yablonsky original." She remembered the pride she'd felt at having the prettiest dress at the dance.

"Most daughters wouldn't have appreciated a homemade dress, but you did. I've always loved sewing outfits and seeing how I can add something to individualize a pattern." Mom chuckled, reached into her purse and pulled out a list. "This is everything I'm going to have shipped back to Florida."

It sounded like the four of them would be busy this week. This visit was exactly what she needed to keep her mind off Jase's return to Denver.

THROUGH HIS BINOCULARS, Jase had Thistle Brook Farm in his sights. Looking out through the barn's loft window, he could see everything from the gravel parking lot to the farmhouse. Jase shifted as he laid on his stomach in his tactical uniform, rather uncomfortably since he'd been in the same position for several hours with a baby chick on his back and Patches curled up next to his ribs.

He focused his binoculars on the nondescript van that Captain Shields occupied near Cassie's neighbor's house. Everything still looked calm. This was a monumental bust. Guess Yablonsky figured this was a stakeout.

Jase reached for the other half of his sandwich and stretched his leg muscles, careful not to disturb either animal. Perhaps this whole mission was a wild goose chase. For all they knew, Yablonsky could have left the state or even the country by now, especially if he'd found the money at the farm. Tips to the hotline had dwindled to one or two per day, and none of them panned out. It was as if the man had vanished.

There must be someone helping him, but who was the mystery person? Jase's career depended on it not being Cassie. He might have thought it was her when he first arrived, but not now. He'd bet what was left of his reputation that she wasn't assisting Yablonsky.

He adjusted the night vision binoculars and caught his breath when an older-model gray compact on the road approached the farm. Something about the vehicle looked familiar, and he searched his mind until the bumper sticker jogged his memory. This car had come to the farmstand several times during Cassie's regular morning business hours. Yet it was evening, far too late for anyone to be inquiring after vegetables.

The car slowed near the posted sign at the farm's entrance, which imparted its name, but kept going. The driver didn't turn around but continued along the gravel path toward the farmhouse.

Jase's walkie-talkie crackled. Shields let everyone on the frequency know he was on alert before several of Violet Ridge's officers relayed their locations and readiness to move in.

The gray compact parked in the first spot. Perhaps this was the break they'd sought for so long.

A woman emerged from the car with her back toward Jase so he couldn't see her face even with the night vision binoculars. Her build and hair color were the same as Cassie's. She wore black leggings under a long coat. His stomach clenched as she pulled a wool cap over her hair and wrapped a scarf around her neck, shielding her features from his view.

No! He couldn't believe it was Cassie.

Jase turned his attention to the passenger emerging from the other side: a man with hunched shoulders, dressed in black sweatpants and a dark jacket. Jase was positive it was Yablonsky. The pair hurried toward the farmhouse.

"I have a visual." Jase described the two people. "Do you want me to confront them?"

"Yablonsky and his sister," Shields pronounced

his judgment over the walkie-talkie. "We'll wait until they come out of the house with the evidence."

The way the woman moved gave Jase pause. He knew the graceful and purposeful stride that Cassie had; this woman was not her.

"Negative. It's not—" Jase caught himself before he said Cassie's first name. "It's not O'Neal."

Besides, Cassie drove a truck, and she'd have no reason to hide her face at her own farm even if she was harboring an escaped fugitive.

"The height and frame are an exact match. I'll cover the front door while Virtue and his squad take the back." Shields delivered more orders along with a caution to monitor the windows. "And take care. They might be armed and dangerous."

Jase extracted himself from his vantage point and took an extra second to deposit the baby chick to the warming pen. Then he hurried and assumed his position with the others.

"I thought you had the tools." The man's voice was laced with frustration as he exited the back door. "I'll be right back."

"Freeze! Hands in the air!" Jase and the officers shouted.

Yablonsky raised his hands. He was in custody at last.

More shouts came from the front of the house where Shields and his crew apprehended the woman. Jase slipped handcuffs on Yablonsky, who wasn't making any effort to resist. He escorted him toward the front of the farmhouse in time to see Shields place handcuffs on the woman, whose scarf and wool cap still covered most of her face.

The woman struggled, and Shields clicked the cuffs into place. "Ms. O'Neal, you should have taken the plea deal when you had a chance."

The woman stilled, and Shields smiled at Jase as if victorious.

"Huh?" Yablonsky asked. "That's not Cassie."

The smile faded from Shields's face while Jase breathed again, his adrenaline still rushing through him.

"Of course it is," Shields insisted. He moved the scarf and gasped. "Who are you?"

The woman in front of them was definitely not Cassie O'Neal.

CHAPTER SIXTEEN

"Are you expecting company?" Cassie heard her mother's question at the same moment she saw the gray compact and scores of police vehicles in the farmstand's parking lot.

"No." Cassie's heart leaped as she spotted Jase among the officers. What had happened here at Thistle Brook Farm while she'd been away?

"Is that..." Her mother's hand went to her chest.

Then Cassie and her mother gasped in unison as they spotted Keith in handcuffs, along with a woman they didn't recognize. Cassie's gaze went to the back seat where Penny and Easton were still sound asleep.

Cassie stopped her truck, her heart racing as she put together the pieces. Knowing that she was headed to Colorado Springs to spend the afternoon and early evening with her mother, the police must have organized this operation in a last attempt to catch her half brother.

And they'd succeeded.

Her hands were quivering on the steering wheel while she tried to think about what to do next. She didn't want Penny and Easton seeing any of this. Maybe reversing and leaving would be for the best.

Except Jase looked her way and made eye contact with her. He motioned for her to cut the engine, and she did so.

Jase's chest seemed bulkier, his shirt stretched over his firm shoulders. Obviously he was wearing a bulletproof vest. The danger of his career coursed through her—but she still would have stood by him if they could have pursued a relationship.

He said something to the officer next to him and then headed in the direction of her truck.

As hard as she tried to quell her nerves, she couldn't. Her whole body shook as the events of the past few weeks boiled down to this. Keith was in custody, and Jase had been in on the apprehension.

So, this was truly the end. He would get that promotion, and she would go on with the farm, just as it should be.

"Sweetie, I think that officer wants you to roll down your window." Her mom's voice brought Cassie out of her reverie.

Sure enough, when Jase arrived at her window, he tapped on it. Cassie made a shushing motion with her hand before she pointed to the back seat where Penny and Easton were rousing from their slumber. So much for protecting them. She needed to start the car so she could roll down the window, but she couldn't stop shaking.

Her mom laid her soft hand over hers. Cassie took a deep breath and turned the key enough so she could lower the window.

"It's over." She said the words, but she hoped Jase might say it was just the beginning.

He nodded in her mother's direction. "Good evening, Mrs. Yablonsky. I remember you, but you might not remember me. I'm Jase Virtue. This is certainly an interesting time to visit Violet Ridge."

Cassie studied Jase's expression, looking for any sign that their last discussion wrought the same havoc on his heart that it had on hers, but then again, he was at work. His face was a model of professionalism, and she expected nothing less from him. She heard her two little ones stirring.

"Jase!" Penny exclaimed. "I knew you'd be back."

"Jase?" Sleepiness marked Easton's voice, but Cassie saw him bolt upright in her rearview mirror. "Blossom misses you!"

Jase smiled and waved to Penny and Easton. "Hey there, I'll be back in a minute." He walked away from her truck to confer with another officer.

Cassie tried to compose herself. She inhaled deep breaths, realizing the ordeal was over. A semblance of peace descended on her, and her hands stopped shaking.

Jase returned and knocked on her mother's window. "Mrs. Yablonsky, do you remember the way to the dude ranch? Is there any chance you could take Penny and Easton there while Cassie and I confer about this recent situation? Ingrid baked pies today, and she could use more taste testers."

Cassie turned to her mother, who was already getting out of the truck. "Great idea. I haven't seen Bridget and Martin in years. I'd like to say hello."

Penny and Easton protested leaving Jase and whatever excitement brought all these police cars to their farm, but the idea of pie soon won them over. Cassie hopped out of the truck and her mother slid in behind the wheel. She mouthed a thank-you and her mom started the ignition. Cassie watched as they drove away just as two state trooper cars passed her family on the gravel drive.

Cassie scanned the scene before her. She waited for some emotion at seeing her half brother for the first time in almost eight years, and she was surprised at the pity and regret that bubbled inside her. Keith could have accomplished anything, and instead he'd chosen the wrong path. Sadness at what could have been filled her. Then her attention was drawn to the woman whose coloring and build reminded her of someone…but who?

"Who's the woman in handcuffs?" Cassie asked. "She looks familiar."

Jase motioned for Cassie to come with him. "The woman in the coat and leggings is Lucinda Stillman."

Cassie stared at the woman, trying to place her. "I've seen her somewhere." Then she snapped her fingers. "At the farmstand. I thought she was being polite letting others go ahead of her and pay first, but, come to think of it, you were always nearby whenever that happened."

"She worked at the prison and knew I'd recognize her," Jase said.

"But there's something else." She searched her memory, a flood of images swirling through her mind, until she realized she'd seen Lucinda before. But way back then, she'd had spiky platinum blond hair. It was long gone now, replaced by long brown hair, almost the same shade as Cassie's. "At Keith's trial. I saw her the day the bank manager testified."

"Clara Abbott? She died of cancer shortly after the trial," Jase said. "Come to think of it, her daughter's name was Lucy. I'll bet Lucy Abbott and Lucinda Stillman are one and the same. I'll check it out."

Cassie placed her hand on Jase's arm. "Captain Shields doesn't look happy to see me. Maybe I should go to the stable and wait there."

Jase's boss approached, his lips pursed in a straight line. "Ms. O'Neal. What a coincidence that you're here right about the same time as your half brother." Captain Shields turned around and told the deputy to escort Keith and Lucinda to separate patrol cars. "Too much of a coincidence if you ask me. Were you here to help them?"

"With my mother and my two children in the back seat? Really, Captain Shields, this is too much." Although she prided herself on taking most things in stride, this campaign against her needed to end. "I assure you this is exactly that, a coincidence. I returned from a round trip to Colorado Springs, and I have the receipt from dinner. My mother's friend had a change of plans, and Mom has come to stay with us for a visit. She just took my children to Jase's family's ranch so they wouldn't see any of this."

Once again, her hands started shaking, the gravity of everything bearing down on her with full force. She took in Keith, standing there in handcuffs. "Why did you come back here?"

"Where's my money?" Keith glared at her. "Where did you hide it?"

Captain Shields raised his eyebrow, and he began telling Cassie her rights.

Her legs wavered, but she straightened. Her spine stiffened. "I'm calling my lawyer. This is wrong."

Jase spoke up. "Everyone. There's a simple way to find out what Yablonsky meant." He turned toward Keith. "Is Cassie part of this?"

Did Jase think so little of her that he believed she could be involved in Keith's criminal activity? Stunned, she felt her heart shatter into a million pieces.

Jase sounded frustrated when he asked, "Why do you think Cassie has the money, Yablonsky?"

"Every time Cindy and I came here," Keith growled, "she'd keep Cassie busy at the farmstand while I searched the farmhouse. I can't find where she moved my stash."

"Stop talking!" Lucinda, or rather Cindy, interrupted Keith. Her eyes sent him a sharp look of rebuke. "You just admitted that I'm involved."

As if being here with Keith wasn't a sure giveaway.

A lone bark from the farmhouse alerted Cassie to Rusty's presence. "My dog needs me."

Keith shook his head. "That dog really got in the way. A couple of times I ended up in the corn maze 'cause he was barking his head off."

"Did you plant the dog as a conduit to pass messages between you and O'Neal?" Shields asked.

Keith tilted his head. "Huh?"

Cindy rolled her eyes. "He's asking if you sent Cassie the dog so you could pass notes to her. Presumably, she'd slip away from the cop who was assigned to stake out the farm and talk to you." She let out a wry chuckle. "If you had come to the farm today by yourself, I'd never have been caught, you jerk. The police would have arrested Cassie instead."

Cassie had trouble breathing. "So you've been together for years?"

"Yeah, and we were so close to getting the money and leaving the country. Forever." Lucinda frowned.

Police officers led the pair away as Captain Shields remained behind with Cassie and Jase. Rusty's barking became more urgent to the point she was having trouble concentrating.

"I'd like to take Cassie inside so we can let her

dog out of his crate." Jase stood tall and faced his superior.

Shields nodded. "Guess the dog's appearance at your farm was a coincidence, same as the two *C* names."

Cassie noted the lack of an apology but let it go. She took off sprinting for the house and rushed into the mudroom. Her emotions were bubbling over, her longstanding calm deserting her just when she needed it the most.

She released Rusty, whose tail thumped once in greeting. He inserted himself between her and Jase, almost as if guarding her.

She had to know whether Jase truly believed in her or not. "You didn't leave. Why did you tell me you were going back to Denver?"

"There are times in my job I can't reveal everything."

She supposed that was true, but something else troubled her. She couldn't put her finger on it, but Shields's willingness to arrest her was crushing. How long had he been convinced Cassie was part of Keith's crimes? And if Shields was this adamant about her involvement, what about Jase?

"When you came here, did you know about Cindy? That there was a second woman whose name started with *C*?" she asked.

He ran his hand through his hair. "Is that as important as my decision about the future?"

He reached out to her, but she kept her hands by her sides. If she touched him, she might lose herself in someone who didn't have any faith in her. He searched her face, but she took a page from his book, staying as stoic as possible.

"Even with everything that's happened in your life," Jase continued, "you were this beacon of hope and trust. No matter why I came here, I fell for your optimism and you."

No matter why I came here.

As easy as it would be to let her heart be swayed by the rest of his sentence, she concentrated on those six words, her suspicions raised. "Just tell me the truth about why you came back."

"I thought I was finished with Violet Ridge, but I wasn't. When I returned, I found so much more than I expected."

"What did you expect to find out about me? You came here to protect me from Keith, right? Or…" She couldn't ask the question, didn't dare say the words aloud.

His gaze met hers, the sadness in those depths too telling. "Shields chose me because of my connection to Violet Ridge. The circumstantial evidence pointed to you as Yablonsky's partner."

Jase hadn't been sent here to keep her safe after all. Her chest constricted as the full impact struck her. A chill ran through her, bringing an iciness to her veins. Feeling she'd never be warm again, she rubbed her bare arms. "So you didn't take up this post to protect Penny and Easton. Or me. You turned up to prove I was in cahoots with Keith."

Jase closed his eyes, his jaw clenched tightly.

She wanted to caress the layer of stubble and comfort him, but she stayed where she was. He opened his eyes, and she saw the truth there. "My first few days here, I thought you were helping him, but..."

"And the stakeout occurred when you knew my mother was coming to Colorado Springs and I would be back on the farm without Penny and Easton."

"I—"

"That's all I need to know." She strode to the pegs on the wall, grabbed a thick jacket and wrapped herself up in it. She wished Jase's arms could warm her, but that would never happen. She deserved someone who believed in her, wanted to stay with her. "Once your investigation is concluded, I hope you get your promotion."

She and Rusty brushed past him, and once outside, she inhaled a deep breath of fresh mountain air. She spotted Shields, who removed his captain's hat when she approached.

"They're taking Yablonsky to the station, but I talked to him first, while you were getting your dog. He maintains you've had nothing to do with any of his crimes."

"I've repeatedly said the same."

Captain Shields looked uncomfortable. "I'd like to get this formally on the record."

"I'll call my attorney, and she'll arrange time for an interview. All further communication will be through her." She kept a careful eye on Rusty, who was close to her side. "May I go check on my horses? I need to make sure this commotion hasn't affected them."

Captain Shields stepped aside, and she walked toward the stable with tears streaming down her cheeks.

CHAPTER SEVENTEEN

THE SUN HAD set hours ago, and Jase acknowledged that it had also set on his and Cassie's relationship. He entered the main lodge of the Lazy River Dude Ranch and acknowledged the night clerk monitoring the reception desk. He climbed the stairs to the third floor where he'd be spending the night in Seth's old suite before leaving for Denver in the morning. Shields had offered him a lift back, but Jase wanted one more night in Violet Ridge.

When the dust settled, Cassie's innocence had become clear. Lucinda Abbott Stillman had more of a connection to Keith than anyone had ever realized; she was also Lucy Abbott, the daughter of the bank manager. Lucy and Keith had dated and planned the robbery with information she gleaned from her mother, Clara. After the trial, Lucinda had married and tried to forget her former boyfriend, who promised he'd never reveal their relationship. When she divorced, she reunited with Yablonsky, who had always called her Cindy.

No one, not Jase or Shields, had ever connected Lucy Abbott to Lucinda Stillman, let alone to

Yablonsky. The pair had come to the farm and searched whenever the farmstand was open. They'd always left empty-handed. The stolen money had been moved, but by whom or where, no one knew.

Jase exhaled a shaky breath as he let himself into Seth's apartment from his bachelor days. A long hot shower and sleep might help him feel human again.

What did he want? That was easy. Cassie. Plain and simple. She was all he needed, and she'd trusted him, but now? The trust was broken beyond all repair.

He blinked and found Seth sitting in the living area, reading a book.

"What are you doing here?" Jase asked.

"Checking on my little brother." Seth placed the book, spine up, on the end table and rose to his feet. "It must be a relief knowing Yablonsky's finally in custody. Good job."

Jase took off his jacket, already having exchanged his tactical uniform and bulletproof vest for sweatpants and T-shirt. He slipped off his shoes. "Thanks for letting me crash here tonight. After breakfast, I'll be leaving for Denver."

"That soon?" Seth came over and stopped short before launching himself at Jase, giving him a hug.

Jase didn't know what to do at first. Then he embraced his brother, letting Seth's strong arms hold him up. For a minute, he stood there, Seth's love and affection sinking into him. The future was before them, and Jase basked in his older brother's unconditional acceptance. No matter where he lived, his family would be there for him. This time he'd be there for them as well.

Cassie could have easily made the choice he'd once made; she could have run, going to Florida with her mother after her father died or her divorce from Brayden. People had sent wary glances her way ever since Yablonsky was convicted, unsure of whether they should associate with her. She'd responded with grace, starting the community garden and then going one step further with Adopt a Grandparent Day. Throughout it all, she became a trusted citizen of the town, so much so that people dropped off animals at her farm, knowing she'd find them a loving home. Unlike Jase, she never lost her trust in people.

Until now.

She didn't trust Jase anymore.

That gut punch hit him almost as much as having to give up the hope that he and Cassie could build on the past few weeks and form a loving, supportive relationship. Like Seth and Amanda's or Daisy and Ben's.

Jase broke away from his brother and shrugged. "I thought about moving back to town, but after today? Cassie doesn't want anything to do with me, and I don't blame her." He collapsed on the sofa. The past few weeks had caught up to him, and he fought the urge to sleep sitting up right here.

Seth's loud sigh brought Jase out of the first

hints of sleep. "I'll still be your big brother wherever you are." Seth sat beside him, but Jase didn't move. "Put Cassie aside for a minute. Where do you want to be?"

It seemed as though today was full of the insightful questions Jase should have been asking himself all along. Like asking Grandpa Martin about the accident. Like connecting Lucy Abbott and Lucinda Stillman. And yet he couldn't overlook one important part of today: Yablonsky was once again behind bars even if they never found the cash.

Now it was time for Jase to finally concentrate on what he wanted.

Everything he wanted was here in Violet Ridge. But could he go about his daily business and see Cassie, knowing they'd never claim the promise of something permanent?

Her hope and optimism had filled him with a new sense of how his life could be, even if she wasn't by his side. Also, it was time to claim his place in the Virtue family again.

"I want to be your brother and be a part of Grandma and Grandpa's lives." Not to mention the lives of his other siblings and extended family members, including all their children.

Seth gave Jase a gentle nudge. "Haven't you gotten that message? You're a permanent part of all of us no matter where you live."

Jase almost choked up from Seth's acceptance of him. "I love you, Seth."

"Right back at you, little brother. You know this family always has your back, right?" Seth handed him a pillow and a blanket. "If you ever need anything, all you have to do is ask."

Seth said goodnight and left the suite, no doubt headed back to the house he and Amanda shared on the other side of the ranch.

Jase weighed his options. He could return to Denver where he'd be a shoo-in for the captaincy once Shields retired. Or he could stay here where he'd see Cassie...and inevitably the man who would one day claim her heart.

He laid out on the couch and let sleep claim him.

AT THE FRONT of the corn maze, Cassie accepted the trowel from her mother and reached for the chrysanthemums waiting to be transplanted into the decorative pickle barrel.

For the past few days, she and Mom had explored every inch of the house for the money or a map. They had searched her mother's sewing machine and dress forms and the back of her father's grandfather clock. They'd also consulted the blueprints she'd retrieved with Jase at city hall.

Nothing. She wanted to get back to her routine, the way life was before Jase arrived.

Except that would never happen. Jase had added so much to her life in the short time he had been here, his kindness and intensity bringing into focus why she did what she did. She loved this farm, the town's residents, her kids. For so long, she'd been focused on proving she was more than Keith's half sister, she'd forgotten why she had overcommitted herself. It had taken Jase and his laser focus to put everything into perspective.

It was hard to believe a week had passed. This time next Saturday would be the grand opening of the corn maze.

She reached into her jacket for her gardening gloves and pulled out a lollipop instead. Jase's favorite. She remembered their time at the watch shop where the clocks around them emphasized the precious nature of each moment. Like the first time Jase held Blossom. Or the fun the four of them had riding their horses. Or those kisses.

"Cassie?" Her mother's voice drew her away from her memories of Jase.

From here on, Cassie would only have memories rather than new adventures with him.

"What, Mom?" Cassie asked.

"I made my flight reservation this morning. I'll be here next month for your birthday." Mom smiled. Cassie was thrilled that her mother wanted to travel back to the farm so soon.

"Penny and Easton will love that." Cassie placed the mums in the barrel and packed the soil around them, before returning her mother's smile. "So will I."

"They can help me plan a small party for you." Her mother handed her the watering can. "I always loved planning your birthday parties."

That was an understatement. Mom was the

birthday queen. "I remember the one where you turned the house into the beach."

Mom nodded. "I loved the retro party when you were in middle school with fun games like pin the tail on the donkey and hide-and-seek."

"That was easy when all the barrels and farm equipment were piled everywhere." Cassie flexed her muscles, recalling the property before she set up the farmstand.

"You were always the last one we found. How you managed to curl up in the pickle barrel was beyond me." Mom chuckled. "That was a great hiding place."

Goose bumps dotted Cassie's arm. *Hiding place.* "Keith still lived at home then, didn't he?"

Cassie didn't have to wait for her mom's answer. The pieces finally fell into place. The tipped barrels.

Keith must have remembered her hiding place when he was looking to stash the money. It would have been easy for him to doctor a barrel with all tools and supplies on the farm. And after his escape, he had searched for and found eleven pickle barrels still on her property, including two she'd converted into household storage bins. That meant…

"Get Penny and Easton! I know where the money is."

Within minutes, the four of them were all piled into Cassie's truck. She drove to the seniors' center where the parking lot was packed. Up and down the aisles she went and then snagged the first available space.

Cassie sprinted into the building where a group of residents were practicing the tango in the lobby. Likely curious, they started to follow as she ran outside to the community garden and the twelfth and final pickle barrel collecting rainwater.

Her mother and children caught up with her about the same time as Zelda and Nelda and the other seniors.

"What's your hurry?" Zelda asked.

Cassie gazed inside the barrel at the rainwater. She handed her jacket to her mother and pushed up her flannel shirtsleeve. Her whole arm should have been wet, but the water only went up to her elbow. "Watch out."

She motioned for the crowd to move away, and she tilted the barrel in spite of everyone's shouts. Rainwater splashed onto the ground, and she reached into the barrel where a false bottom greeted her. "Anyone got a screwdriver or a pry bar?" she asked.

Doc Jenkins handed her his multitool, and she dislodged the piece of wood only to discover a huge metal box. She yanked it free and opened it. Money spilled out everywhere, the bills fluttering around her feet.

The onlookers gasped as did Cassie. This was what a million dollars looked like.

She reached for her phone to call the police, but Zelda shook her head.

"Theresa, take Penny and Easton home," Zelda said. "I'll go with Cassie and deliver this in person. They'll take my word that Cassie was as surprised as all of us."

Hours later, Cassie and Zelda walked into the Denver police station with Zelda holding the metal box. They introduced themselves to the dispatcher and waited for Jase. Finally, Cassie would be able to clear her tarnished name, and maybe she and Jase could discuss the future. Nerves welled in Cassie's stomach. Did Jase love her? Could they commit to making a relationship work?

To her dismay, it wasn't Jase but Captain Shields who greeted her and Zelda, who introduced herself as the former mayor of Violet Ridge.

"Follow me." His curt voice cut off any chance of asking to speak to Jase.

Shields escorted them to his office where Zelda placed the metal box on Captain Shields' desk.

"My mother is visiting from Florida," Cassie began, "and remembered my birthday party when I hid in a barrel. That was when I thought of how I'd donated one to the seniors' center. We found the money, and I brought it straight here." Despite the joy she felt from making the discovery, Cassie looked around, half expecting to be arrested at any moment.

"I was there along with my tango class buddies and saw her find the money. We'll all vouch for Cassie," Zelda added.

Captain Shields raised an eyebrow. But he opened the metal box and then picked up his phone, relaying an order to bring him an evidence bag. After the commotion died down, and the money had been properly dealt with, he steepled his fingers and stared at Zelda, then Cassie. "Detective Virtue isn't here right now, but it seems I owe you and him an apology."

An apology from this man would count for a lot, especially to Jase. "Why Jase?"

The captain flexed his fingers, the cracking sound echoing in the small space. "Detective Virtue went to bat for you. He said that if you were Yablonsky's accomplice, he'd resign. As hard as it was for me to admit, he was right. And to his credit, you returned the money when you found it."

"Darn tootin' she did." Zelda nudged Cassie's side. "You should get that apology in writing."

Cassie patted her friend's hand and turned back to Captain Shields. "I'd really like to talk to Jase. It's important. Something personal."

Captain Shields shook his head. "I'm sorry, he's not here at present, but I'll let him know about this."

He accompanied Cassie and Zelda out of the building and shook their hands. Together, the women headed to her truck.

Cassie wondered if she should visit Jase's condo. Captain Shields had only confirmed what she believed in her heart. Jase might have thought she was guilty at first, but he had come to trust her and have faith in her innocence, in them. Jase loved her.

Sliding into the driver seat, she realized it had been easier to shut Jase out of her life rather than risk someone else leaving her again. With a long lingering glance at the police department, she recognized it had been fear that kept her from hearing everything he had to say to her.

Officers emerged from the building and headed for their squad cars.

It might have been fear that stopped her before, but now it was something else. Jase had so much to bring to this department and the residents of Denver.

She let him go, and she and Zelda started back home to Violet Ridge.

CHAPTER EIGHTEEN

At last, the corn maze was going to have its grand opening tonight. Most of Violet Ridge had arrived at Thistle Brook Farm, yet the one person Cassie wanted to be with was in Denver. While understanding the importance of Jase's career, her heart still ached with missing him.

Cassie longed for a hot soak in her tub, her body almost as tender as her heart. Today had been packed with farm chores and last-minute preparations for the grand opening. Last night's rain had left puddles in the main parking lot and overflow area, but spreading hay everywhere had helped give her farm a festive air.

She looked around in satisfaction at the hay bales, scarecrows and pumpkins near the ticket booth and entrance to the maze. Her seasonal employees had set up tables near the farmstand, which had been converted to a concession area with kettle corn and homemade praline pumpkin spice fudge. Extra spotlights had been installed and were now shining bright as dusk settled over the mountains.

Cassie smiled at the two hundredth guest to buy a ticket that night and slid their receipt across the counter. Then her walkie-talkie crackled with a request to come to the concession stand.

Waving at the other ticket taker, Cassie exited the booth with Rusty following close behind. Although the mystery of the missing bank robbery money had been solved, she had accepted she would never know who'd tied this wonderful retriever to her mailbox. She stopped and rubbed his side. "You fit in at the farm." The words almost stuck in her throat.

Jase had fit in as well, but she supposed that was part of his trade. He would have to adapt to different environments in order to gain trust and do his job. She wanted to believe she had been more to him than part of a case, but she'd never be sure.

She arrived at the farmstand, the queue of people waiting to order dessert or a drink most encouraging. While she didn't expect to recoup all her expenses this first year, especially after delaying the opening for the past two weekends, this was a positive sign she was heading in the right direction. Agritourism was daunting at times, but nights like tonight with satisfied guests made it worthwhile.

DeeDee, a mother of one of Penny's classmates who had jumped at the chance to work part-time for extra holiday spending money, waved Cassie over to where she was ringing up a customer's purchases.

Cassie recognized the customer. It was Emma Martinelli, the newly married owner of the Rocky Mountain Chocolatiers, which happened to be Easton's favorite business in downtown Violet Ridge.

"Hi, Cassie," Emma Martinelli greeted her.

Cassie returned her big smile, although deep down, she couldn't help but feel a little disappointed. She stifled a wry chuckle. What did she expect? For Jase to show up out of the blue.

"Do you have a minute?" Emma asked. "I don't have long since Dominic and Macy should be done with the corn maze any time now." Dominic was Emma's husband, whose construction company had done some work on the farm, and Macy, her daughter, was in Penny's class.

"Sure." Cassie helped Emma transport her purchases of hot apple cider, apple doughnuts and caramel kettle corn wrapped up in a waffle cone to a nearby picnic table.

"I had a sample of your pumpkin fudge, and it's delicious. Better than my fall flavors. Any chance you'd consider consigning some of your fudge at my shop? We could brainstorm some new offerings, too. You don't have to answer now, but I wanted you to think about it."

Cassie took Emma's number before hurrying back to the ticket booth, Rusty at her side once more. But before she could resume her post, Penny and Easton ran toward her with their grandmother a good distance behind. Her mother had extended her stay, which they'd all been glad about, but would be leaving tomorrow.

Penny slowed down just short of colliding with the customers in line for tickets, then stopped in front of Cassie.

"Did Jase come after all?" Her daughter's eyes looked full of hope. "We mailed him a special invite. He wouldn't want to miss the fun."

Easton nodded, his face reflecting that same longing. "And Highlander's still here. Jase must be coming back."

Cassie's heart ached that they'd gone to the trouble of mailing him an invitation, no doubt with their grandmother's help. Until now, she hadn't realized her children were still holding out hope Jase would return. This type of optimism was exactly what she'd been trying to instill in them for years, and now? This was a test of the worst kind. She didn't want life's setbacks giving them a negative view of the world, but neither could she shield them from everything.

"I'm not sure when you might see Jase again. And the next time I see Amanda, I'll ask her when someone can transport Highlander back to the Lazy River Dude Ranch."

"Did I hear my name?" Amanda appeared at her side.

"How about some corn dogs and caramel apples?" Mom asked Penny and Easton suddenly. Offering Cassie a wry smile, she and the children were gone again, joining the crowd.

Cassie noticed Rusty checking out another dog, the pair getting on well. She focused on Amanda. "Where's your fiancé?" Cassie leaned over the ticket booth and tried to spot Seth.

Amanda released a long breath. "Seth is helping someone with a problem, evidently, but he promised me we'd go through the maze together. I'm expecting him any minute."

Cassie mentioned the idea of Highlander returning to the dude ranch, and Amanda agreed that she'd take care of it. Rusty gave a long howl, and Cassie glanced down at him. Rusty was sitting on his haunches, his head curled upward as the plaintive strains of his howl reached a crescendo.

Startled, Cassie turned back to Amanda. "He's never been like this before. I'll have to put him in the farmhouse."

Amanda chuckled. "It's almost like he's hearing Seth play the guitar for the first time." She held out her credit card. "Twelve tickets, please."

Cassie frowned. "Why twelve?"

"Two for me and Seth, two for my grandparents, one for my sister, one for Crosby and five for Daisy and her family." Amanda pointed to the growing line of customers at the booth. "You know what? I've helped at the farmstand before, and I'm great with people. Why don't I just take over for a minute so you can calm down Rusty?"

Before Cassie could correct Amanda on her faulty addition—she'd listed eleven people, not twelve—Amanda entered the booth and swiped her own card. Just then, Rusty took off like a rocket toward the corn maze.

Cassie sprinted after her dog, taking care to avoid guests in her way. She shouted a hasty hello to Doc Jenkins and Zelda Baker as well as several other senior citizens from the center, thankful they'd come to support her. She was almost out of breath trying to keep up with Rusty.

The sounds of a country band reached her ears. She hadn't hired anyone to perform. Maybe she should have. This band wasn't great, the harmonica particularly off-key.

Cassie halted, Jase's words echoing in her mind. *I don't play the harmonica in public, much to everyone's appreciation.*

It couldn't be…could it?

Cassie's heart soared as she hurried toward the music.

JASE KEPT HIS lips relaxed while he and his siblings performed. No matter what else happened here at the corn maze tonight, his heart soared at Seth, Daisy and Crosby delivering for him like this. There was Crosby, concentrating on his fiddle, while Daisy plucked the banjo and Seth strummed his guitar. While the four of them would never land a professional gig, that wasn't the point. They had dropped everything and agreed to their public musical debut simply to help him.

His grandparents looked on with pride. Grandma

Bridget was tapping her cane in rhythm to the tune while Grandpa Martin curled his arm around her.

It was as if the crowd parted when Rusty arrived, adding his howls to their playing, with Cassie on his heels.

Jase had almost forgotten how beautiful she was as she stood there in a gold sweater, indigo jeans and well-worn boots. Her business acumen was in full force tonight; everyone he'd passed had complimented the corn maze and concession stand. Cassie O'Neal was one amazing woman.

Jase was only too aware he'd lost her trust. Somehow, during his tenure as Violet Ridge's new detective, he'd find a way to regain her faith in him. At least he had to try, and this was the right way to begin. He had always intended on coming back, but the invitation from Penny and Easton sealed the deal.

The song came to an end, and he and his siblings stopped playing. The crowd whistled, and someone shouted out a request.

Seth chuckled. "Thank you, but the Virtue Family Band has played its one and only gig."

Cassie tapped her chin. "Do you know 'Heart of Gold'?"

She wasn't talking to Daisy, Crosby or Seth; she was talking to him.

It was a start. Jase brought the harmonica to his lips and played the song for her and her alone.

As he hit the last few notes, he spotted Easton and Penny, and his heart grew full again.

"I knew Jase would be back! It was our invitation that did it." Easton ran up to hug him as soon as the song was over. Penny followed suit. "I knew you couldn't stay away."

"Blossom misses you, and so do I." Penny clung to his side and looked up at him. "When do you have to leave for Denver this time?"

"I don't." Jase met Cassie's gaze and took a deep breath. "I accepted a position with the Violet Ridge Police Department, and I start next week."

Cassie's mother approached and put a hand on Easton's shoulder and Penny's. "I think your mother and Jase need a minute to talk." They started to protest, but Theresa nipped that in the bud. "You'll get to see Jase soon, come on, there's still lots to do."

The rest of the crowd moved on until there was only him and Cassie. She hadn't kicked him off the property yet, so he was taking that as a good sign that she might be willing to listen to him.

"Just so you know, I intend to be the first person in line at your farmstand every morning until you hear me out." Jase closed his eyes, bemoaning the fact he wasn't good at delivering romantic lines.

He opened them again to find Cassie standing before him. She folded her arms and tapped her boot on the ground. "Why don't you save me that trouble and say what you have to say now?"

Her tone didn't give any indication of whether she'd be willing to give him another chance. Although he had a feeling Penny and Easton were ready for him to play a larger role in their lives again.

Jase glanced over and found his grandparents and siblings trying to be unobtrusive. Seth placed his guitar in its case while Daisy and Crosby did the same with their instruments.

Jase reached for Cassie's hand, the instant zap of energy confirming he'd made the right decision to come here. He pulled her into the corn maze, passing people debating which way to go. He knew every inch of the maze and headed for a quiet corner in a wrong-way section with Rusty right beside them, the bright floodlights casting a pretty glow.

They stood there, staring at each other, and his mind went blank. The speech he'd so carefully rehearsed had left him. Only the words resting in his heart remained. "Cassie, initially, I did come here under false pretenses."

"You came here searching for Keith, and you found him." She grinned and raised her index finger to his lips. "The day you captured him, I asked the wrong question. It's not important if you came here thinking I was guilty. What matters is that you changed your mind."

He nodded. "Once I got to know you, I realized you could never have been involved in those crimes."

"I've spoken to Captain Shields, he must have told you. He said the same." She moved toward Jase and slipped her hands in his. "Why did you quit your job in Denver? I can't stand in your way of being the next captain when he retires. Your career is too important."

"My heart's here, and so are you. And Penny, Easton and Blossom. I couldn't stay away. Chief Gutierrez is a good man, and it's a good department. I'm proud to be working here in Violet Ridge."

This time she brought her lips to his, silencing any further explanation. One kiss led to another and Jase couldn't believe she was in his arms.

Everything he'd always wanted was here in this moment. For too long, he'd known life could change in an instant, but it had taken Cassie's innate optimism to convince him that life could change for the better. And this was one of those moments.

Cassie paused and leaned back. "I lashed out at you because I was scared of someone leaving me again. Then you did, and well…"

It was his turn to silence her fear with a kiss. He poured his heart, forever hers, into the embrace before he broke away. "I'm back for good, if you'll have me?"

"Blossom would peck at my boots if I didn't give you another chance." She chuckled.

He looked deep into her hazel eyes and hoped she was feeling the same as him. "What about you?"

She snuggled against him. "I think I'm falling in love with you." He wrapped his arms around her, knowing that he'd come home for good.

EPILOGUE

THE OPENING CHORDS of the birthday song echoed in Cassie's dining room, and thirty candles on her cake winked at her. With her happiness brimming over, Cassie looked around at everyone gathered together.

True to her word, Mom had flown back to Violet Ridge yesterday, taking the weekend off from her college classes. She had wanted a theme for Cassie's party and thrown out ideas like disco, winter wonderland and even luau, but Cassie nixed them all. It was enough to have her loved ones around her, her good name intact.

Penny and Easton crowded around Jase, who was settling into his new job as detective nicely. Jase's rich baritone rose above everyone else's, and Rusty could hold back no longer. He howled his contribution, much to Easton's delight. Her son's face radiated joy and contentment, exactly what Cassie felt inside.

Bridget Virtue's sweet soprano blended with Martin's deep bass, the pair standing next to their granddaughter Daisy and her husband Ben. Their triplets had just found their way through the corn maze along with their uncle Seth and soon-to-be-aunt Amanda, who had volunteered to keep the trio on track so no one missed the cake being cut.

Not only had Jase's family welcomed him into their fold in the past month since his move back to Violet Ridge, they had also treated Cassie like a cherished member as well. Bridget had even taken it upon herself to give Cassie knitting lessons.

Cassie pursed her lips and tried to think of a wish. Everything she could have ever have wanted was here at Thistle Brook Farm. With that in mind, she blew out the candles in one fell swoop.

Everyone clapped, and her mother flipped on the light switch, bathing the room in soft light once again. Within minutes, everyone was enjoying cake and ice cream.

Jase motioned to Cassie, setting his plate on the table. She received his hint instantly; they hadn't had a minute to themselves all day. They donned their jackets and opened the front door, only to find Jase's brother Crosby rushing up the porch steps. He thrust a present toward Cassie and frowned. "I'm late again and missed the party, didn't I?"

Cassie chuckled and thanked Crosby for the gift. "You only missed the singing. There's still cake and ice cream."

"Thanks, Cass." Crosby waved and started inside before Cassie asked him to take the gift with him and place it with the others for later.

Crosby complied, and Cassie turned her full attention to Jase.

He shrugged. "At least he arrived on the right day. His shoes didn't match, though. Maybe I should talk to him and make sure everything is okay. He seemed preoccupied."

Cassie reached for Jase's hand and squeezed it. "He's fine. He's always preoccupied with the stories of Violet Ridge's past."

Jase replied with a return squeeze. "I just feel like I have to make up for lost time. I'm happy, and so are my other siblings. I want my brother to find someone to love, too."

Cassie's heart soared, basking in Jase's love. She adored this protective, caring side of him. Even better, he was showing everyone this facet of his personality now. She looked forward to seeing it for years to come.

"Crosby will get his act together. You'll see." She hugged Jase's arm. "Let's try the corn maze together. It's hard to believe it's over for the season."

The three weekends she'd opened the maze to the public had been a huge success. She was already planning for a bigger and better design next year.

Jase steered her toward the other side of her porch. "I thought we could sit for a spell on your new present."

Cassie gasped at the beautiful swing hanging from the eaves. "I love it! When did you install it?"

Jase smiled, a sight she never grew tired of seeing. "This afternoon, when your mother was fitting you for your Christmas dress."

She ran her hand over the cypress wood painted in a rich, walnut stain and then threw her arms around Jase. "It's perfect."

Before she could kiss Jase, a plaintive howl broke through the night. What was wrong with her dog? He only made that sound when it was important like when the police had apprehended Keith and Lucinda, who were now safely behind bars.

Cassie sprinted to the front door and opened it for Rusty. The dog bolted outside and ran toward the farmstand. Cassie went after her dog with Jase keeping up beside her.

Rusty stopped beside a shivering retriever mix huddled in the shadows next to the stand.

Cassie's heart went out to the poor animal, and she reached into her pocket for one of Rusty's small liver treats.

Jase stiffened beside her, but he held out his hand. "May I?"

She nodded and deposited the treat in his palm. Jase approached the dog with caution, and the animal emerged from the shadows. And quickly gulped down the offering. She focused her big brown eyes on Jase, who reached out and petted her.

He turned to Cassie. "She's so friendly. How can she already trust me so much?"

Rusty nudged Cassie's hand until she rubbed

his ears. "Dogs have a way of sensing when someone's right for them."

The retriever mix sniffed Jase as if deciding whether or not he was worthy of devotion. At last, she sat before him, and Cassie knew this dog had bonded with Jase.

"I'm sure any dog this beautiful and sweet has an owner," he said. "I'll take her to the vet tomorrow and see if she's microchipped."

Cassie wasn't convinced. In fact, she'd bet the dog had just found a lifetime home with Jase. "We both know someone abandoned her here, but she won't be abandoned for long."

Rusty left Cassie's side and sniffed the newcomer, who did likewise. She wagged her tail, and Rusty glanced at Cassie as if asking if they could keep this new friend. Cassie was already deciding where the dog would sleep.

The retriever whined and nudged Jase. He obliged by petting her, and Cassie bit back a laugh.

Jase sent her a questioning look. "What?"

"It seems as though it wasn't that long ago when a certain detective didn't believe a bond could form so fast." She smiled at Jase, then at Rusty.

"Lucky for me you showed me the error of my ways," Jase said as the new dog let out a sigh of contentment. As well she should, given her forever home was likely right here at Thistle Brook Farm.

Jase moved away from the dog, toward Cassie with his arms outstretched. She accepted his embrace, her head resting comfortably on his shoulder, and reveled in the feeling of having him close. Over the past three weeks, they'd spent every free moment with each other. He'd finish his shift in time to arrive for dinner, saying hello to Blossom before joining her and the children.

Out of the corner of her eye, she caught the retriever lying down, and Rusty curled up beside her, as if protecting her. "I've become a two-dog household," Cassie noted.

"Can you find room for one more addition?" Jase broke their contact and reached inside his jacket pocket. "Cassie O'Neal, I love you, your children and your farm. Will you add this cowboy cop to your family? Will you marry me?"

Her hand flew to her mouth, and she nodded. "Yes, I'll marry you! I love you, Jase Virtue. Let's go tell Penny and Easton and everyone."

He slid the ring on her finger, and she welcomed another new member into her family. He'd shown her that his word was his bond, and they'd learned to trust each other and fallen in love in the process.

She walked hand in hand with him toward the farmhouse and their future. Rusty and the new dog were following closely behind. She'd never forget this birthday—the day Jase claimed her heart and a place in her family.

For always.

* * * * *

For more great romances in the
Violet Ridge miniseries from Tanya Agler
and Harlequin Heartwarming,
visit www.Harlequin.com today!